HAT TRICK

BRAD KEENE

Second Edition 2016.

ISBN-13: 978-0-9965014-2-2
ISBN-10: 0-9965014-2-8

Cover Design by Michele Catalano
michelecatalanocreative.com

Chapter 1

Ash

SOUTH OF PALOMA. Beach side. Next to the buckets of bath salt.

Those were the directions Ash had given him. When Gordon called earlier that morning to say he wanted to move in, she had sounded relieved, like she was about to say yes to someone else, but Gordon was her preferred choice. She told him where to find her. She'd walk him to the loft and dig up the spare key.

Gordon found a parking space and made his way up the Venice Beach Boardwalk, weaving through the crowd past tables offering incense, Eastern religion trinkets, psychic readings, political conspiracy literature, and the chance to have your name written on a single grain of rice. The denizens were wildly eclectic, coming in all sizes and colors, as if the entire world had drains emptying on Venice Beach.

He spotted a wooden rack lined with plastic cement buckets filled with bright, chunky salt. Gordon had never seen bath salt before, but assumed this was it. Packed sandwich bags of the stuff sat in front. He approached the ragged stand that also held pyramids of body lotion and organic soap.

"Three bags for ten bucks," said a soft-spoken voice.

Gordon turned and saw a thin man with dreadlocks let out a protracted yawn.

"You bathe?" asked the man, shaking off the remainder of the yawn.

"Not really," said Gordon.

"You're missing out," said a female voice.

It took a moment to realize where it was coming from.

Looking up from the grass next to the booth, sitting on a low beach chair on top of an Indian rug where a collection of handmade figurines were on display, was Ash.

"Baths are therapeutic," said Ash. "You get to submerge. A portion of every day should be spent underwater."

"With my salt," said the man, tapping the bags.

Ash's red hair was cropped, save for the scattered bangs that hung in whatever direction the wind nudged them. Tattoos branded her pale, freckled skin. On the back of her neck, a rose with its fair share of thorns. On the side of her calf, the sun with twisting rays that resembled pubic hair. A baggy, paint-stained shirt hung over pants sheared at the knees. No noticeable make-up for her face which was adequately accented by a tilted smile.

Ash introduced Gordon to Toby, the vendor selling the bath salt, who soon turned his attention to a gaggle of Italian women who were bent over the buckets, inhaling deep whiffs.

While Toby's booth was marked with a fluorescent green banner promoting his products and web address, Ash's area had nothing. Not even a cardboard sign.

"If they ask, I tell 'em," she said.

Ash made her meager living selling tiny figurines made of wood, wire, and whatever other materials she felt like gluing on. The figurines varied in design, each reflecting the mood she was in during the moment of their creation.

Her total business consisted of the chair, the rug, the figurines, and a flimsy box of supplies. Like most artists who made a living on the boardwalk, she created while she sold.

When Gordon asked if she had a license to sell, she said she didn't need one. Artists don't even have to pay the city if they're located on the beach side, but they're not allowed to set up before nine (not that it mattered to Ash, who usually appeared well after eleven). Though vendors come and go, the locations of booths are usually respected. Some have occupied the same patch of grass for decades.

"Watch my stuff, Toby?" said Ash, standing up. "Won't be long."

"Sure thing," said Toby, counting the cash from a sale to the Italians.

Ash lit a cigarette and took Gordon by the hand, leading him away.

***

Standing in the cramped loft that resembled more of a workshop than a place to live, Ash showed Gordon where he'd be sleeping.

"I use it for storage," said Ash.

It was the closest thing the place had to a bedroom—a space the size of a small office with a sliding wooden door.

"It's supposed to glide on the track," she explained, demonstrating how the door wouldn't budge more than halfway.

"It's cool," Gordon said. "I got nothing to hide."

"You're in the minority."

Gordon placed his canvas bag on the old Army cot against the wall. A red velvet cushion sat on top.

"'Case you don't have a pillow," she said.

"You like sleeping out there?" He had to step over a mattress when they came in.

"That I do. Right under the skylight. Below the stars."

"Can you see the stars?"

"No. But I know they're there."

The place was fraught with various art projects, but none more striking than the line of tombstones leaning against the wall. Not cardboard replicas, but the real deal. Heavy cement and marble pieces, all in different phases of being painted.

"Morbid, huh?" said Ash.

"Interesting."

"That's what people say when they think it's morbid."

Gordon shrugged; grinned. "I like 'em."

"I'm trying to change the perception of what a grave marker should be."

"How? They are what they are."

"Meaning?"

"Grave markers mark graves."

"Is that it?"

"Well…"

"They're *much* more than that. Tombstones represent people. When your kids, lover, spouse, whoever, comes to visit your final resting spot, it's the thing they look at, the thing they talk to. And they're usually boring as fuck. Except for some of the cool gothic ones, they're all cookie-cutter slabs. Is that what you want your eternal symbol to be?"

Gordon didn't answer. He thought the question was rhetorical. It wasn't. Ash was waiting.

"I hadn't given it much thought," he said.

"That's the problem."

"But they have words."

"Loving Husband. Loving Daughter. Quotes from the Bible."

"Right."

"I want to take it beyond that. Show people they have choices."

Gordon nodded. It was one of those things that made sense, but also one of those things that no one *he* knew would give a fuck about.

"You sell 'em?" Gordon asked.

"Not yet. They're for a show."

A large, oscillating fan circulated dry wind, but he could still smell the pungent odor of paint. Windows were open, but Gordon guessed the ventilation wasn't adequate for the amount of chemicals being exposed. Dangerous? Oh well.

"That all your stuff?" Ash asked, anticipating a second trip to Gordon's rented car.

"Yep."

"Ain't much."

"Don't need much."

Ash nodded to the paint cans. "Don't mind the smell, do ya?"

"Not at all."

"Liar."

Chapter 2

Shawn and Cedric

"HE AIN'T HOME," said a voice through the door.

Gordon looked through the window, but the glare was too much.

"I'm Gordon. The new roommate."

"Shawn ain't here," the voice said.

"He said I could move in today."

Finally the door opened. A man in his early thirties with a cap pulled down to his eyes stood in the archway. He glanced at the canvas bag sitting at Gordon's feet.

"Didn't say he found someone," said the man.

"He said today would be good to—"

"Cedric," said the man, extending his hand. They shook.

"Gordon Lake. I assumed Shawn—"

"He didn't tell me shit."

Cedric turned and walked back in, leaving the door open.

Gordon entered and closed the door, noticing that Cedric had already disappeared. He found him in the kitchen, scooping protein powder into a Lakers mug.

"Great place," said Gordon.

Without looking up, Cedric asked, "He tell you about the rat problem?"

"No."

"That's Shawny. Sell 'em the good stuff, they'll find out the rest soon enough."

"You guys have rats?"

"Uh-huh."

"I didn't know areas like this had rats."

"Where you from?"

"Chicago."

Cedric smirked. "Jordan fucked y'all by goin' to the Wizards, huh?"

"I've let it go. How many rats?"

"Enough." Cedric poured milk into the mug, then mixed it with the protein.

"Is this place, like… infested?"

"Worried you're gonna be takin' a dump and have one bite your ass?" This made Cedric laugh. He wasn't altogether wrong in his assessment.

"I prefer my bathroom visits to be uneventful, yeah."

"They live in the yard. Exterminator came out a few times, but it didn't do shit. Ask me why."

"Why?"

"'Cause Nature Boy Shawn keeps puttin' food out for the squirrels. The food, in turn, attracts the rats. They think this place is the fuckin' Farmer's Market." He downed the protein shake in a series of gulps, then wiped his mouth with his forearm. "What d'you do for work?"

"Just moved here."

"What d'you *wanna* do?" asked Cedric, letting out a belch.

It was a question Gordon hadn't really thought about.

He had no intention of holding down a job. He didn't need to. It'd just waste time. He wanted to live as much as he could, as differently as he could, and embrace whatever that entailed. Work had consumed him his whole life. It was the last thing he wanted to think about. But the question was bound to come up again, so he had to think of something to say. Besides, the excuse of a job would help explain where he was when he wasn't home, in case curiosity led them to ask. He had to come up with a fake job with flexible hours and no set schedule.

"Freelance," said Gordon.

"Freelance what?"

He was in Hollywood, so—

"Editor," said Gordon.

"That's cool," Cedric said, losing interest.

"What about you?"

"Retail. Discount Sports Village. In the mall. But I'm a musician," said Cedric. "Ever hear industrial? House? Trip-hop?"

"Yeah." Not really.

"That's what I do. Got an album comin' out."

"You sing?"

"Nah, man. Shit's all music. I mean… I could sing if I wanted to. I'm multi-talented like that. But I don't."

Cedric went on to say that he was going to be world famous, that people already talked about him online, that his new album of progressive dance mixes was called *Blast Your Bone*, that every club on the West Coast would be playing it before the end of summer.

He spoke of the deal that he would soon sign, of his coming fortune, of the women and respect that would come with it.

Watching Cedric expound on his career was like watching an infomercial at three in the morning. He was ready for Cedric to rattle off a toll-free number: Order now and receive, absolutely free of charge, your very own *Blast Your Bone* orange peeler.

***

Entering his new bedroom (his second of the day), Gordon set down the canvas bag and took in the space.

It was four times the size of his area at Ash's, but then again, the house was ten times as big. The room was clean and fully furnished. Although he didn't recognize the make of furniture upon first glance, (probably California made—not the type he was accustomed to seeing), he could tell it wasn't flimsy.

The room was so orderly in fact, Gordon was hesitant to disrupt anything. It felt like a showroom. Look, but don't touch. You break it, you buy it.

But then his eyes noticed something on the wooden floor, and the feeling of residential bliss vanished.

Were those specks of dirt… or drops of rat shit?

He walked closer and leaned over. It was dirt. Had to be. Probably. Hopefully. Maybe Cedric was fucking with him about the rats. Busting the new guy's balls. He'd ask Shawn when he got the chance, when Cedric wasn't around.

Chapter 3

Dean

THERE WERE TWO DRY erase boards in Dean's apartment in Pasadena; one for daily goals, one for weekly goals.

"All people want things," said Dean, having stopped in from work to supervise Gordon's move-in. "Ask anyone on the street if they want something, they'll say, 'Sure.' But then ask them what they want *exactly*. If they say happiness, that's too general. They didn't answer your question. Everyone wants happiness. But how are you going to achieve it? You need a game plan. You need goals. You need to figure out what they are and write them down. That's what I do. And that's what works."

The list on the daily goal board was written in exquisite penmanship:

cardiovascular cycle

review inventory

roommate move-in

schedule sales meeting

brainstorm new employee bonuses

"Hourly breakdown," said Dean. "Keeps me focused."

Built like an athlete, impeccably groomed, and reeking of self-confidence, Dean was a man on top of his game. He seemed a *little* high strung, but Gordon had to admit—he liked his attitude, and he liked the goal boards. It reminded him of the chalkboard in his high school locker room. Back then, the goals were football oriented—limit turnovers, minimize penalties—but the similarity was comforting.

"Can get you one if you want," said Dean.

Dean patted him on the shoulder, already taking pride in the fact he was shaping his new roommate for the better. He led Gordon into the bedroom where he'd be staying. It wasn't as big as the room at Shawn and

Cedric's, but it was a far cry from the closet-like space at Ash's.

A framed motivational poster hung on the wall. It featured a bare-chested man dangling from a rope next to a mountain. "Never Stop Climbing" were the words underneath, although the man didn't seem to be climbing. He was just hanging there, as if waiting to be rescued.

"I took the liberty of supplying you with some essentials," said Dean. "Storage boxes, list of nearby stores, two rolls of toilet paper, to ease your transition."

Gordon heard a gurgling sound. He noticed a five gallon water cooler near the window. A large bubble wobbled up and burst at the surface. Dean beamed a proud, fatherly smile, as if it was an infant speaking its first words.

"Got your cold, your hot, your easy-dispense paper cones," Dean said, in full salesman mode. "Thought you'd like one, so I had the guys bring it in. Like it?"

"Gotta have water," said Gordon.

"That's why I've committed my life to it. This isn't the horse and buggy trade. It's the nationwide distribution of an element necessary for man's survival. You can get your bigger TV, your faster car, your new, whiz-bang, digital device—but water's water."

"I grew up drinking from the tap."

"Absolute poison."

"We had a filter."

"Filtered poison is still poison. Would you drink filtered cyanide?"

"No…"

"Then you see my point," said Dean, patting the cooler. "Give me reverse osmosis or give me death."

When Gordon asked Dean how he became a peddler of water, Dean said that he nearly drowned four years earlier. He was jet skiing off the coast of Santa Barbara, jumped a wave, landed awkwardly, and slapped his head against the jet ski. Knocked him silly. He sank twenty feet before a friend who saw the mishap pulled him up. It was during that descent that he had an epiphany.

Turn his life over to God? No. Reconcile with a childhood enemy? Nope.

Sell water.

As the same substance was doing its best to drown Dean, all he could think about was selling it. According to Dean, when his head broke the surface, he started choking with a huge smile, his destiny realized.

"At that moment, I thought to myself, 'Dean Monroe will be the greatest seller of H_2O this world has ever seen.' Two years later, I became Assistant District Manager at Pure Mountain Pacific. Never looked back."

Dean filled two paper cones and handed one to Gordon. They toasted and drank. Dean studied Gordon's reaction as if he'd just sipped a top shelf, single malt scotch. Gordon noticed he was being scrutinized and tried his best to look impressed.

"Reverse osmosis," said Dean with a new level of smugness.

Gordon was surprised Dean wasn't dizzy from the overdose of pride, but the guy knew who he was. It was a quality he wanted for himself.

Dean's generosity was overwhelming in contrast to the indifferent attitude he received from Cedric just a few hours earlier. But that was good. Contrast was good. He wanted each living condition to be different.

"I'll be back at 8:15," said Dean. "Call me if you have any questions." He handed Gordon two keys, each color-coded with plastic covers. "Red's the bottom lock, blue's the top." He was in a hurry and already shuffling out the door. "You eat yet?"

"No."

Dean reached into his jacket and produced a prime rib coupon for Gilroy's Chophouse in Old Towne Pasadena.

"On me," said Dean.

"You sure?"

"Sure I'm sure. Promise me you'll go."

"I'll check it out."

Dean walked out, disabling the alarm on a black BMW Roadster. A crunchy guitar riff from the stereo blasted as he started the engine, then faded as the Roadster pulled out and turned the corner.

Dean seemed to have his shit together, all right. He was a model of self-discipline.

Gordon didn't figure Dean would be living in an apartment for long. An annual goal board wasn't visible, but if it existed, Gordon was sure "purchase house" would be at the top, written neatly in black marker.

Gordon couldn't help but be envious. He envied any person who knew where they were going.

Chapter 4

GORDON DROVE AT a casual speed, thinking about what he had just done.

The idea had come to him that morning when trying to decide who to live with. He wouldn't choose one roommate above the others.

He'd choose *all three.*

He had paced feverishly, allowing a brief smile as he figured out what his mind was telling him. He could live in all three residences simultaneously. He had the resources, so why not?

Each choice offered its own set of possibilities. Each choice allowed him an opportunity to explore different aspects of himself.

But there had to be a time limit.

He couldn't let the months unravel indefinitely. This was an experiment of sorts, and all experiments had a framework. So how long should this one be allowed to proceed? One month? Two, maybe? Three?

Three seemed like a good number. Assuming he split time equally amongst the residences, that would be more or less one month for each.

And walls had to exist.

Each life had to be kept separate from the next. Each roommate couldn't know about the others. That was necessary. That was critical. He had to be careful in that regard. Nothing could be tainted.

Going ahead with the plan also meant he had to split his belongings into three groups: one pile for Ash, one for Dean, one for Shawn and Cedric. He didn't have many clothes to begin with, so dividing them made him look poor, but that was okay. He'd buy more in the coming days.

Gordon thought about the experiment as he drove. It was the craziest fucking thing he'd ever done in his one-note life.

So that was it then.

He'd let the random variables of multiple homes rain down on him with his mouth wide open and his arms outstretched. And when the downpour stopped three months from now, when the experiment was over, maybe he'd finally be the person Gordon Lake was meant to be.

It would be a forced birth, but it was fucking time something happened. His life never had the chance to take shape on its own.

From the crisp January morning he was born, he'd been raised to be his father.

Same beliefs, same schools.

Same sports, same job.

Same fucking life.

Gordon had planned to check out of the hotel that morning, before he started moving into the multiple homes, but a new element of the plan had cropped up in his brain.

He wouldn't check out at all.

He'd keep the room for the duration of the experiment.

The more he thought about the prospect of living in different places simultaneously, the more he figured he'd need some sort of home base.

He would need a location where he could be objective, where he could evaluate the progress of the experiences. He thought about using the rental car, but that was no good. There had to be a place that allowed him to keep evidence of the lives out in the open without the risk of a roommate finding it.

So he had decided to maintain a *neutral place*, as he took to thinking of it. That neutral place would be room 116 at the Starlight Inn.

But the idea no longer stopped there.

Dean's strict adherence to organization had inspired him to maintain a daily, written record. A journal.

After dinner, he'd stop at a drug store and buy a composition journal to record his thoughts, feelings, reactions… anything. Then, after ninety-three days, when the experiment reached its conclusion, he could review the entries.

The idea of keeping a journal filled Gordon with hope that he could indeed pull this off.

Chapter 5

THE HOSTESS OF GILROY'S Chophouse had seated him in a back booth after he told her he didn't feel like eating in full visibility of other customers. Turns out this wasn't a problem. The restaurant's layout consisted of wooden panels that divided its massive square footage into clusters of tables, making it seem like you were dining in an intimate café, not a publicly traded franchise establishment.

Gordon perused the overpriced selection, more out of curiosity than anything else. He was here because of the coupon, and it didn't say pick whatever you like. He was going to be eating prime rib tonight, and that was fine with him. It was—

"Hey there," said a woman's voice.

Gordon looked up, and the world stopped spinning.

Her name tag said "Naomi." Blue eyes, dirty blonde hair tied in a bun, snug shirt that pressed against her breasts. Gordon found himself captivated. She set down a basket of wheat bread and said, "Can I get you something to drink?"

"Vodka on the rocks," said Gordon. Her eyes were melting him.

"Any preference?" asked Naomi.

"Stoli."

"Coming right up."

Not wanting her to leave just yet, he dug into his pocket for the coupon and said, "It says I gotta show this up front."

She took the coupon and looked it over. "Prime rib it is. How'd you like it?"

"Medium-well."

Naomi jotted down the rest of the order, took the menu, and smiled as she walked away. Gordon leaned back, recovering. The planet resumed its rotation.

He'd never been hit over the head like that. Whatever he was feeling, it went beyond physical attraction. There were intangibles at work. She was… she was…

Maybe he was tired.

No, there was no maybe about *that* —he was fucking exhausted. It had been a grueling day that had him zig-zagging around town.

And now this girl made his head spin. Maybe he was just lonely. Or horny.

He tore into a warm roll.

For the rest of the meal, Gordon analyzed his exchanges with Naomi the waitress. Was her charm exclusively for him or was it simply her waitress-persona?

Funnier the lip, higher the tip?

He recalled how his friend Mike used to flip for every female bartender. Once the bartender flashed a smile and asked if he wanted a cold beer, Mike was in love. Was this the same sort of misinterpretation of professional friendliness?

Gordon didn't think so. At least, not on his part. He didn't share Mike's history of instant infatuation. Gordon had ordered countless buckets of wings from gorgeous girls before, but he never felt like this.

Gordon examined Naomi's every word, every expression, every gesture. He studied her as she waited on the adjacent tables. Was she the same for them? Was it a performance?

What if fate had led him from the cold confines of Chicago, all the way across the country, to find love? Maybe *that* was the path. Maybe that's what was missing from his life. It was idealism at its highest level, but screw it.

Magic happens, right? It happens all the time. Just not to him.

Gordon decided to ask her for her number. He took out some cash for the tip, but he'd leave it on the table after he spoke with her. Asking for a number and handing over cash at the same time would make it seem like he was paying for the number.

Naomi walked over with the leather billfold. He smiled. She smiled. There was definitely more at work here. He could feel it.

This was the start of something special.

"Gordon?" asked Naomi, tilting her head slightly.

He hadn't given her his name.

"Dean's new roommate?"

"Yeah," said Gordon. "How'd you—"

"He just called to see if you came in. Described you dead-on!"

"He called?"

It was like a doctor discussing a test, but who hadn't given you the results yet. But by your gut, you knew it was bad.

"Dean's a total control freak," said Naomi. "If he sets something in motion, he *always* follows through."

Gordon felt sick.

"Guess we're gonna be seeing a lot of each other," said Naomi, extending her hand. "I'm Dean's fiancée."

Touching her skin was both exhilarating and heart-breaking. He tried to read her in that instant. Was she feeling even a tinge of regret? He couldn't tell. And then the handshake was over.

A smattering of polite conversation followed, but Gordon didn't register much of it. He wanted to crawl away.

The knowledge that Dean was engaged to Naomi didn't stop what he was feeling, as much as he wanted it to. That wasn't good. He told his brain to forget about her. It was only thirty minutes worth of emotion after all; a mere half hour of naïve giddiness.

But a light had been turned on and he couldn't find the switch to turn it off. He had a feeling he'd better find it soon. This was a light that could burn through everything.

Chapter 6

A COMPOSITION JOURNAL lay on the table in room 116.

He'd just returned from his free dinner (and complimentary heartbreak) at Gilroy's and wanted to get started on the day's entry. The sooner he finished, the sooner he could go to bed. And the location of tonight's bed would be at Ash's.

Each night, he would rotate where he slept. His excuse of being a freelance editor with an unpredictable, ever-changing schedule would provide a digestible excuse for his absence from whichever two residences were denied his presence on any given night.

Sitting at the small, round table under a weak light, Gordon opened the journal and on its first page wrote:

March 1

He looked at the date.

It didn't feel right. He wouldn't be maintaining this journal forever, just for three months. Was the date relevant? As a measure of time, sure. But this was an experiment with a set time schedule.

Three months.

Thirteen weeks.

Ninety-three days.

That was the time limit he had to work with. That was his canvas.

Gordon drew a single line through the date and embraced a new way to judge time. Perhaps the way it should always be judged—as fleeting, depleting, shrinking. So instead of the date, Gordon placed the tip of his pen at the top of the page and wrote:

93

As in ninety-three days.

An easy reference to how much time he had remaining in his trio of existences.

It was a countdown. Quite possibly the most important countdown of his life.

He let his mind drift back to that morning, to his initial impressions of each move-in... of Ash... of Cedric... of Dean... of himself with all three.

Gordon began writing.

Chapter 7

WHEN GORDON FINALLY RETURNED to Ash's loft, the place was in darkness. He called out, but received no answer. He didn't remember her mentioning a boyfriend, but maybe she was on a date.

For all he knew, she was out stealing tombstones. There's a thought. He never did ask if she made those things. He could picture her dressed in black, sneaking across a cemetery in the dead of night, shovel in hand, bag slung over her shoulder, pillaging for the sake of art.

Gordon didn't bother turning on a lamp.

Moonlight streamed in from the skylight, providing more than enough illumination. He made his way to the back, navigating around scattered paint cans and brushes, to the little room with the sliding door that didn't work.

The walls of his space were bare. Should he decorate? A poster maybe? A bookshelf? A plant?

He didn't want to make any more choices for the day. It felt like he reached his capacity for decision-making hours ago.

He sat on the Army cot. A yellow flyer rested on the velvet cushion Ash had given him. He picked it up and squinted to read...

6ᵗʰ Annual Dripping Head Acid Art Exhibit
Eagle Warehouse off Hollywood Blvd.
Free Admission - Free Drinks - Free Mind Fuck

Underneath, scrawled in purple ink:
You're Going! Tomorrow Night!
Ash's writing, he assumed.

This was the exhibit she mentioned. He'd be there. The flyer had already sold him on that. He stretched out on the cot, kicked off his shoes, and let the piece of paper drift to the floor.

Chapter 8

Then

Chicago

SUCK IT UP.

That was what Gordon Lake was taught to do when the temperature plunged and the cold sunk its teeth into his skin.

So he stood inside the furniture truck and tried his best to ignore the miserable weather. Acknowledging it would only give it power, and he was taught *not* to give it power. When you think about something, you feed energy into it.

So bury it. Pissing and moaning ain't gonna make the sun come out.

Gordon's father, Ollie, a stout man in his late fifties and proud owner of Lake Furnishings, emerged from the company warehouse and waved to him. By the style of the wave, Gordon knew he was fucked. It came in a large arc, a gesture only used before back-breaking hauls.

Gordon hopped from the truck and jogged to the loading bay, watching his footing on the black ice. When he found his father amidst the rows of crates and saw what he was nodding to, his worst nightmare was realized. It was the piece of furniture known as—

"The Beast?" said Gordon.

"Yep."

"You gotta be kiddin' me."

"Wish I was."

"I thought she ordered a night table."

"Mike wrote down the wrong number."

Just looking at it made Gordon's back ache. Formally listed as the Grand Cayman Summer Mahogany Dresser, it was perhaps the most awkwardly designed and heaviest piece of furniture in existence.

"Grin and bear it," said Ollie.

Gordon bent at the knees and wrapped his gloved hands around the sides of the dresser. His father slid a banged-up hand truck under the other end.

Like synchronized swimmers, they tilted the Beast in one motion, grunting in unison. Gordon could feel his back tighten as they started the journey to the truck. Taking baby-steps through the warehouse, Ollie's breath was already becoming frost as he half-muttered, half-hummed the words to "Summer Wind." He grimaced, repositioning his grip.

They waddled into the swirling snow, across the wet pavement, up the truck ramp.

"Okay," said Ollie. They eased the behemoth down. Ollie leaned against its brass bordered mirror, sweating and out of breath.

"You okay?" asked Gordon.

"Just winded," said Ollie.

"You sure?"

"Yeah…"

Ollie closed his eyes for a moment to steady himself.

They should've waited for Mike and Tom to come back from lunch, the two guys that rounded out Lake Furnishing's staff of four. But their richest client, Carol White, had called in a fit of anger, insisting they move up the delivery time, because she had to leave for her cousin's baby shower.

"About time," said Ollie.

Gordon followed his gaze as Mike and Tom came rolling up in Tom's pick-up. Mike hopped out the passenger side door, wearing shorts and a faded Walter Payton jersey. It was a miracle he was wearing that much. The man loved to defy the elements.

"Can't see shit out there," said Mike, holding a bag sagging with grease.

"You can see your watch, can't you?" asked Gordon.

"Deli line was a bitch."

"Carol White called," said Ollie. "She's pissin' herself."

Tom climbed from behind the wheel and noticed the dresser sitting in the truck. "You two slayed the Beast on your own?"

"Like I said, Carol White's got piss runnin' down her leg."

"Fuck that cunt," said Mike.

"She's in a rush," said Gordon.

"She's always in a rush," Mike said, digging his hand into the bag. Gordon could smell the roast beef cut through the air. His stomach churned.

"She's our best customer," said Ollie.

"Cunt's had three orders in the last year. Busted our balls for all three." Mike chomped into a bacon cheeseburger, spraying grease on his jersey.

"All three," nodded Tom, unwrapping a bologna sub. "Let her wait. It's Friday."

"That's why I want to get there and unload. Beat the traffic home."

"And throw your back out?"

Ollie shrugged. His back was killing him lately, but work came first. Pain was treated the same as shitty weather. You ignored it. You sucked it up.

Oliver Henry Lake was a machine who never missed a day of work in his life, and expected the same tenacity from those he employed. Gordon felt the brunt of it. He was his only son, a boy poured from the same mold and instilled with the same relentless work ethic. His mother died when he was six, leaving the child-rearing duties to Ollie (save for the occasional weekend visit by Ollie's sister who frowned upon her brother's hard-nosed fathering, but did nothing to soften it).

Because of this, Gordon had grown into a twenty-six year old version of his father.

Same crew-cut hair, with Ollie sporting the half-gray version. Same mustache which always looked like it needed trimming. Same tall, sturdy physique that could easily accumulate layers of fat if it ever stopped moving. (Neither saw the inside of a gym; hauling furniture was more than enough.)

It was as though Gordon had inherited absolutely none of his mother's features. But most importantly, as his father was keen to point out, they were men who flat-out ignored pain.

Bad back? Bad knees? Bad headache? No one gave a fuck. Furniture came in, furniture went out. The work never stopped.

So suck it up.

Other warehouses used equipment to lessen the burden of moving furniture, but not at Lake Furnishings. Ollie ran the show here, and he always thought it was quicker to just pick up and go. The way he'd been doing it his whole life. A hand truck was the only thing you'd find to ease the pain of transport (and it was practically an antique).

Man invented the wheel, and Ollie conceded its usefulness. Man also invented the hydraulic fork lift, but Ollie waved it off. The wheel was enough.

It was agreed that Mike and Tom would follow them to the White residence, help unload the shipment, and then everyone could go home for the day. The idea of getting a jump on happy hour lit up Mike's face. If it meant he had to endure angry, incomprehensible ramblings from the resident cunt, Carol White, so be it.

Ollie and Gordon climbed into the truck's cab with Ollie on the driver's side. He cranked the engine. Gordon looked out the window at the snow gathering on the roof. It seemed as though snow never came without a purpose, like it fell with the goal of smothering everything. People took to the ground with shovels every day, but it didn't matter. The snow would come again, and maybe one day, it would win.

Ollie shifted gears, and the truck rolled back, the *beep-beep-beep* sound alerting pedestrians that a shitload of steel was coming their way, even though there was no one in sight. Gordon watched his father drive, his eyes trained on the side-view mirror, his right hand on the wheel. Ollie's face was shiny and pale, his breathing shallow. Gordon had seen him like this before. Ollie pushed himself every day, and when you get to his age, it takes longer to recover.

Suck it up. Don't feed energy into it. Ignore it.

The truck was moving forward now, pulling out of the lot, its wipers snapping back and forth. Tom's pick-up followed. They passed the chain link fence into the field of gravel that led to the road.

Ollie wiped sweat from his face and rolled down the window a notch.

"You okay?" Gordon asked.

"Just wanna get this load off our backs."

***

The truck rumbled through sparse traffic, its headlights bouncing off a white haze.

"You gonna take that girl out again?" asked Ollie.

"Which one?" said Gordon.

"Oh, that's right. I forgot my son's a swingin' bachelor. I'll be more specific. The one you met at the thing downtown."

"I called her," said Gordon with a laugh.

"And?"

"She hasn't called back."

"So call her again."

"Why?"

"Maybe she didn't get the message."

"Nah. She's done with me. Should've let it go days ago. We were dead on arrival."

Ollie glanced at his son, sensing disappointment. "Know what you should do? Hit a bar with Tom. Pitcher and some wings'll make you forget about her."

"I've already forgotten about her."

"Knock a few back anyway."

"Just in case?"

"Just in case."

The two lanes narrowed into one. A blinking arrow was pushing all the vehicles to the right. There wasn't an accident, nor could Gordon see any signs of construction. It was as though the city just felt like having the lanes merge at that point.

"Asshole," said Ollie.

There was a black Mini-Coop right in front of them, moving too slow for Ollie's taste. A burst of the truck's horn sounded, but the car kept creeping along.

"Jerk-off's never seen snow before," Ollie said, this time wiping sweat from his upper lip. He exhaled, exasperated.

The mysterious merge ended after a mile or so, then widened back into two lanes. Gordon felt the rev of the engine as Ollie proceeded to navigate around the asshole in the Mini-Coop. As they passed it, Gordon could see down into the car.

"It's a woman," said Gordon.

"'Course it is," said Ollie.

The woman had her hair pinned back. Her red, gloved hands clutched the wheel. She was alone, but chatting away, a smile on her face. Cell phone user in her own world.

As they overtook her, Ollie punched the horn again.

She glanced up to Gordon. He stared back through the frosted glass. She was driving carefully and didn't deserve the dual honking, but in his father's eyes, cautious driving wasn't going to get them to Carol White's house on time. Still, the woman's smile was now gone, and that was a shame.

Ollie cut the wheel hard.

When you're overtaking someone to make a point, there's no sense doing it with subtly or the point is lost. You have to appear in front of them like a ghost materializing. You want their heartbeat to quicken. You want them to think about the reason you're being so intrusive into their space.

The truck cut into the right lane, only allowing a few feet of clearance for the Mini-Coop.

"Bitch," Ollie said, as he leaned purposefully with the turn.

The truck didn't cooperate.

The "fuck you" maneuver backfired horribly as the truck's tires skid. Ollie jerked the wheel to compensate, but it was too late. An ear-ripping *screeeech* served as the truck's scream as the whole thing tilted...

Gordon reached for something, anything, as the view outside the window rotated. Ollie's body, with no seatbelt holding it, fell onto Gordon as the truck landed on its side. The crashing of furniture compounded the array of violent noise.

Then it stopped.

The thought that Carol White was going to be pissed actually went through Gordon's head before his mind tried to get a handle on what the fuck happened. He heard a groan from his father next to his ear, as the windshield wipers dutifully continued wiping. Snow fell through the driver-side window.

Was he hurt? Were either of them hurt?

Gordon felt pain, but it wasn't severe. He adjusted his body, moving his shoulder so it wouldn't press so hard against the door. He was on his side now, the whole truck was, like they were going off to sleep for the night.

"Dad..."

Ollie didn't answer, his weight pressing against Gordon.

"Shit... Dad!"

The door above them opened. Mike peered down.

"Holy shit…" said Mike.

"He's not moving," said Gordon.

Mike shifted his view to the outside. "Ollie's hurt!" Gordon could hear Tom shout something back. Mike nodded, then, "You okay?"

"Call 911."

"Tom's on it."

Seconds later, Mike and Tom were leaning into the cab, pulling Ollie free.

They set him down on the snow as Gordon climbed out; his shoulder was sore, but he was otherwise fine. He hopped into the snow and ran to the spot where Mike and Tom were bent over his unconscious father, talking to him, trying to get a response.

"You know CPR?" asked Tom.

"No," said Gordon. He knelt by his father, taking his hand.

Tom noticed the woman in the Mini-Coop standing by the freeway thirty yards away. She was staring at them, chatting on her cell. He screamed to her, waving his arms. "Hey! You know CPR?!" The woman shook her head.

"He's still breathing," said Gordon.

"He don't look hurt," said Mike. "I don't see no blood."

Ollie's face was pale. His chest rose and sank in increments so slight, they were almost unperceivable.

"His heart?" asked Mike.

"Maybe," Gordon said, then to Ollie, "Hang in there, Dad. Help's comin'."

He wiped snow from his father's face as a gust of wind pushed against his back, nudging him forward. He adjusted his body to shelter Ollie. Mike and Tom were speaking behind him, but Gordon didn't hear a word.

The snow felt so cold, colder than it had ever felt in his life. He couldn't ignore it anymore. He couldn't shut it out. In that moment, it was as though he felt its sting for the first time.

"Hang in there…"

Looking down at his father, Gordon felt something else. Waiting for the ambulance to arrive, he was overtaken by an unfamiliar, disorienting sense that pushed him more off balance than the fierce wind.

Holding his father's hand, the feeling ran through Gordon, pure and overwhelming.

Watching his father die, Gordon felt utterly and completely lost.

Chapter 9

Now

THE SHOUTING COULD be heard from outside.

Parked on the street in front of the Pacific Palisades house, Gordon locked the rental car and looked around to see if any neighbors were reacting to the very audible argument. He saw no one and headed up the lawn. Shawn's voice was the loudest, though Gordon couldn't make out what was being said until he opened the door.

"I'm late. Do you fucking understand that?" said Shawn, pacing with keys in hand.

Shawn was in his mid-twenties. He moved with an awkward gait and had slender eyes that made him look Asian at a glance.

Cedric was on the couch watching SportsCenter and only raising his voice when he felt like mocking Shawn's outrage.

Gordon stood by the door, curious to what the commotion was about. They didn't acknowledge his presence.

"Move— *your*—fucking— *car*," said Shawn.

"We had an agreement," said Cedric.

"Stop fucking around!"

"We had an agreement."

Shawn was shaking with anger. "Fine. *Okay?* But I'm late."

"Then go."

"I can't go, asshole, 'cause your piece of shit is pressed against my bumper."

Shawn finally noticed Gordon. A moment passed as he wondered if he should bother to put a spin on the shouting match. Gordon was the new roommate after all, so this wasn't something he needed to be privy to. But then again... fuck it. Welcome to the fucking family! He decided to drag Gordon into the spat.

"You think it's fair to block someone's car from leaving? I came home to change for a job interview, and while I was inside, Cedric pulled in behind me. Now I'm stuck."

Gordon didn't want to get involved. "You're stuck?"

"His fucking bumper is touching mine. I can't back out. And I'm fucking late!"

"See…" said Cedric, finally turning his attention away from the television. He directed his words to Gordon without looking at Shawn. "What Shawny here forgets is, it's my driveway. *My* driveway."

The narrow driveway was able to fit just one car.

"You own it?" asked Shawn.

"We came to an agreement when I moved in," said Cedric, still addressing Gordon. "If *he* got the bigger room, *I* got the driveway. If *I* got the driveway, *he* couldn't park in it."

"I said, I was sorry."

Cedric's head snapped in the direction of Shawn. "And what'd I say?"

"I said I was—"

"And what'd *I* say? I said, no more, didn't I?"

Cedric went back to watching NBA highlights, once again calm. Detached. Shawn took a deep breath and tried one last time.

"Cedric. I'm asking you again. Please move your car."

No reply.

Gordon watched in silence, unsure of what to expect. He didn't know either of these guys. A tense moment passed as Shawn stared at Cedric. Then Shawn turned and stormed out, brushing by Gordon.

The door slammed.

Within moments, an engine revved to life.

Gordon went outside to see what his new roommate was up to. He was greeted by an arcing spray of dirt as Shawn's Celica tore into a line of ferns, the only route to escape the driveway without ramming through the garage door.

Gordon caught a glimpse of Shawn's enraged face through the windshield, his mouth locked open, letting out a yell which was impossible to hear over the engine. Tires ripped through ferns, cut across the lawn, then finally touched pavement as the Celica tore down the street.

The neighborhood, which seemed downright abandoned only a few minutes earlier, was now filled with people stepping from their homes to investigate the asshole destroying their suburban peace.

They looked to Gordon, trying to elicit shame as if he had something to do with it, but Gordon didn't comply. His mind was elsewhere...

The tension between Shawn and Cedric was uncomfortable, and—as much as he hoped the driveway incident was an isolated event—there were too many signs to suggest otherwise. And now he was living with them.

Where did he fit in?

Maybe he should take a side. Maybe he should get in the mix of things if such an argument should happen again. This seemed right, and it pointed to something that had been bothering Gordon all morning...

Throughout his first meetings with all his new roommates, he'd been reserved.

He'd listened and complied to every request made of him. But it wasn't enough. He had to get *involved*. The experiment would only be valid if he engaged in total immersion in the three lives.

Wasn't that the point? Didn't he want to explore the separate personas?

To do that, he needed to embrace all of them. He couldn't be Gordon Lake from Chicago, ex-furniture worker nice guy just looking for a place to stay. He had to amplify aspects of himself.

He had to be three different people.

He had to act different in each life, feel different, *be* different. He chose his new roommates for their contrasting personalities, and from this, he needed to construct contrasting lives for himself.

Gordon brushed soil off his pants and headed inside.

Chapter 10

"KICK-ASS RIB EYE, huh?" said Dean.

"A perfect pink," said Gordon.

They were in the middle of mounting two dry-erase boards in Gordon's bedroom. Dean had insisted on providing him with the necessary tools for improvement. He even gave Gordon something he called a goal pad, but it was just a spiral notebook, the kind you could find in any drugstore.

"My girl take care of you?" asked Dean.

My girl. A phrase of possession. It made Gordon sick.

"Yeah, she's great."

"We're getting married, y'know. She tell you that?"

"Mentioned it."

"We're going to make a dynamic team. I'm molding her into something great."

Molding her.

After they finished hanging the boards, Dean offered to help prioritize Gordon's personal objectives, but to this, Gordon declined. He wanted a coach, not a therapist.

When Dean returned to work that evening, Gordon took a peek at the weekly goal board that hung in the kitchen. He wanted to get an idea of what to jot down on his own "tools for improvement."

Glancing over Dean's writing, something caught his attention.

He'd seen initials in a few spots on the board that didn't make sense at first— *N.H.* Now it was clear.

They stood for Naomi Hill: the fiancée, the love of Dean's life, the woman he was molding. Dean's matter-of-fact attitude toward her was reflected in the listings. Everywhere her initials appeared, the accompanying notes came across as amazingly impersonal:

Set up N.H. account.

N.H. miscommunication discussion.

N.H. trip logistics.

N.H. relocation.

The formal choice of words made Naomi sound like government legislation, not a woman you were planning to marry.

Gordon wondered what she thought of the reminders. Gordon didn't care for them. He admired the sweeping organization Dean adhered to, but this was too much. The way Dean talked about her was the only apparent flaw he had, but he was a results-oriented guy. Maybe he couldn't turn it off.

Gordon stared at Naomi's initials.

Sooner or later, he'd see her again, and that would answer a lot of questions. He was hoping the inevitable meeting would drown the infatuation he still felt. Because to him, she was more than a listing on a board.

Chapter 11

THE 6 ᵀᴴ ANNUAL DRIPPING Head Acid Art Exhibit showcased eclectic pieces from local artists. The crowd was mostly young and well on its way to being inebriated thanks to an open bar that greeted guests once they brushed aside four shades of garbage bags that were cut to serve as curtains.

A slide projector blasted photographs on the wall in quick succession: An auto accident. The White House.

A flaccid penis. The Face on Mars.

A stillborn fetus. A supernova.

Gordon figured observers were supposed to draw correlations, so he tried, but the images overwhelmed him, so he gave up.

He asked the bartender which artist was responsible. The girl slid him a rum and Coke and said she wasn't told.

"It's like a mental stimulant," she said with a shrug.

Gordon shrugged back, then made his way into the warehouse, passing a DJ at a dual turntable spinning a mix of trance, just loud enough to elevate the pulse but not interfere with the proper absorption of art.

People were clustered throughout, laughing and drinking. Ash's exhibit was on the roof, but Gordon took his time getting there. He'd never been in a setting like this. School field trips had exposed him to sterile museums with their paintings and statues and pottery. But this was different. This was *alive*. (Not coincidentally, this realization coincided with the first rush of Captain Morgan.)

The lighting was dim with tiny bulbs positioned to illuminate the pieces.

A woman in an orange jumpsuit stood next to a bathtub filled with gravel. She handed Gordon a pair of yellow dishwashing gloves and instructed him to slide his hands in. She held his drink as he put on the gloves and thrust his hands into the gravel.

"Deeper," she said.

He wiggled his hands downward. The gravel was up to his elbows. He suddenly felt a patch of fur, as though he was touching a dead animal. The woman saw his reaction and nodded as if he was now in on the truth.

When he removed his hands and returned the gloves, she put her lips close to his ear and whispered, "Progress." She made the word sound so dirty, he could feel the stirrings of an erection.

Gordon took his drink back and eased away. Another guest stepped up and was handed the gloves. Gordon could see the woman mouth the word *deeper*.

***

Ash's cemetery occupied half the roof.

The altered tombstones Gordon first saw stacked in the loft were spread out, forming no distinguishable rows. Visitors were allowed to enter the graveyard via an iron archway that served as the sole entrance. Next to the archway was a basket of roses. Each person was allowed to take a single flower and place it on the grave of their choice. A layer of soil within the perimeter added to the feel of authenticity. Everything adhered to realism except the tombstones themselves which varied wildly:

Day-glo painted, soaked in oil. Covered in diapers, layered with mirrors.

Smeared in Vaseline, built with Lego. Made from glass, plastered with dollars.

Visitors scattered in whatever direction they were pulled.

Rose in hand, Gordon sauntered behind a couple who were whispering. Their lowered exchange brought him back to the day of his father's funeral. Grieving family and friends had spoken at the same subdued level, save for the occasional outburst of tears. The memories were fresh. Just recently, he walked with the same sluggish pace through snow covered grounds to reach the service, the whole morning having felt as though it transpired in slow motion. It was something he never wanted to think about again.

Gordon brought his mind back to the present.

He lowered himself onto one knee and placed the rose in front of a smooth, coral white tombstone. He heard someone approach from behind.

"You got the flyer," said Ash, her voice quiet, but excited.

He stood, and they hugged.

"I had no idea you were gonna do this much," said Gordon.

"Yeah?"

"Yeah. I love it."

"You're a sweetheart," she said, kissing him on the cheek.

Ash wrapped her arm around his and guided him out the cemetery.

They leaned against the railing on the edge of the roof, the lights of downtown LA glimmering behind them. Ash took Gordon's drink and finished it in one swig.

"You mingle with the crowd?" asked Gordon.

"Not at all."

"Why not?"

"Attention should go to the *art*, not the artist. Anyone who says otherwise is a spotlight-whore."

"Then why be here at all?"

"Curiosity."

"For?"

"People's response to my work."

"Should it matter?"

Ash squinted, thinking about it. "Guess not. But I'm human. Besides, people steal, so consider me security."

Gordon nodded as he watched a heavyset woman place a flower in front of the tombstone covered in Vaseline.

"You get a response from the other artists yet?" he asked.

Ash grimaced at the notion. "Fuck 'em. They've been working against me since day one. They didn't want my exhibit on the roof. Thought it would draw the crowd away."

"How?"

"They think LA people *love* the roof. They bring booze up, hang out, talk on the phone, network, fuck in the corners, who the fuck knows...?"

"But you got it up here."

"I was a stubborn bitch."

Leaning in the shadows, Ash and Gordon watched people wind their way through the cemetery. As visitors exited, some paused, searching for the artist to compliment or question, but Ash stayed back. She wasn't here to shake hands.

"Which tombstone do you think will get the most flowers?" asked Gordon.

"So far, the one with the mirrors is the clear leader."

"Any theories as to why?"

Ash shrugged. "I'd say they look at it, see their reflection… makes 'em think about dying. Reminds 'em their little cocktail party ain't gonna last forever."

***

Three hours later, Ash and Gordon were back at the loft, tipsy from the complimentary drinks.

Ash poured two bowls of Frosted Flakes. They ate in the kitchen standing up.

Gordon let his eyes gaze over her. There was a definite attraction, but it was different from what he felt for Naomi. There was no magic here, no poems to be written, no melody to be composed, no mystical force weaving blissful joy through his soul.

No… this was as basic as it got. Good, old fashioned, instinct-driven, sexual urges. He watched Ash munch on cereal, milk on the corner of her lips.

He didn't get any similar vibes from her, but then again, he didn't get any "stay away" signals either. He admired her lack of inhibitions and fuck it attitude. It was a quality he wanted for himself.

Just as life in Dean's world offered him a chance to embrace self-discipline, life in Ash's world presented an opportunity to explore just the opposite.

This was a place to cast rules aside.

Fueled by alcohol and an active libido, Gordon's thoughts manifested into words.

"I want to be like you," he said.

Fairly direct, but it was too late to take the words back.

Ash was amused. "No. You don't. Trust me."

"What I mean is…" said Gordon as he set the empty bowl in the sink, "I don't want to be restrained."

"Then don't be."

"It's not that easy."

"Sure it is."

"Teach me then."

"Teach you?"

"Yeah."

She wondered if he was serious.

"I'm not a cult," said Ash.

"Give it a try."

"No thanks."

"Be a cult of one," said Gordon. "The Secret Society of Ash. I'll pay annual dues."

"All I want outta you is the rent. Let's see if you can handle that first."

"You know what I'm sayin' though?"

"No…"

"I feel trapped."

"No more late-night cereal for you. I think you got a sugar rush."

"It ain't the sugar."

Ash yawned, sized him up, and despite her intoxication (or perhaps because of it), she humored him. "The thing of it is… this society doesn't…" She laughed. "I can't believe I called it a society. Lemme start over…" She took a breath. "The thing of it *is*… people deny their urges. They deny their urges, all their urges, for many reasons… follow me?"

Gordon nodded.

"Be it religion, government, peer pressure, spousal expectations, health issues, moral issues, what their horoscope says that day… they deny. Deny, deny, deny."

"So the choice—"

"The choice…" Ash steadied herself against the counter. "The choice you make *is*…" Her tone had become serious. "You don't deny."

Though the declaration was heartfelt, he could see it was a philosophy she struggled to follow herself. But she wanted to so much, the tension bled through her voice, as if she was instructing herself and not him.

"Don't deny," she continued. "Anything. Hungry? Eat. Horny? Fuck. Sad? Cry. Tired? Sleep. Angry? Lash out!"

"That's anarchy."

"So?"

"So if everyone did it, it'd be chaos."

"Fuck everyone. I thought we were talking about *you*."

"We are."

"Then don't worry about the rest of the world. All you control is you," Ash said, poking him with her finger.

"So I shouldn't deny."

Ash clenched her fist. "Repression suffocates the soul. It squeezes and squeezes and squeezes... until..." She opened her fist, revealing an empty palm. "The will to fight is gone. Until you submit. Until all you care about is paying your bills on time and avoiding pain." She watched him closely, her balance unsteady. "That's basically it. Think you can handle that?"

Her words sounded more like a challenge than a question.

"I think so," he said.

"Well then..." She stepped close. He could feel her warm breath against his skin. "Welcome to the cult."

91

I thought about calling home, but didn't. I'm not sure I want to.

Things remind me of home all the time, but I don't want to think about it. It's behind me now. I want to put it out of my mind. My whole life has been masked. I've been trying to live up to people's expectations of me. I'm through with that shit. My new roommates are the tools to shake me free.

Dean brings me discipline, and I will embrace it.

Ash brings me freedom, and I will embrace it.

Shawn and Cedric... now those two are a fucking trip. At first I thought I made a mistake with them. I wasn't sure what I was going to be in that life. What part of me would I explore? Those two fucking hate each other! That house is a war zone. But fine.

Shawn and Cedric bring me hate, and I will embrace it.

But I won't embrace it by hating. I will be the peacemaker. For once, I won't do nothing when other people fight. I will fix it. I'm not sure why there's so much tension. They're uncomfortable around me. Like they regret bringing me in. Cedric snapped at me for not removing the lint from the dryer's filter. He took the lint and threw it on the ground. It's still there. No one will pick it up. Three men refusing to pick up lint. But I will. Next time I'm there. Petty shit, but it matters.

Ash wants me to help pack up the tombstones and bring them back to the loft. I asked if she thought the show was a success. She said she didn't know. She seems bitter. I'm not sure if she's pissed at the other artists. She thinks they're out to get her.

Dean says he likes my progress. I'm not sure what he means, but he's excited. The guy never fucking stops. I feel like his little brother sometimes. He makes me face

reality. He says you can't taste life if you cover it with fantasy.
    I want to taste life.

Chapter 12

THE TIP OF THE PEN hovered above the page.

Gordon was unsure if he had anything to add to the day's entry.

No. That was enough for now.

He capped the pen and closed the journal.

Room 116 at the Starlight Inn was the neutral place, the spot for Gordon to collect his thoughts and gauge his progress. He was only a few days in, but things were already starting to take shape.

The maid hadn't visited for a while, nor would she. Gordon kept the "Do Not Disturb" sign permanently attached to the outside and made sure the elderly manager knew of his insistence to not be bothered. At first, the man was hesitant to grant this, but once Gordon fanned out the three month stay in cash, his mood changed considerably.

Gordon assuaged the man further by saying he was seeking isolation to study for an important medical exam. The manager had mumbled something about education being the backbone of something or another as he counted the money.

Gordon stashed the journal in the bottom drawer of the night table. Reaching across the mattress, he picked up the art exhibit flyer Ash had left for him. Tearing off a piece of Scotch tape, he put the flyer on display.

Each of the three residences had been designated a wall.

Collages were growing on them. Only now, the distinct collages consisted of images that would compliment his journal entries.

Ash's wall showcased the flyer, a picture of the loft, and the words *Don't Deny* written at the top, each letter taking up an entire piece of notebook paper. It was the philosophy that was the center piece of his life with her, so Gordon thought it should serve as its headline.

Shawn and Cedric's wall displayed a photo of the house, a fern branch from one of the plants Shawn had flattened when he ripped his car across the lawn, and the word *Peacemaker* at the top, written in the same fashion as Ash's headline.

Dean's section consisted of a napkin from Gilroy's Chophouse, an apartment photo, and the word *Achieve*. Gordon wanted to add a picture of Naomi, but didn't have one yet. He could snap one of her under some lame pretense or perhaps from a distance, like a stalker squatting behind a bush. Or he could steal one from Dean's room, but Dean only displayed a single photo of Naomi—a full-figured, glossy image of her in shorts and a tank top, smiling on the Santa Monica Pier, framed and hung next to a "Pure Mountain Pacific Employee of the Quarter" certificate, which was bigger and in a nicer frame.

Gordon stood in the center of the room, gazing at the collages.

He wanted his time spent in room 116 to be productive and limited. He wouldn't sleep here, wouldn't use its bathroom, wouldn't watch TV, wouldn't masturbate, wouldn't take a nap. He was here to document and reflect. That's all.

Already, it was time to go.

Chapter 13

Then

KNEELING IN FRONT of the casket at St. Matthew's Funeral Home with his hands clasped and eyes closed, Gordon didn't know what to say to God.

He pressed on with a few requests anyway, as if the Almighty might lose interest if he didn't come up with something fast. So he asked God to take care of his father, to let him be at peace, to grant him entrance into Heaven to live for all eternity by His side. Of course, he assumed entry into Paradise wasn't an issue given his father's sometimes shaky, but otherwise solid track record of being a good human being, but he asked nonetheless.

To assume anything when it comes to God would be foolish.

Gordon opened his eyes and looked at his father's suited body tucked neatly into the coffin. He felt like he should say more. But what?

He kept his hands clasped, as if to let God know the line was still open and that he wasn't through yet. Gazing at his dad's face, something came to him. Gordon closed his eyes again and thanked God for allowing him to be part of his father's life. It was a good run, but all things must come to an end. So thank you.

Amen. Line closed.

Gordon opened his eyes and, placing a hand on the wooden railing, climbed to his feet. He adjusted his jacket and stepped away from the casket, allowing room for another mourner to take his place, to open their own line.

The crowd was modest. He didn't expect too many people. It wasn't like the Mayor died. It was only his dad. Oliver Henry Lake. His viewing attracted only a small group of family and friends. He was someone who had a fatal heart attack. Happens every day.

He saw Aunt Rena standing near the wall. She was holding up remarkably well. That morning, she announced to a kitchen full of grieving relatives that she planned to swallow a Valium before the viewing, otherwise she'd make a blubbering fool of herself. She told Gordon most of the women in attendance will take some sort of sedative in order to maintain a modicum of composure.

Gordon found it funny that he wasn't offered any drugs to alleviate the grief, that he was expected to see his father's corpse without any medication to steady his nerves. He was supposed to be tough, but that was a joke. Gordon had never felt less tough than in the funeral parlor at that moment, watching Aunt Rena dot her face with a tissue. She patted him on the arm, but didn't say a word. The valium was doing its job, but she still couldn't talk about her dead brother.

Gordon made his way to the back of the room, glancing at faces. Some familiar, some not. This was the first viewing he could remember attending. He was told he saw his grandfather's body, but he was only three at the time.

Gordon leaned against the back wall, unsure of what to do next.

This was the time of day he unloaded the new shipments. It was always boring work, but for the first time, he craved it. Boring, unemotional work. With his father at the other side of a white leather couch, crooning some Sinatra standard, as they lifted it off the truck. The next thing Gordon was scheduled to help carry was his father's casket. The man spent thirty-nine years of his time on Earth hauling furniture, and now his journey to the grave would be inside something everyone else would have to burden.

Gordon had a fleeting, morbid thought that they should load the casket onto the furniture truck, then back it up to the grave on the day of the funeral, the piercing *beep-beep-beep* of the truck alerting mourners to the arrival of Oliver Lake. Gordon would hop out of the cab, along with Mike and Tom, and together they'd unload the coffin, sleeves rolled up, fresh morning sweat on their arm pits, Mike's piece of shit radio balanced next to the ramp, playing *My Way*. His father wouldn't mind. He had a sense of humor. He—

"Hey, Gordon." A whisper.

Gordon looked up from the carpet and saw Tom and his wife, Maria.

"How ya doin'?" asked Tom.

Gordon shrugged. He didn't feel like talking.

"We miss him so much," said Maria.

"Me too," said Gordon.

"Gonna be by the house later?" asked Tom.

There was a gathering scheduled after the viewing. Not exactly the official wake, but close to it. A pre-wake, if there is such a thing.

"I'll be there," said Gordon.

Tom touched him on the shoulder and led his wife away. Tom seemed different to Gordon, like he didn't know him anymore, like they just met, like Gordon just conferred with a stranger.

Is it possible to have worked with Tom for eight years and not know him? All those deliveries, all those backyard barbeques. The Super Bowl Sundays, the bowling nights, the happy hours. And Gordon suddenly felt like he didn't know Tom at all.

Ever since the doctor told them at the hospital that they had done everything to save his father, but he had passed away... ever since then... Gordon felt like he knew *no one*.

That feeling in the snow. Of being lost. It had stuck with him. It had blossomed. He felt blank, as if the person he'd been his whole life had died with his father. He felt like an impostor, someone who looked the same, but had been replaced on the inside.

Replaced with *what*? He didn't know. Everything felt new.

Despite the available chairs, Gordon sat on the floor. He slid a finger into his right leather loafer. It was too tight and itched his ankle.

He could see Mike in front, taking his place in front of the casket. Mike's two little boys, Michael Jr. and Keith, plopped down next to him. Together, the three prayed.

Gordon watched from the back, wondering what Mike was saying to God.

Chapter 14

TOM WANTED GORDON to take some time off. There was no sense in rushing back to work. Grieve in peace, he said. Grieve in privacy.

But Gordon went back the following week. He thought he'd feel closer to his dad at the warehouse where they shared endless days together. If his father's presence was anywhere to be found, anywhere to be felt, it would be there. Besides, Mike and Tom needed him (whether they realized it or not).

So Gordon went back to work.

But he was wrong. He didn't know it for the first few days, but the realization finally came to him as he was looking over a clipboard of paperwork, standing in the darkest corner of the warehouse, where a stack of crates blocked light from a window.

His father wasn't there at all.

There was no presence. No feeling of being watched over. No feeling that his dad's spirit was leaning against the door, nodding approvingly at business rolling along. Not even a hint that he was hanging around in some protective, fatherly, angelic, supernatural form.

Gordon stood like a statue and admitted it to himself. The place felt empty because it *was* empty.

His father was gone.

Mike, Tom, and Gordon had discussed hiring extra help to lighten the load. To make matters worse, with Ollie dead, it wasn't clear who was in charge. There was no line of power to speak of. Gordon was the Prince in a way, but he was also the youngest. So it had always been Ollie and everyone else. Only four days had passed since the funeral, but it was clear someone had to step up to the plate and take charge, and Gordon didn't want to be the one. He was fine doing what he was doing.

"Gordon?"

Tom's voice. He was standing in the doorway, but Gordon didn't bother to face him.

"Find that lounger?" asked Tom.

"Still looking." Gordon flipped through the pages of the clipboard.

"Maybe it never arrived."

"Thought I heard Dad mention it. Before. Maybe it's…"

Gordon looked at the stack of crates like he was thinking about the possible location of the lounger. But he didn't give a shit. Instead, his eyes were drawn to the metal frame of the blocked window. He thought about the light on the other side that wasn't allowed to come in.

"Look…" Tom stepped forward. "It's okay if you don't have your shit together. It ain't gonna be the same for a while."

"It's never gonna be the same."

"No, but… what you're doin'…" Tom glanced to where Gordon was staring, but didn't register the blocked window, figuring Gordon was just looking off into space. "What you're doin' is good."

"Good?"

"Being here. Working. Your dad didn't stop for nothin'. Didn't take a sick day in all the years I knew him. The time I ate the bad shrimp, you remember that? The time I puked my guts out all night? Crawled my ass into work the next day feelin' like dog shit run over, 'cause I knew Ollie would'a done the same. Shit, anytime I had a cold, he looked at me like I was a pussy."

This last remark was intended to make Gordon smile. It didn't work.

"Look," said Tom, "All I'm sayin' is, it's noble that you're here. You feel like shit, but *you're here*. The old man left us for a better place, but we're all here. We're workin'. That's how we honor the man. We keep the train movin'."

"Yeah?"

"Yeah."

An exchange of yeahs. An affirmation between two men. They were on the same page, and nothing more needed to be said.

"Fuck the lounger," said Tom, his tone lighter now. "I'll call the factory after lunch."

"I think it's here," said Gordon, this time actually checking the labels on the crates.

"It ain't here."

"Maybe it's over with the—"

"Furniture intuition, Gordy. It ain't here. After lunch, I'll call." Tom headed out, then without looking back, added, "Keep the train movin'."

It looked like Tom was the one stepping up to the plate. He was taking control. He strolled in, gave his morale speech, followed it with a work plan of sorts, then a battle cry (however lame), then strolled out. Not bad, Tom, not bad.

***

Weeks went by like this.

Identical blocks of days passing by like widgets on an assembly line. No progress was made with the company. No growth. In fact, they lost a number of customers when news of the death circulated.

And the snow didn't let up. It seemed to sense their weakness and was moving in for the kill. The weather channel delighted in reporting the record snowfall. Every day, the hosts of the inane morning shows joked about the cold, each remark punctuated with a fake laugh.

Gordon accepted sole responsibility for keeping the pavement in front of the warehouse clear. He shoveled every morning, first thing. His muscles ached, but he liked that aspect of the job. The pain was good. The soreness gave him something to think about.

It took some time, but Tom and Mike fell back into their routine. Their laughter returned. A framed picture of Ollie from a picnic three years ago hung in the office. He was fast becoming history. Things were getting back to normal for Tom and Mike.

Not for Gordon.

He knew less and less about the world with each passing moment.

***

At the end of the day, Gordon stepped from the warehouse, zipped up his jacket, and pulled down his Bulls cap. The sky was darkening quicker than usual.

"Happy time," said Mike, locking the door behind him. Tom had left early, a new perk ever since he considered himself in charge. "New bartender's got tits like you wouldn't believe. Real too. You ask for ice, she'll bend over to scoop it, and you can get a view that'll give you a stiffy."

"Yeah?" said Gordon, hardly listening.

"Sometimes I ask for a glass of ice, just to see her tits."

"What d'you do with the ice?"

"Nothin'. I let it melt, then ask for more."

"She gives you more?"

"What's she gonna do? Refuse me ice?"

"She know you look at her?"

"They *all* know. They love the attention."

"Yeah?"

"Fuck yeah. Let's go."

"I'm takin' the train."

"To Drake's?"

"To home."

"Drake's *is* home. C'mon…"

"I'm not up for it tonight."

"My ass."

"Serious."

Mike studied him. "You sick?"

"No. Just—"

"It's happy time, Gordy, and you don't look happy. Which means you gotta *get* happy. Which is why they invented happy time."

Mike never called it happy hour. To him, it was always happy time, as if the thought of limiting it to an hour was not only absurd, but insulting.

"I'm burnt," said Gordon. "Next time." He started walking.

Mike shouted a stream of insults at him, all designed to pressure him back.

Gordon let the wind fill his ears and drown out Mike's voice.

Chapter 15

Now

THE RAT WAS IN Shawn's bedroom.

He'd been downloading "Piece of My Heart" by a local punk band when he heard a faint, rapid clattering. He ignored the sound at first, hoping he imagined it, but it persisted. He turned and saw a plump rat scurrying across the floor, over a pair of prewashed jeans, and into the closet. Shawn leapt up so fast, his chair flipped in the air as though he were Jerry Lee Lewis launching into a blazing piano solo.

The exterminator was dialed immediately.

Shawn wasn't the type to grapple with a rat one-on-one. He needed professionals and told them he didn't care if they used poison, gas, bullets, or if they coaxed it out with a song and dance. He just wanted the fucking thing gone.

Gordon waited with Shawn on the front porch as the exterminator rummaged about. Shawn had refused to remain inside.

"You believe I gotta pay for something that's essentially the city's problem?" asked Shawn. "There should be a tax-funded extermination unit. We found a dead one in the pool once. Right before I had guests over. I was too embarrassed to say anything. So they swam in ignorance, frolicking in rat fluid."

The exterminator exited the house holding a plastic bag with a lump at its bottom. Shawn jumped to his feet.

"Got it," said the man, enjoying the reaction.

"Is it dead?" asked Shawn.

"Yep."

"You didn't leave any blood stains or anything?"

"Everything's sanitary."

"I'm gonna use Lysol," said Shawn. "Was that the only one?"

"Only one I saw, though it's hard to be one hundred percent sure. These fellas can squeeze through a hole the size of a quarter."

"Well, you're on speed dial…" Shawn squinted to read the man's name tag. "Eric."

"I wouldn't worry about it. This happens from time to time," said Eric. "Rats're cheap pets, so parents buy 'em for their kids… or for a snake to eat."

"No, no," said Shawn, like he was correcting a two year old. "These things *live* around here."

"Maybe…" said Eric, holding up the bag with the lump. "But this fella's bred."

"Bred?" asked Shawn.

"For pet stores."

"Who buys a rat for a pet?" asked Gordon.

"They're as affectionate as dogs. They'll even come to you when you call their name."

"And that's a good thing?" asked Gordon.

"You're not listening," said Shawn. "This house has *wild* rats."

"I don't doubt it. Field rats have been booming around here. In Beverly Hills too. Stroll right into mansions like they own the place." The man lifted the bag. The lump swayed back and forth. "But this fella's bred. White coat, pink eyes, clean."

"Then how'd it get in my room?"

"Kids free 'em, or they escape, then they go lookin' for food and water."

Shawn fell silent, forcing Gordon to wrap up the conversation. He took the invoice, bid the man goodbye, and waved as the Hillside Extermination van drove away.

"*Cedric,*" said Shawn, as if answering a question.

"What?" said Gordon.

"He put the rat in my room. He blames me for the rats in the backyard. He says the seeds I leave for squirrels attracts them. So he buys one and puts it in my room."

"Could be someone's pet."

"It's Cedric."

Gordon had to smooth this over. Every human had the capacity to make peace, to quell conflict, and this was a chance. *His* chance.

Gordon said, "I don't think Cedric—"

"Because you don't know him. I've been living with the cretin for two years. This sort of thing *reeks* of him."

"Then why be roommates?"

Shawn gave a quick rundown on the history.

The house was first rented out a decade ago to two girls. One girl left, another was brought in, then they left and two guys took their place… basically the turnover of roommates had been somewhat high, even for LA standards, and people were often left living with someone they barely knew. When someone gave their thirty day notice, the person who replaced them was often a stranger—a friend of a friend of a friend, someone referred by someone else, or a hastily picked schmo from a roommate service. But this revolving door of occupants was tolerable since the house was magnificent, and everyone was thankful to have a place to live.

So it was then, by coincidence, that two people (actors, of course) moved out simultaneously—one turned over their keys to Shawn, the other to Cedric. Neither man knew each other, and neither man particularly liked each other, but the house was big enough and nice enough for them to endure their differences.

Or so Shawn thought.

Cedric turned about to be a nightmare, or as Shawn put it, "An uncouth bane." He never demonstrated any form of manners and never once cleaned. Anything. It was as though he expected clumps of dirt and layers of crusted food to simply evaporate if given enough time. He was a man who expected the world to come together around him without any effort on his part. He was a man that Shawn held in contempt.

"Why not move?" said Gordon. "If you hate him that much."

"And let him push me out?"

"So what? Why stay if you're miserable?"

"'Cause I moved in first. May have been only a day earlier, but that still makes me first. And I like this place. And you seem cool, right? You and me are two-thirds of this house. The majority. We gonna let him ruin our lives?"

"We?" That was a new wrinkle.

"How long before you find a rat in *your* room?"

"He's cool with me."

"He's a selfish asshole. Let *him* move out. I'm not going anywhere." Shawn shook his head. "… put a rat in my room. Sick fuck. Fuck him. *Fuck him.*"

Shawn seethed and headed in the house. Gordon followed.

Inside, Shawn marched straight to Cedric's bedroom, opened the door and paused, taking in its contents:

Mattress on the floor, stereo, torn condom wrappers, TV, scattered clothes… and a computer.

This last item held Shawn's attention. Gordon stood a few feet behind him.

"Think he has anything on his hard drive?" Shawn asked as he crossed the threshold and planted himself at Cedric's desk.

"Shawn…" said Gordon, entering the room.

Shawn was swift on the keyboard, scanning Cedric's files, email addresses, and the array of website cookies.

"Probably doesn't know they're here," Shawn said of the little digital footprints websites leave behind. "Cars, porn, sports… mind-boggling sophistication."

"This isn't cool," said Gordon.

Shawn was typing fast. Gordon wasn't sure what he was up to, but he wanted to—

A car door shut outside.

Cedric was home.

Gordon evacuated immediately, but Shawn couldn't. He had to return the computer to its found state. Gordon hovered in the hall. It was taking forever.

The front door opened.

Gordon decided to intercept Cedric.

"Hey…" said Gordon as Cedric saw him, a lame attempt at sounding casual.

Cedric nodded, brushing right by Gordon and headed toward his room.

Gordon had to say something. "See the Lakers last night?"

"No defense, no win," said Cedric, now turning into the hall…

… in time to see Shawn in front of his bedroom, trying to make it seem like he was examining a bulb fixture.

Cedric considered Shawn, then went into this room. Shawn sighed and walked away.

"Hey!" said Cedric.

Shawn turned back. Cedric was there. Glaring.

"You been in my room?" asked Cedric.

"No," said Shawn, as if he was just accused of murder.

Cedric shifted his attention to Gordon. "What about you?"

Gordon shook his head. Cedric returned his glare to Shawn.

"Better come clean, yo, while I'm still in a calm mood," said Cedric.

"Why would I go in your room?"

Cedric stared at Shawn, weighing the sincerity in his voice… then returned to his room. The second he was out of sight, Shawn wasted no time leaving the area. Gordon followed him into the kitchen where they collected themselves. Gordon wanted a beer. He went to the fridge as Cedric suddenly entered and said, "Cool thing about my monitor is…"

Gordon could see the color drain from Shawn's face.

"It turns itself off when no one's using it. Power saving feature. Clicks off after thirty minutes. Interesting thing about *that* is… I've been gone six fuckin' hours." Cedric stepped deeper into the kitchen. "Why were you in my room, Shawny?"

Shawn went on the offensive. "Why'd you put a rat in *my* room?"

"A rat?"

"From a pet store."

"You think I put a rat in your room?"

"The exterminator found it."

"Bitch, I wouldn't step one foot in your room. I'd slip in semen."

Shawn's eyes shot to Gordon for just an instant, but Cedric saw it.

"You didn't tell him?" asked Cedric.

"Whatever," said Shawn.

"Man, that's like… failure to disclose or something."

Shawn turned to Gordon, "I'm gay." Then back to Cedric. "Happy now?"

"Gordon, you care that you're living with a man who sucks dick?"

Shawn took a step toward Cedric. A sign of aggression. In a flash, Cedric closed the rest of the distance, getting in Shawn's face.

"Make a move," said Cedric.

Shawn stood his ground. Gordon stepped in to separate them. Cedric let himself be pushed back by Gordon.

"Cock suckin' bitch," said Cedric.

Shawn turned away and left.

"I catch that bitch in my room again, I'll kill him," said Cedric. "You tell him that."

The front door slammed.

Cedric snorted laughter and left Gordon alone in the kitchen.

Gordon's initial goal was to be the peacemaker, but the root of the animosity was deeper than he had suspected. Shawn was right about one thing: Cedric did seem to genuinely hate him.

Gordon retrieved a beer from the fridge. As the first gulp went down, he thought about how close they were to ripping each others' throats out.

He had to make things right. He had to make a difference.

But he was off to a shitty start.

Chapter 16

GORDON HAD AGREED to meet Ash at the warehouse to help her pack up the exhibit.

When he arrived, he saw her car parked outside. The moment he entered, an unsettling feeling came over him. A space that was so alive and rippling with energy when he first set foot in it was now lifeless, quiet, and dark. Letting his eyes adjust, he was disappointed to see that the other displays were already gone. He looked for the bathtub of gravel, the one with the dead animal (or something that *felt* like a dead animal) at its bottom, and was let down to discover that it had been removed. He wanted to dig one more time.

Gordon climbed the stairs and stepped onto the roof.

Ash was on her knees, slumped over, face buried in her hands. He couldn't hear her crying, but her back convulsed in a short, rapid rhythm, a sure-fire sign of sobbing. When Gordon looked beyond her, the source of grief was evident.

The cemetery had been destroyed.

The tombstones were piled in a single, messy lump. Broken, shattered, cracked, and torn apart. The fence had been knocked down, the archway snapped in two, the basket shredded, the roses crushed and scattered.

Ash noticed Gordon, but didn't try to pull herself together. To do that would be to mask an emotion, and she was firmly against masking emotions.

"Less work for us, right?" said Ash. "Someone already started taking it down."

"I'm sorry," said Gordon. "This is… we gotta call the police."

"Already did."

"How long you been up here?"

"Not long."

"Any idea who…"

"Plenty of ideas who. But no one I think would actually do it. I haven't pissed anyone off… lately… that I know about." She laughed, wiped away tears.

"Can it be fixed?"

"Nope."

"You sure? Fence doesn't look *too* bad. Basket can be replaced, same with the roses."

It sounded encouraging, but he knew the whole point of the exhibit was the tombstones, and they were decimated beyond repair.

"I'm not sure I'd even want to fix it. Once you give birth to something, it's kinda hard to do it again," said Ash. "There'll be other babies. But this one's dead." The first strains of acceptance crept into her voice. "Fuck it."

Gordon sat next to her.

A light breeze kicked up, drifting a few rose stems. It was then Gordon noticed it.

Lines of paint on the ground. He stood up and walked closer. "What's this?"

Ash strolled over with the languished pace of someone walking through a crash site.

Gordon used his foot to push aside a piece of tombstone, exposing the lines of paint.

Three feet in length and brush-drawn in orange was a single letter: *E*

"The fuck?" said Ash.

"Was it there before?" asked Gordon.

"Not that I noticed."

"Maybe it was put there by whoever did this."

"Like a signature?"

"I guess."

"E?"

Gordon considered the letter for a few moments. "Maybe it was the start of a word or phrase, but they got scared off."

They stood, breeze blowing, eyes on the *E*.

"Eat shit?" ventured Ash.

"Good guess," said Gordon. "Could be a name."

"Ernie? Emanuel? Eddie?"

"Or a gang tag."

"East-coast? El Salvador Playaz?"

"Those real gangs?" asked Gordon.

"Fuck if I know."

The mark was clean, its strokes measured. There were no traces of additional paint that might hint at an additional letter.

"Maybe that was it," said Gordon. "Zorro only leaves a Z."

"Thanks for taking this serious."

"Look at it this way. This could help. Maybe the cops can match it to other cases of vandalism."

"I wouldn't hold my breath." She spit on the mark as the police arrived.

After talking to the cops, Ash and Gordon went back to the loft and got shit-faced.

They didn't discuss the destruction of her exhibit. Ash insisted they didn't. She wanted to keep the energy positive. Gordon asked if that meant they were denying feelings, thereby breaking the golden rule of *Don't Deny* (their golden rule, anyway). She said they weren't, because they left the anger on the roof in Hollywood. At least for that night.

But there were times when Gordon's mind wandered back to the discovery of the *E* painted on the ground. He didn't believe it was a random strike, and for some reason, he didn't believe the situation was over.

Chapter 17

"I NEED TO BE CHECKED into a hospital for exhaustion," said Naomi.

"That's a rich person's illness, and you're not rich," said Gordon.

"You're saying poor people don't get exhausted?"

"Of course they do. But they deal with it."

"No hospital then?"

"No."

"Party pooper."

Naomi was lying under the covers in Dean's bedroom. Gordon sat by her side.

Dean, the guy who should be attending to her, was at work. It was the middle of the day, and Gordon was hungover from drinking with Ash, but this was fine by him; sitting next to Naomi was the perfect tonic.

"What you got is the flu," he said, producing a bag from Rite-Aid, "And it's treatable in this very apartment."

Naomi watched as Gordon took out items, enjoying the attention.

"Tylenol Gel-Tabs. Easy to swallow. Sudafed. Non-drowsy. Tissues. *With* aloe vera and Vitamin E lotion. And this…" Gordon took out a tiny, stuffed, puppy dog toy. "This is Fernando."

"Fernando?"

"He's gonna sit right here…" Gordon placed the puppy next to the bedside lamp. "… and watch over you." He knew it was corny, and the gesture crossed over into boyfriend-territory, but it was only a few bucks, and who wouldn't want a little puppy watching over them when they were sick?

"Hey there, Fernando," said Naomi, petting the toy. She looked to Gordon. "Why don't you have a girlfriend?"

Gordon laughed, but didn't find the question funny. The laughter was a ploy to buy him some time. This seemed like a trick question. He had to be careful. The true answer was— *'Cause Dean is dating the woman I want.* But somehow, Gordon thought that reply would complicate things. He let his laugh peter out. He only had a few seconds now. He had to say something.

"I'll leave Fernando to look after you," said Gordon.

"Why are you single?" she asked.

She wasn't going to let up. "I don't know."

"Waiting for the right girl?"

"I guess," Gordon said, standing up. He headed for the door. He had to get out of there. "Feel better, okay?"

Naomi thanked Gordon for the cold medicine, waved, and clicked on the TV.

Gordon shut the door gently and stood there for a moment. This particular life was about achievement, not destruction. Shaking up Dean and Naomi's relationship would be counterproductive.

Then again, isn't destruction of anything technically an achievement?

Gordon grinned at the thought, then mentally made the adjustment; it's about *positive* achievement. But couldn't some forms of destruction be seen as... he broke the thought, thinking of the bigger point that was coming to mind.

He had to keep his behavior consistent. In all the lives. He had to view the three philosophies as hats he could slip on and off.

Time with Ash was self-indulgent. It was about not denying.

Time in Dean's world was about responsibility and consequences for your actions.

So why the *fuck* was he sitting on a bed flirting with Dean's girlfriend?

A slip up. That's all. A bit of Ash residue.

Hats.

Had to be like hats. Slip 'em on and off.

Then at the end of the experiment, he would know which fit and which didn't. He would know *himself.*

He wondered why everyone didn't pick a time to live multiple lives.

Gordon never went to college. According to his father, Gordon's future was in the family business, and "You learn the business by doing the business."

But college isn't just about picking a vocation, it's about finding out who you are. It is a place to try on hats. A place denied to Gordon. He never got to search for the right hat. He missed the time of his life when confusion is considered normal.

He thought about Naomi. It was sickening that fate would slide her right under his nose at a time when she was no longer available, but that was reality. Gordon could view her as a test. This portion of the experiment was an exercise in self-discipline, and she was there to test him. So it was *good* that the unattainable was in a bed under the same roof.

Gordon retreated to the living room. He sat on the sofa and, for the first time, felt a tinge of hatred for Dean. Ugly, but it was there. Gordon shook off the feeling, tried to think positive.

He was in control here. Control of himself, of his emotions, of his actions. It was a control he didn't want to lose.

62

I think the maids are getting suspicious. Not only did I ban them from entering my room, I don't ask for clean sheets, toilet paper, soap. Nothing. I don't use any of that stuff. I don't sleep here, I don't eat here, I don't shit here. I just write in this journal.

Whatever.

It's weird coming back to the hotel. I've gotten used to being three different people, but here is different. Here, I'm back to being Chicago Gordon, and I don't know who that is. It would be easier to be one of the "new guys" in this space, but that would defeat the purpose. I have to put aside the other lives while I write this.

So on with my daily report—which hasn't been daily by any means, but driving all the way down here is a hassle. So if I've missed a day or two, fuck it. I've written over sixty pages, and that's more than I've written in the last ten years—not counting inventory orders, but that's not really writing, is it?

So where are we? One month in.

Ash can be a moody bitch, but I don't complain. I act like an asshole if I'm feeling worn. A bitch and an asshole! She asks where I go for long stretches of time. I say work, but that doesn't make sense to her since I disappear sometimes in the day, sometimes in the night. She knows I'm full of shit. I'm either at Dean's apartment or Shawn and Cedric's place or here. None of which I can tell Ash.

So I lie. I tell her I'm spending my time editing some video for some company. When she asks for more info, I say I don't want to talk about work.

Shawn and Cedric haven't spoken to each other since the rat blow-up. But I've stuck to my guns. I'm doing what I can to make the place livable for everyone. It's not about me there, it's about them.

The world of Dean is like boot camp. He expects results. Even in lame shit like finding out the best diet for me. It's easy to down a shot of wheat grass in front of him when I know a cheeseburger is waiting for me at Ash's. Dean has been consumed with helping Naomi plan their wedding. It's like he's laying the groundwork for an invasion. Food, transport, movement, sleeping quarters. I half-expect uniforms to be issued to guests, maybe color-coded to tell who's with the groom and who's with the bride.

Chapter 18

THE SMELL OF MOTH balls was overwhelming.

It was like the guy literally crawled out from under a stack of grandma's clothes in the chest stored at the back of the attic.

His name was Serrick. He was short, in his thirties, and wore a black suit jacket adorned with patches. His hair was messy. Not a stylish, self-aware messy but an authentic, I-don't-tend-to-my-hair-that's-why-I-wear-a-hat messy. The hat, a black bowler, was currently in his hand, twirling on a finger.

Serrick stood over Ash and Gordon who were both lying on the mattress in their underwear. It was early morning, not a favorite time for either of them.

Gordon had crawled in next to her since she didn't feel like rising. This wasn't unusual. They cuddled from time to time, without ever having sex or even fooling around. Ash was perfectly comfortable changing clothes in front of Gordon, completely fine with letting him gaze at her naked body, but for some reason, sex hadn't come into the picture. But with Ash, it always seemed like an option. Like the first time could happen at any moment.

When Serrick knocked on the door, Ash had called for him to come in, but made no effort to get up.

"It's like fucking *Trainspotting* in here," said Serrick. "You guys high or what?"

He had a slight Russian accent that sounded like it could be fake. Back in Chicago, Gordon knew an English guy called Clancy that frequented the bars. Turns out, he wasn't English, and his name wasn't Clancy. It was all an act. The "I'm from Manchester" act got him laid. Most of the guys knew he was full of shit, but they never told the women. If girls want to spread their legs because of a flowery accent, then let them. More power to Clancy. (His real name was Tony.)

"Want some Cheerios?" asked Ash.

"You said you were gonna come over and look at my photos," said Serrick, more whiny than angry.

"When?"

"At eight."

"I've never been *anywhere* at eight."

"You said."

"I said I'd *call* at eight."

"You didn't even do that."

"'Cause I was sleeping," she said, sitting up. "But I dreamt about calling."

"This is important. I gotta submit my portfolio to the magazine guy after lunch."

It was amazing to Gordon that Serrick could carry on a conversation without once acknowledging the fact there was a man lying next to Ash.

Did a man in Ash's bed not seem unusual? Was Ash a slut? He didn't think so, though he was positive she didn't screen her partners as stringently as the common woman. So maybe she was a semi-slut. Semi-sluts aren't so bad.

"I don't know why you want to get involved with a trash publication anyway," said Ash.

"Money," said Serrick. "I read somewhere it makes the world go 'round."

"Fuck the world," said Ash, yawning.

"That's lovely, but can you bottle your global resentment for one hour and come to my place and give me your opinion?"

"Can I bring Gordon?"

Can I bring Gordon? It made him sound like a dog.

"I don't care," said Serrick, giving Gordon the once-over. "But we need to go."

Ash turned to Gordon. "Wanna see some pictures? Serrick's a kick-ass photographer."

"Sure."

***

Serrick lived in a third floor apartment on 4 th Avenue.

Cracked stairs led to a doormat with *Go Away* woven-in. Inside the apartment was dank and dark with a smell that matched the odor seeping from Serrick's clothes.

Serrick flicked the lights on. Glossy, professional-looking photographs were piled everywhere, along with photo albums. Various lenses and cameras rested wherever there was space.

"Sit," Serrick commanded, nodding to a blue loveseat. He disappeared into the bedroom. They sat.

"Found this by the highway," said Ash, patting the sofa. "I helped him carry it up."

"What's this?" asked Gordon. There was a yellow splotch on the arm rest.

"We don't know. But we poured vodka on that part when we got it up to kill anything that might've been growing."

"Why not cover it?"

"Serrick isn't ashamed of the stain, so he doesn't want to hide it."

"I'd hide it."

"You're ashamed of imperfections?"

"If the imperfection is the crusted remnants of human fluid, yeah, I might be a little hesitant to have it on display."

Ash shrugged. "I think it's brave of him."

Most people would define brave as something a little bit more ambitious, like charging a hill in battle or raising a child in the inner city, but what Ash was really saying was: Serrick didn't hide the truth. And that was brave to Ash, even if the truth was a yellow splotch.

Serrick emerged with a large, leather portfolio. He placed it before them on wine crates stacked to form a table.

"What I need from you is order suggestions. Content is pretty much set," said Serrick, then, as an afterthought, looked to Gordon and added, "You too."

Gordon leaned forward, careful to keep his elbow off the stain.

Page one of the portfolio featured a black and white picture of the desert.

"You're opening with a landscape?" asked Ash.

"So?"

"It's not you."

"That's good. I don't want them to see *me*. Landscapes are safe. This is the shit they want to see."

"It's bland."

"It's innocuous. A palate cleanser."

Ash turned the page. The next photo was awash with soft colors: a cute, little girl peeking out from behind a sand castle.

"*Jesus,*" said Ash.

"If you're gonna be like this—"

"Where are *you* in all this?"

"I'm there."

"Where?"

Ash flipped past pictures of trees, children on a playground, sunsets...

"There," said Serrick. "And there."

... past a sunflower, an old man on a ten-speed, a bowl of salad...

"A fucking bowl of salad?" asked Ash.

"Look at the symmetry of the vegetables, how the colors align."

"It's a salad."

Serrick took the portfolio back in one motion, slammed it shut.

"Forget it."

"Now you're pissed?"

"I said I needed *order* suggestions, not a snotty critique. I just wanted to know if I should lump the food together, cluster the children in the middle, whatever..."

"There's a million portfolios like that out there."

"It's what they want."

"Fuck what *they* want. Give them who *you* are."

"You don't understand the marketplace."

"Where's the picture of the man getting shoved by a gang-banger with a Gap couple watching from their café table and doing nothing?"

"Filed away."

"Why?"

"Because I'm applying to be the community photographer."

"That *is* the community."

"Not the one they want between make-up ads. They want palm trees and street performers and museums, not bums lying in piss," said Serrick, walking back into the bedroom.

"It's bullshit!" Ash called out. She looked to Gordon. "Let's get a breakfast burrito."

"What about—"

"My stomach's crying out the ingredients. 'Gimme bacon, Ash. Hot eggs and spicy salsa and shredded cheese and—'"

"Ashley!" said Serrick from the room. "C'mere a sec!"

Ash sighed and disappeared down the hall. Maybe Serrick was trying to isolate her from Gordon to get an uninfluenced opinion (as if Gordon had the power to sway her mind).

Gordon stood up, stretched. He needed coffee.

This jaunt to Serrick's lair wasn't the most heart-pumping experience, and he was still groggy. He peeked into the fridge—an ancient Frigidaire humming loudly and covered with magnets of bears copulating, a baby in camouflage, a fat woman sunbathing topless—and saw a lot of products with the word "soy" on it. Fair enough. The guy's healthy. But he probably does ecstasy and acid, and if so, that kinda negates the soy.

Gordon noticed a stack of glossies resting on the counter and flipped through them.

People screaming at cops during a war protest.

A woman peering through a barred window of her home.

A street-cleaner truck coming within inches of crushing a homeless teenager sleeping on the curb.

Definitely not bowls of salad. Ash was right. Serrick *was* holding back. But he had his reasons. He was trying to get hired, and the job called for the mundane. So he was delivering a collection of the—

Gordon stopped at a picture of an angel statue with the wings broken off. Police tape cordoned off the area around the damaged statue.

Something caught Gordon's attention. He held the photo closer to a light.

On the ground, amidst chunks of plaster, was a painted—*E*

"*Holy shit,*" said Gordon, barely above a whisper.

Ash and Serrick strolled out of the bedroom, still bickering.

"Then have it go from land to food to people," said Ash.

"Why?" asked Serrick, portfolio still in hand.

"'Cause people live off the food which comes from the land, right? So you're showing progression."

Serrick was genuinely impressed with the reasoning. "That sorta makes sense."

"That's all I can offer you with that dreck. I say dump it and submit the real stuff. *Your* stuff."

But it was too late. Serrick was already shuffling the order of the photos, intrigued by the idea of progression.

"When was this taken?" asked Gordon, holding up the statue picture.

Serrick glanced up. "Last week. In Burbank."

"How'd you find it?"

"Heard there was a report of vandalism in front of Target. Couldn't resist. I was hoping it was something extreme. Like smashed windows or bullet holes. Target's got that bull's eye as its logo. You'd think someone would make use of it."

"What was vandalized?" asked Ash.

Gordon handed her the glossy.

"An angel?" asked Ash. "Serves it right for shopping at Target."

"Look by the feet," said Gordon. "On the cement."

Her eyes widened.

"Should I put the filet mignon *after* the salad?" asked Serrick. "Is that being anal?"

Gordon kept his focus on Ash and said, "Think the cops know it's happened before?"

"Cops?" asked Serrick.

Ash looked to Serrick. "This has the same tag we found when they trashed my work." She handed him the photo and pointed out the mark.

"This?" asked Serrick.

"That," said Ash.

"An *E*?"

"It's identical," said Gordon.

"It's tacky," said Serrick, handing back the photo.

"Did they catch the person who did that to the statue?" asked Ash.

"Not that I know of," said Serrick. "But…"

"But what?"

"A friend of mine said he *thought* he knew who did it," said Serrick.

"Who?" asked Ash.

"Didn't say."

"Who's your friend?"

"Philip. You met him at the Greek Festival that time. He said he knew someone who was talking about busting up one of those angels."

"Fuck, Serrick. Can you call him?"

Serrick tried calling Philip's cell, but voicemail picked up. He left a message instructing him to call back, that it was urgent.

The destruction of her cemetery exhibit was obviously a sore spot for Ash, but she had managed to get over it fairly quickly. Gordon recalled how fast she made the transition on the roof that day. She wasn't one to linger on bad emotions, but now the incident was alive again; the fire of her anger was breathing fresh oxygen.

Gordon and Ash left Serrick's soon after and ate breakfast burritos by the beach. Between bites, she asked him what he thought the odds were of catching the guy that demolished her exhibit. He said slim, but that didn't dampen her growing excitement of not denying an instinct Gordon had yet to see her carry out.

Revenge.

Chapter 19

Then

GORDON WALKED INTO HIS one bedroom apartment and tossed his only piece of mail, the phone bill, onto the ironing board. When you live alone, you can do things like leave the ironing board in the dead center of the living room. When you live alone, a different set of rules apply.

But it was also draining. The silence. The isolation.

Gordon thought a girlfriend would cure this, but that brought another set of problems. Couples are rarely compatible, a fact he kept learning the hard way.

Ingrid lived with him while her apartment was cloaked in a plastic tent in order to wipe out its vast civilization of termites. The extermination ended up taking three weeks longer than expected. Ingrid was pleasant for a few days, then decided to change a few things. Nothing big, just enough to throw off Gordon's rhythm.

If you love a woman, you'll adjust to accommodate her. But Gordon didn't love Ingrid. He barely liked her. The sex quickly became tedious, and her conversational skills were on par with that of a thirteen year old. By the time she moved out, he couldn't stomach her. He went from infatuation to resentment in twenty-five days.

So Gordon had learned to tolerate the isolation, but now everything was changing.

He heard that people who lived alone kept the TV on for company, even if they weren't watching it. They just left the thing running. Gordon tried this, but felt like an idiot. He wasn't interacting with the thing, it couldn't give two shits about him, and all he was really doing was filling his subconscious with garbage. Instead, he would come home from work, exhausted, and sit on the couch in silence, letting the setting sun cast him in darkness before he clicked on a light.

To say the décor was minimal in Gordon's apartment would be pushing it. There were exactly three things hanging on the unpainted walls:

A Chicago Bulls 1998 championship banner that he won in a raffle at Drake's.

A Red Bull poster with a calendar at the bottom, below a model in a leather skirt.

And a postcard of the Russell Crowe movie *Gladiator*. It was a miniature version of the official poster, a freebie from the postcard rack at Drake's. (The postcard was taped above the stereo. He was not sure why he put it there, but it seemed like a good place for a gladiator to be.)

Gordon sat on the couch in the fading light and looked at his surroundings. He was looking for *himself* in his surroundings.

Does a person's home always reflect who that person is? He was twenty-six years old, and the only things he contributed to his apartment, excluding appliances and furniture, were free items he got from a bar.

Fuck. Was he *that* lazy? Couldn't he find time to put up a family picture? A painting from the mall? A vista of an Italian shore? Maybe he *did* need a woman to share his space. Maybe he should've handed over the keys to Ingrid and just said to hell with it.

Gordon shared his daylight hours with his father. And in many ways, Gordon was who his father was—a simple man with a simple view of life. But this was home, and his dad didn't live here. So in a space exclusively belonging to Gordon, shouldn't it offer *some* clues to who the fuck Gordon was?

Maybe it couldn't. Maybe Gordon just carried around nothing but his father's qualities. For lack of his own.

But since the day of the accident, Gordon didn't feel like anyone anymore. He felt like a hard drive that had crashed and lost all its data.

He was empty.

And having the TV on for company wasn't going to help.

Chapter 20

GORDON COULDN'T HAVE picked a worse day to deliver the news to Tom and Mike. Everything felt bad in the air. All the omens were there.

When Gordon approached the truck, Tom was giving a serious tongue lashing to the new guy he hired a few days earlier. A guy named Bill. Fucking great. Tom was already pissed. This was just going to make things worse. Gordon could wait until tomorrow or even later in the day, but he wanted to get it over with. He couldn't stomach another hour in this place. It had to be done now.

"Gordy, thank Christ," said Tom with a sigh. "Help me out here. We got two orders mixed up. Two loads went to the wrong—"

"It was the same name," said Bill.

"Same name, *different orders*. One was for his *home*, one for his *office*," said Tom, keeping his eyes on Bill. "All you had to do was fill out the right paperwork."

"I filled out the—"

"You filled out shit, Bill. You filled out shit. Now the customer's got a pole up his ass. He's pissed, wants a discount, and we *still* haven't shipped his shit."

Tom coughed, a string of saliva sticking to his hand. He wiped it on his coat, turning to Gordon. "Go help Mike, would ya? We gotta get the rest of this over there ASAP. We can't lose this guy's business. I won't let it happen."

"Tom…" said Bill.

"I don't wanna hear it."

Gordon found Mike in the back of the warehouse. He was strung out almost as bad as Tom. It hadn't been a good morning for anyone.

"Shit, man," said Mike. "So much shit's hittin' the fan right now, you would not fuckin' believe."

"Tom told me."

"Where the fuck you been? I've been waiting. I didn't wanna slay the Beast with the new guy. He's a fuck-head."

"Why'd Tom hire him?"

"He knew him from Drake's. I told him, 'Just 'cause you drink with a guy, don't mean you can work with him.' Two different worlds."

"There's plenty of good people out there."

"Preachin' to the choir, pal. Now we're up to our heads in shit 'cause fuck-head can't take an order." Mike positioned himself at the back of the dresser. Crouching down, he said, "Let's slay this fucker."

Gordon had to tell him. He had to get it over with.

"Mike…"

"I'll walk backwards," said Mike, trying to get a grip.

"It's not—"

"I know it's my turn."

"It's not that."

Mike looked at him.

"I'm quitting."

Gordon said it with such conviction, Mike straightened and didn't say a word.

"I'm through," said Gordon.

"Stop fuckin' around."

"I'm serious."

"You tell Tom?"

"Not yet."

"You can't quit."

"I got to."

"Tom told you to take time off."

"It's more than that."

"You're depressed. It's normal."

"I can't work here anymore."

"Take some time off."

"No…"

Mike let out a laugh, the reality of Gordon's announcement dawning on him.

"This is your father's company," said Mike.

"I know."

"Your father."

"I never meant to stay here my whole life."

"Oh really?"

"Yeah."

"Then what was your plan?"

Gordon glanced at the blocked window, searching for an answer, but none came.

"That's what I thought," said Mike.

"I'm not getting into this…"

Gordon headed for the door. Mike followed.

"What's so bad you gotta leave?" asked Mike.

"I put in my time," said Gordon without breaking stride. "I'm ready to move on."

"To something better?"

"To something different."

"That's bullshit, and you know it."

"I'm done, Mike."

"You can't do this to your father."

"Stop bringing my dad into this."

"Hey."

Gordon stopped and turned back. Mike got in his face.

"We all loved your father. My old man don't give two shits about me, but Ollie did. You're not the only one fucked up by his death."

"I know…"

"No, you don't. This place is a monument to that man. He put his life into it."

"That don't mean I gotta put mine."

Gordon turned his back on Mike and walked outside, pushing the door shut. Mike slammed it open. The reverberation of metal on brick caused Tom and Bill to look up from the loading bay.

"You can't just walk away," said Mike.

Mike grabbed a hold of Gordon's shoulder, but Gordon twisted quickly, pushing away his arm. Mike shoved him. Gordon slipped on the icy pavement and fell to his knees.

He didn't want to fight. He just wanted to leave. But when he got up, Mike shoved him in the back.

"Hey," said Tom, walking over at a fast clip.

Gordon spun on Mike and pushed back, his adrenaline pumping now.

Mike threw an awkward punch that glazed off Gordon's shoulder, then connected with his temple. Gordon planted his foot to maintain his balance as Mike struck again.

The second punch *wasn't* awkward. It was textbook, and it tore the skin on Gordon's cheekbone.

"Enough!" said Tom.

He reached them, but not in time to prevent Gordon from tackling Mike.

Gordon tried to get in a few retaliatory blows, but it was hard when he was grappling. Mike got him in a headlock. Their feet kicked wildly, trying to get leverage.

Tom grabbed Mike by his coat. "Get the fuck off him!"

It took a few seconds, but Tom managed to pull them apart.

"The fuck?" asked Tom.

"He quit," said Mike.

"What?"

"He told me he's quitting. Ain't that right?" Mike went for Gordon again, but Tom restrained him.

"What's he talking about, Gordy?"

"I'm done," said Gordon, touching the cut on his face.

"See?" said Mike.

"That's why you two decided to beat the snot outta each other?"

"He's disgracin' Ollie's memory."

"You know shit about my dad."

"I know he'd be ashamed of his son."

"Fuck you."

"No. Fuck you!"

"All right, all right," said Tom, one hand still locked on Mike's coat. To his credit, he was taking control of the situation and not fanning the flames. He pointed at Gordon. "Go home. We'll discuss this later."

"Fuckin' disgrace," said Mike.

"Mike. Shut the fuck up!" said Tom. "Take Bill inside and finish the order."

Mike tore his coat from Tom's grip, spit in disgust, then headed toward the loading bay. When Tom looked back to Gordon, he was already on his way home.

"Hey…" said Tom.

But Gordon kept walking.

Tom watched him go. He wasn't surprised at the outburst. He knew it was too early for Gordon to come back to work. He turned his attention to his clipboard.

There was work to be done. With or without Gordon, there was a job to do.

***

On the way home, Gordon revised his plan for changing his life.

Quitting the warehouse was essential, he knew that, and now that was behind him. But it wasn't enough.

He didn't just have to leave his job, he had to leave this city. He was going to go all the way with this, and in order to do that, he had to escape.

Chapter 21

Now

STANDING IN HIS BOXERS, Gordon looked in the bathroom mirror in room 116 at the Starlight Inn and thought about his posture.

His looks were his looks. He could gain weight, lose weight, get a tan, dye his hair, cover his skin with tattoos. There was always something he could do to change his appearance.

But his posture. The way he carried himself. The way he stood, walked, sat, moved. He never spent much time thinking about those things. How much did they affect the way he felt? The way other people judged him?

Looking at himself in the mirror, Gordon loosened up, shaking his hands and rolling his neck like an athlete before a game.

He tried to stand like Dean. Upright. Confident. He imitated Dean as best he could, even shooting out a few gestures. The nod. The thumbs up. The smile.

Not bad. Gordon already felt better.

He then stood like Cedric. Arms folded. Head tilted. Eyebrow raised. Gordon felt cocky, like he was tolerating some fool.

Not the best feeling.

He changed his posture to mimic Shawn. Hands on hips. Lips curled. Narrow eyes. Gordon felt suspicious, like he was waiting for someone to confess.

It gave him a weak sense of authority. He felt anxious, like he was slowly losing control.

Who was left? Of course.

He shifted his body to imitate Ash. Relaxed. Slight grin. He leaned against the wall, ran a hand through his hair.

He could feel his breathing slow down, like he was at ease watching the world go by. It didn't give a fuck about him, so he didn't give a fuck about it. The feeling made the grin open into a smile.

He then returned to his own posture, but the transition was strange. He had to take a few seconds to remember what it was.

Of all the people he was mimicking, he found himself the hardest to imitate. He changed the way he stood a few times and found himself feeling uncomfortable.

Uncomfortable. That's when he knew he got it right.

Chapter 22

EVERYTHING IN THE ROOM had order.

Dean had suggested this, of course, but he wasn't specific with how Gordon should take it, so Gordon took it as far as it could go. A first time visitor might conclude that Gordon suffered from obsessive-compulsive disorder, but he was only building a success foundation, as Dean called it.

Not only did goal boards hang in Gordon's bedroom, Dean also put up a massive calendar. Gordon didn't know they made calendars that big; it must be for corporate use or to hang in a factory. Each twenty-four hour cycle was broken up into segments of thirty minutes.

Gordon struggled to fill the spots, but wanted to impress Dean should he inspect it.

Most of the entries were fictitious, of course. He couldn't write *Stop By Secret Hotel Room* or *Spend Night at Other Homes*. So he concocted vague activities like *Meet with Sam* (there was no Sam) or *Transfer Funds* (there were funds, but they didn't need transferring).

The closet was arranged in perfect order. Not by color, or type of garment, but by days of the week. Yes, this was sick stuff.

The shower and toilet were immaculately clean—mostly because he rarely used them—and the carpet was regularly vacuumed.

Books were alphabetically arranged above a desk, all deemed required reading by Dean. *Think and Grow Rich* by Napoleon Hill, *Self Matters* by Dr. Phil, *Unlimited Power* by Anthony Robbins, *How to Get Rich* by Donald Trump, and a series of sports-related, self-help tomes written by head coaches. Not one piece of fiction was to be found.

When spending time in this life, Gordon made sure his appearance reflected the right attitude. So he kept his hair combed, pants ironed, shirt tucked in, and made sure he was freshly showered with just the right splash of cologne. (The fact that Naomi was sometimes around only made this effort easier.)

All this was quite the contrast to his appearance when hanging out with Ash. With her, he just *was*. No effort to look like anything at all. Over *here* was different, and sometimes that meant he had to change clothes before seeing Dean.

Gordon filled a paper cone at the water cooler. As he drank, he could hear Naomi and Dean arguing in the living room. He crumpled the cone, threw it in the trash, and decided to intrude.

He exited his bedroom, strolled by them, and acted like he was looking for something near the couch. They hardly paid him any attention, but he soon picked up on the subject they were fighting over.

Wedding plans.

Gordon was split with how to treat this.

One part of him wanted to give the couple their privacy, let them hash out the ceremony on their own. But another part wanted to get involved, and he knew that if he lingered, either Dean or Naomi would snap and ask his opinion, giving him a guilt-free entry into the conversation. So Gordon lingered, and—

"Where would you rather exchange vows, Gordon?" asked Naomi. "A small, quaint chapel or a massive, cold church?"

"It's not cold," said Dean.

Gordon wanted to side with Naomi for obvious reasons. "A chapel's nice."

Naomi beamed at the support and turned to Dean. "See."

"You failed to mention that your quaint, little chapel is actually a dilapidated, part-time crack house in a crime-ridden neighborhood."

"No, it's not."

"The priests wear Kevlar vests."

"It's where I grew up."

Dean looked to Gordon. "Ever hear of Our Holy Lady of the Immaculate Heart? It's a majestic piece of breath-taking architecture located on a mountain peak. You can feel the presence of God."

"I promised my mom I'd get married in the family church," said Naomi. "It's where I was baptized."

"Flea-infested junkies sleep under the pews," said Dean.

"Where'd you hear that?"

Dean returned his focus to Gordon. "Does this make sense to you?"

"He already picked the chapel," said Naomi.

"*Before* he knew it was a haven for crack smokers."

"Listen to you. Mr. Positive."

"I'm… honey… I want the best possible location for our wedding."

"I think St. Augustine's would be perfect."

Dean sighed. "Our Holy Lady of the Immaculate Heart is the number one ranked wedding location on four different websites."

"I promised my mom."

"So you want to hire armed guards to set up a perimeter around the chapel?"

"It's not that bad."

Dean wasn't going to tolerate this anymore; he wanted an answer from Gordon. "What do you think?"

"They're both nice," said Gordon.

"Don't ride the fence, Lake."

They were both staring at him.

He took a breath. "Tradition, in my opinion… can add to things," said Gordon. "For the good. Make it better. Fuller…" It was like he forgot how to talk.

"Gotta do better than that," said Dean. "Use those communication skills we went over."

"Let him talk," said Naomi.

She looked at Gordon and for an instant her eyes said something else (what exactly he didn't know), but there was a change, and it meant he had to step up to the plate.

"If I were you…" Gordon said to Dean, "I'd go with the chapel. Sometimes, big weddings can overshadow the true purpose of the day."

Dean steamed.

"It's about love, right?" said Gordon. "About a life long commitment. You don't need a huge building on a mountaintop for that."

Gordon stopped right there. He felt like he was endorsing the relationship, which he didn't want to do. But Naomi… oh, did he score points with Naomi.

She nodded her thanks to Gordon, then looked to Dean who was clearly facing a situation of two-against-one.

"The most majestic cathedral you've ever seen," said Dean. "You'll love it."

That was Dean's response. As if Gordon hadn't spoken at all.

The wedding discussion wound down. Naomi had to leave for the restaurant. There was no goodbye kiss.

After she was gone, Dean confronted Gordon about the incident.

"What you did today…" said Dean, in full lecture mode. "You undermined me."

"How?"

"We're roommates, Lake. Fellow men. A team. Since I let you move in, we've been working together to improve each other. To strengthen each other's positions in life. Haven't I made a difference?"

"Yeah." He had, though Gordon didn't like where this was going.

"So when you openly and aggressively disagree with me by taking the side of my girlfriend, you undermine me."

"I'm not trying—"

"Trying means jack. It's what you *did*. You know how I became the top manager for three consecutive months? Teamwork. I strengthened the unit from within. Because I'm a leader. Because I don't undermine my fellow workers. You're an editor, right?"

"Yeah…" He almost said no.

"That's part of the problem. You work alone."

"I don't work alone. I got producers on my back about what to cut, what to add." All bullshit, obviously.

"Not the same thing as teamwork. You work alone. It leads to shit like this."

"You believe my job led to me voting for the chapel?"

"Everything's connected, Lake. That's what I've been trying to teach you. If you let one part of your life slip, it has a ripple effect into the others. So yes, the fact that you're an isolated person inexperienced with the benefits of teamwork, I believe led to you undermining me, your roommate, thus weakening our greater goals."

Dean was good at slinging shit like this. He lived for it. Gordon could only imagine the diatribes he subjected his coworkers to.

But was he right?

Gordon was second guessing his own opinion on the chapel.

By voting against the majestic cathedral—as harmless as this seemed—was he undermining his relationship with Dean?

This is where Naomi complicated things. Gordon had decided to view her as a challenge that would help sharpen his self-control, but she was causing problems.

She was taken.

"I've given you a lot to think about. Choose success," said Dean, once again taking on the tone of Gordon's high school football coach. Gordon had liked this at first, but now it was wearing thin.

The tension between him and Dean made Gordon think of Shawn and Cedric and how they didn't speak anymore. He had to do something about that. Maybe he could use what he was learning *here* to help *there*.

He could take a philosophy from one life and apply it to the other.

Was he screwing with the rules? No. As long as he didn't mix who he was in the three places.

Gordon could feel his mind shifting. When it came to time allotment for each life, he tried to follow his instinct rather than a strict hour or day rotation.

And since his thoughts were on Shawn and Cedric now, that told him one thing…

It was time to change locations.

Chapter 23

CEDRIC WAS CLEARLY trying to provoke Shawn.

He'd half-eat Shawn's food, leaving the remaining half in the fridge. He'd turn off the washing machine when it was filled with Shawn's clothes. He'd move Shawn's car keys. He'd unscrew the bulbs in Shawn's room, just enough so they wouldn't turn on.

He'd even let his friends shit in Shawn's bathroom. Full-on, no-holds-barred, colon emptying without the use of the tangerine scented spray that sat conspicuously on the toilet lid. And when the Feces Droppers decided to piss and nothing more, there were always drops of urine dotting the toilet seat and floor. The better part of Shawn wanted to believe that it was an accident, that their dicks simply weren't capable of precise aim, but the better part of him was usually wrong, thus he *knew* they were doing it on purpose.

Each act was inconsiderate and rude, and Gordon had to do something about it.

So he wrote a letter.

It was a list detailing the current state of affairs and a set of proposals to fix things. Taken as a whole, it was, in essence, a treaty.

A degree of civility had to be reached. A degree of respect.

And that's what the treaty addressed: mutual respect.

Yeah, it was mainly directed at Cedric, but Gordon wrote the words carefully so it'd seem like Shawn and Cedric were equally guilty of cohabitation transgressions (a phrase he included). If the letter seemed titled toward Cedric, it would make him defensive, and if he got defensive, then chances of both parties signing the treaty were over.

Oh, yes. Gordon wanted them to actually sign the letter.

Two lines were drawn on the very bottom for their signatures. He wanted the document to be an official declaration of peace. After all, he too had to live under this roof (sometimes anyway).

When Shawn returned home from an interview at a temp agency, Gordon showed him the treaty.

"He won't sign it," said Shawn.

"He may," said Gordon.

"He won't even read it."

The first draft took up two whole pages, but it had looked like a business contract, so Gordon edited it down to one.

"Even if he reads it, even if he signs it—which he won't—it doesn't mean he'll change," said Shawn.

"Maybe he needs to know it's for the benefit of all," said Gordon.

"Sad, really. That it's come to this."

Gordon held out a pen.

"Jesus, are you a lawyer or what?" Shawn took the pen. "Just here?"

"Just there."

"No initialing?"

"Just your name."

And so, Shawn signed the treaty.

It was a historic day in the House That Anger Built, but the difficult part was still to come, getting Cedric to sign.

Gordon carried the letter with a certain amount of pride to Cedric's bedroom and taped it on the door, right at eye level.

Shawn watched, worried. "Sure we're not instigating?"

"Look..." said Gordon. "If this blows up, it's on me."

"No, no, amigo. If this little treaty of yours blows up... it's on *both* of us."

***

After a few hours passed and Cedric failed to show, Gordon decided to leave for...

Well, that was the problem.

He didn't know whether to spend time with Ash or Dean. Any sane man would choose Ash, but Gordon wasn't exactly the poster boy for sanity.

He was in the middle of exploring who he was, and some clues were rising to the surface, though not as fast as he had hoped.

He could see potential in all three lives; they all worked on some level. So he had to crank it up a notch. Less than two months remained in the experiment.

Since he was caught up in confusion, he decided to get dinner, and what better place to eat than Gilroy's Chophouse in Old Towne Pasadena?

And what better place to be served than in Naomi's section?

This was only the second time he'd been in there to eat. He'd been keeping away from Naomi.

Don't put yourself in temptation's path, he told himself. But here he was. Smack in the middle of the path with a perfectly cooked tenderloin in front of him. He savored the taste.

The restaurant was swamped, so he couldn't mingle as much with Naomi as he would've liked. But a little mingling was better than none. Plus, he got to watch her. He chewed slowly, observing her interaction with customers, adoring the way she squatted next to a table to take an order. Gordon looked around to see if any of the other servers were squatting. Yeah. Squattage everywhere.

But no one else had her smile.

He thought about how he felt the first time he saw her; almost giddy. For a moment during that initial encounter, it seemed like the experiment was going to end before it had a chance to begin.

Naomi had the power to define him in that instant, and he was ready to let her. But the affection wasn't mutual. If it was, then maybe his triple-life wouldn't have proceeded.

After a second drink, Gordon flirted with Naomi. He couldn't help himself. And she even flirted back, and that led to the third drink. Then the fourth. Naomi wouldn't bring him the fifth. She said he was spinning enough, and she didn't want him sleeping in the booth.

And she was right, his world *was* spinning, a fact he didn't appreciate until he stood. He was probably too drunk to drive to Venice, but he was going to try. (The decision was made to stay with Ash since he couldn't stomach seeing Dean and was too tired to deal with the Shawn/Cedric war.)

Naomi walked him to his car, trying to get him to sit at the bar and down some coffee, but he politely refused. If he stayed any longer, he was bound to tell her how he felt about her. He wasn't about to do that.

As he drove away, he could see Naomi in the rearview mirror, standing in the parking lot, watching him.

Chapter 24

"YOU'RE DRUNK," said Ash.

"A little," said Gordon.

He sat against the wall of the loft, drained from his below-the-speed-limit-avoid-all-cops drive from Pasadena.

"Who were you drinking with?" asked Ash.

"Work people," said Gordon. "People from work."

"Celebration type thing?"

"Kinda."

"You lying to me?"

"Yeah," said Gordon, thrown by her suspicion, but trying not to show it. He slowed his voice to sound sullen. "Friend of ours got fired. He has a kid, and… we were cheering him up."

Gordon was impressed he could roll with the question even though he was sloshed, but why did she question his honesty? He hated lying to Ash, but this small fib was merely a humble servant of the larger, big lie. And that lie didn't count. So if a little lie served the big lie, it was permissible.

"Is he okay?" asked Ash.

"Who?" asked Gordon.

"Your friend."

"Yeah… he'll be fine." *Please* no more questions.

Ash sat next to him and put a hand on his knee. In the same quiet and serious voice she'd been using since he walked in, she said, "I know who it is."

"Who?"

"The guy who ripped apart my exhibit."

"You know who it is?!"

"Serrick got the info from his friend who was at a party at a guy's house. This guy was bragging about busting up the angel statue, and get this: The guy's name is *Earnest*."

"Earnest?"

"As in a name beginning with E."

"You think it's the guy?"

"Are you listening, drunk boy? He was boasting about busting up the angel. The first letter of his name matches the mark. Hello? Smoking gun?"

"You call the cops?"

Ash thought about her answer, then said, "No."

"Why not?"

"I got the address from Serrick." She held up a folded piece of paper. "We're gonna confront this asshole ourselves."

"When?" asked Gordon.

"Right now."

"I don't know if I'm in a condition to—"

"I've been waiting for your ass *all day*," said Ash. Not angrily. Determined. And though forceful, her tone didn't bother him; he liked the fact that he was needed for a mission. "I don't give a shit if you're wasted. We're gonna confront this fucker. Right the fuck now."

***

The address belonged to a house in Silver Lake. The trees on the property made it feel isolated, but this was an illusion. Nothing is isolated in LA.

Parking on the street, Ash and Gordon trudged up the steep driveway.

As for the plan, Gordon was following Ash's lead, and she was going with her gut, which meant there was no plan.

She rang the doorbell.

They heard a deep cough. The door opened, revealing a grizzled man in his sixties with shoulder length hair and a grayish-blond beard. He wore a faded red robe and was shirtless underneath.

"Company!" said the man in a welcoming, rough voice.

"Can Earnest come out to play?" asked Ash.

"Earnest," said the man, as if he was jogging his memory. "Earnest isn't home. He's out playing already."

Ash looked past the man, peering into the house.

"You don't believe me," said the man.

"We're eager to see him is all," said Ash.

The man sized up his visitors, never dropping his friendly stature.

"Myron Scott," he said. "Earnest's father."

He extended his hand. Gordon shook. Ash didn't. She glanced past him again.

"*Really* wanna get in here, huh?" asked Myron. "Okay." He cleared the doorway. "Come on in."

Ash stepped into the foyer and Gordon followed, imagining the glee she felt at infiltrating the culprit's house without his knowledge. God, if he could only come home when they were there. It'd be an ambush!

"You two got names?" asked Myron.

"I'm Ash, that's Gordon."

"Ash and Gordon. You're not friends of my son, are you?"

"Why d'you say that?" asked Gordon.

"Hostile vibe," said Myron, leading them into a sunken den filled with paintings, sculptures, and a variety of eccentric art pieces. None of which matched the immediate impact of what was standing in the corner.

A suit of armor sporting an enormous strap-on dildo.

Ash and Gordon glanced at each other. *Freak.*

"We're not entirely hostile," said Ash, prying her eyes away from the rubber penis. "But we're definitely not his friends."

"Enemies?" asked Myron.

"We need to talk to him," said Ash.

"He break your heart?"

"Hardly."

"You break his?"

"Not yet."

"But you're angry with him?" asked Myron, gesturing for them to sit on a wooden park bench. The bench had been coated in orange paint that had begun to chip off, revealing the original green.

Sitting next to Ash, Gordon took in more of the eclectic décor.

There was a painting of an eagle in flight. Prison bars had been drawn over the canvas, carefully applied, but clearly not part of the original image. The bars made it look as though the eagle was flying within a jail cell.

"You have an issue with my son, I'd like to address it. He's only seventeen. He's still my responsibility."

"We'd rather talk to him," said Ash.

"That's not possible," said Myron, sitting on an old TV that wasn't plugged in. "Anytime soon anyway."

"You said he was out playing."

"He is. In Europe. His mother lives in London."

"When's he coming back?"

"Never can tell with that boy."

On the coffee table in front of Gordon was a snow globe. He picked it up and shook it. Under the swirling specks of white was a clown juggling bowling pins. But there was something else—painted on top of the globe were storm clouds. The black and grey swirls seemed part of the design at first, but were obviously added.

"He did something, didn't he?" said Myron.

"That he did," said Ash. Contempt in her voice.

"If my son's been a source of pain, tell me…"

"Doesn't matter if he's not around."

"It always matters, sweetheart," said Myron. "Just 'cause I didn't do the damage, doesn't mean I can't mend it. That's what this world needs. Less people saying 'It wasn't me' and more people saying 'How can I help?'"

"He was destructive," said Gordon.

"Destructive?" Myron laughed.

"If you're surprised, then you don't know your son," said Ash.

"I am, and maybe I don't. His mother pours stuff in his head," Myron said. "And I gotta dig to find out the extent of her corruption. I gotta excavate that boy's skull every time he visits. Ask questions. Probe. Make sure he's still on the level." He stroked his beard. "She's insane, you know. I tried to tell the lawyers that. I brought in a doctor from Oregon to prove it. He came up with squat. Waste of money. But I knew. I knew."

Gordon got a closer look at the man's robe. He could see a jagged outline of a patch that had been torn off. Myron caught him looking and winked.

Ash grew impatient, and despite the man's insistence they stay for a generous slice of lemon meringue pie, they bid farewell.

The visit was a failure.

The guy who destroyed Ash's exhibit wasn't in the country, so they would have to wait until he came back to confront the prick.

Unless the father was lying. He could be protecting his son. The little fuck could've been in his bedroom playing video games for all they knew. They should've asked to look around.

Gordon didn't think he was lying, but it's hard to tell with older people. They have different methods of dancing around the truth, and Gordon wasn't familiar with them. He was pretty good at detecting bullshit from the under fifty crowd. But over fifty? Forget it.

Ash swore she'd deal with this soon enough. Even if she had to wait for the fucker to return from Europe. She couldn't let a fucking teenager fuck with her.

When Earnest came back, she'd be waiting.

Chapter 25

Then

THE RED BULL POSTER was the first thing to go. A clean tear right down the middle of the blonde in the leather skirt. Another swipe to remove pieces still taped to the wall.

Gordon's heart was racing. Part rage, part relief. He wasn't going to wait.

He ripped away the Chicago Bulls banner, then the *Gladiator* postcard. He tore them to pieces. He wasn't taking this stuff down to pack. He wanted it gone. He wanted new surroundings. He was sick of this life.

He had to leave. He had to move away.

But to where?

There were less dramatic options than what he was considering. He could stay in some local, luxurious hotel suite for a few weeks until he got his shit together. Order room service, get a morning massage, sip cocktails at the piano bar. Life on cruise control.

No.

He had to leave Chicago. He had to start over. New surroundings meant more than leaving his apartment. He wanted a new city to navigate. New buildings, new people. And yes, for the love of God… *new weather*. If he was going to do this, he had to be free of this shitty weather.

The snow was after him. It was trying to bury him. Okay, maybe not literally (he wasn't losing his mind in that regard), but it sure seemed that way.

Maybe he could go to an island. Isn't that where people go to escape? He could go to Jamaica or Bermuda or Hawaii. He could lounge in the hot sand, stare at the ocean, absorb the melodies of a steel drum band.

No.

As good as that sounded, that would be a vacation. He didn't want to sit around. He just wanted out of Chicago. He'd already been idle his whole life, living each day with thoughtless repetition.

Gordon dug out a canvas bag from a closet shelf and started stuffing clothes in.

There were loose ends to deal with. He'd write a letter to his landlord saying he was moving. He had four months left on the lease, but fuck it. He'd pay the fee. He'd shut off the power, the phone, the cable, even his cell. As for the furniture, he didn't care. The landlord could sell it, keep it, dump it, whatever.

As Gordon folded a shirt, a drop of blood fell onto the cotton. He'd forgotten about the cut Mike ripped open with his fist.

Gordon walked into the bathroom and looked at the cabinet mirror.

A thin line of red trailed from his cheek to his chin. Another drop fell, plopping in the sink.

Gordon stared at his reflection. He looked tired, but didn't feel tired. He dabbed some toilet paper on the cut, but that was the extent of his medical treatment. He'd deal with it later. He wanted to keep moving.

He wanted out.

***

Taking two canvas bags full of clothes and nothing else, Gordon took a cab to O'Hare International Airport.

He didn't have a ticket. He didn't have a destination. He was traveling on impulse. He wanted to make sure that the location he would eventually settle on felt right in his gut. And for that, he wanted to wait until he was inside the airport to make up his mind.

With the bags at his feet, he stared at the bank of monochrome monitors listing the departing flights. After a few moments, he found what he was looking for. A flight that left in an hour.

Delta. Nonstop.

As for the city... well, he'd never been there before, but at the moment, it felt like the perfect place to be.

***

The plane lifted off the runway and with its ascension, a weight lifted off Gordon. He was leaving Chicago behind, and he couldn't be happier.

Not all burdens make themselves known. Some apply pressure so consistently for so long, you don't realize they're there. You just think *that's the way things are.*

Gordon no longer believed this.

Gazing out the window at the shrinking city, he was sure his family and friends (even Mike) would be worried about him after his sudden disappearance. But he wasn't planning to hide. He'd call Aunt Rena to explain that he was taking a little getaway, and that she shouldn't worry about him. He'd be back eventually. He'd change apartments and resume the business of everyday life.

This wasn't true, of course. He wasn't going to return. But to make things easier for his family in the short-term, he'd simply say he was taking their advice after all and taking a break.

It was permanent, but they didn't have to know that yet.

Leaning his head back, closing his eyes, letting the hum of the engines fill his ears, Gordon cleared his mind of the past.

Chapter 26

THE CAB DROPPED HIM off at the Starlight Inn.

Gordon had requested an inexpensive place to stay, so this is where the cabbie took him. One mile from Los Angeles International Airport.

LA wasn't an unusual destination, considering his desire to escape. He wasn't blazing any new trail, but it seemed the right place to start over.

It was the official city of runaways. Warm. Sprawling (that was important). Gordon wanted big. He wanted choices. California was the state of choices. You could do anything here. Be anybody. It was a vast canvas upon which he could paint whatever he pleased.

Whatever he *chose*.

The Starlight wasn't a five-star hotel by any means, but it also wasn't a dump with stained sheets and a mysterious odor.

He didn't want to live alone. He wanted a roommate. He wanted to interact with people as much as possible. This was the way to dig and probe, because for all his recent anger and confusion and feelings of being lost, and his desire to tear his life apart, a single notion kept creeping up in his mind...

He didn't know who he was.

He had the whole plane ride to think about it, and he kept coming back to that. He didn't know who the fuck he was.

He was built and engineered to be a replica of his father, and he had marched along with that design. But from the instant his father went away, the design went with him, leaving Gordon without any direction, any form, any substance. There should have been two caskets lowered into the ground on the day of the funeral, because whoever Gordon Lake was, he wasn't that person anymore.

He knew there was someone *else* inside, lurking; the true him. Dormant, undeveloped, unused. And he felt, if he really tried, he could figure out who *that* person was.

But time was an issue. He'd already wasted twenty-six years rolling down the path of his father, and he didn't want to waste more years trying to decipher, through the course of normal life, what kind of person actually dwelled without the suffocating mask of his father, the one that fit so snug for so long.

So he didn't want to live alone.

Being isolated wasn't the answer. Interaction was.

Paying cash, Gordon checked into room 116—king-sized bed, landscape paintings, floral carpet—and didn't bother unpacking; he'd do it in the morning. He took a shower instead. The hot water stung the cut on his cheek. The tussle with Mike already seemed like an eternity ago, but it was just that morning. He realized how utterly spent he was. He yawned as he squeezed shampoo gel from a tiny bottle.

Toweled off with his hair still wet, Gordon sat nude on the edge of the mattress and flipped through TV stations. He stopped on a local weather report. The computer graphic of the West Coast caught him off guard. He wasn't accustomed to seeing the Pacific Ocean in a weather forecast.

All over Southern California, the temperature seemed constant. In LA, it was seventy-two degrees, and not one fucking cloud in sight.

***

The next morning, Gordon looked at himself in the bathroom mirror.

It started as a cursory glance, the type where you look at your face for a second or two while brushing your teeth. Nothing special. A thousand mornings can go by like this where you make eye contact with yourself with no real thought.

There I am. Spit toothpaste. Wipe mouth.

But this morning was different. His reflection froze him. Who he saw looking back was his father. The similarity was striking, one that went beyond physical characteristics. Throughout his life, Gordon always had the same expressions as his father, the same gait, the same cadence.

Anger would lead to clenched teeth and a wrinkle above the nose. Disgust meant a furrowed brow and raised upper lip.

Walking was accomplished through short, quick strides that reflected the importance of not wasting time. It was an efficient rhythm that was almost impossible to break, even when strolling through a grocery store.

Laughter came out in sharp, machine-gun bursts that never faded. It just stopped cold as if the gun had ran out of ammo. If someone heard laughter from inside the warehouse, they couldn't tell if it was Ollie or Gordon doing the laughing. Same when they answered the phone, sneezed, coughed, or cursed.

Gordon stared at himself in the mirror.

At his father.

He picked up the razor next to the sink and brought it down against the top of his mustache. No shaving cream, no hot water. Just blade and skin. Whiskers fell. A few drops of blood followed. Gordon didn't stop until the space under his nose was a strip of smooth, raw white.

It wasn't plastic surgery, but it helped. He looked different, and that's what mattered.

He dabbed toilet paper against the razor cuts.

***

Gordon sucked down two Egg McMuffins and walked to a car rental place a few lights down from the hotel.

Since he was near the airport, cars were being rented every thirty feet. He'd considered buying a car, but that was a choice he wasn't ready to make. People chose a car based on their personality, and he couldn't do that. He didn't know what his personality was. What would the *real* him want to drive? What if he bought an SUV only to decide later that he'd rather skirt around town on a motorcycle?

So he rented a white, four-door Ford Contour. Picked on impulse. He could switch it out tomorrow if he wanted.

When inquiring about apartments, the attendant referred him to Southland Rentals. When asked if she knew the cost, she nodded to the growing line of customers.

"Call and ask," she said with a go-away smile.

***

The map of the Los Angeles area covered the entire wall, each city in a different color.

Gordon stood in the Santa Monica office of Southland Rentals, studying the streets and realizing he knew nothing about the layout of

LA. Upon a suggestion from the rep, he purchased a *Thomas Guide*. LA was basically laid out under a grid, so tracking down a location was, in theory, fairly simple: just find the address in the index and flip to the corresponding page number, using the coordinates. The rep, a young, bubbly Asian woman, assured him with a wink that he'd know his way around in no time at all.

"All done," the rep said.

Gordon turned and saw the woman holding a print-out of apartment vacancies. The stack was normally thinner, she said, but since he indicated no preference to location, he was given the works.

The leads had only one thing in common—they were roommate situations. Other than that, rent varied from four hundred per month for a studio to four grand per month for a house.

It was a solid start, and if this batch didn't work out, fresh leads became available every day at three. The paid membership was good for sixty days, but Gordon didn't need that much time. He wanted to find a place to live, and fast.

So he got to work.

Chapter 27

Now

FUCK OFF FAG.

That was Cedric's response to the treaty.

Paper torn from a spiral notebook was taped to Shawn's bedroom door, containing those three words written in large block letters.

So much for diplomacy.

The treaty itself was nowhere to be found. Gordon had left it for Cedric to sign. It was safe to assume that never happened.

"See what we're dealing with?" asked Shawn, ripping the paper down and crumpling it. "We try to be civil, and he responds with *this*."

"Kinda harsh," said Gordon.

"Par for the course."

"But still—"

"Still nothing. He's relishing this. Basking in the attention."

"We had to try," Gordon said.

"Unabashed homophobia. That's what I'm living with."

Gordon couldn't understand why Shawn would tolerate such things in his own home. He could move out. Problem solved. But Shawn refused to retreat. He was dug in like an enemy soldier, prepared to see this conflict through to the bitter end.

Shawn tossed the crumpled sign toward a trash can in his room. It bounced off the edge and fell to the floor.

"I'll call a meeting," said Gordon. "We'll get together, the three of us."

"Why bother?"

"If I get him to sit down, will you talk with him?"

"You're spinning your wheels."

"Will you?"

Shawn considered the effort Gordon was putting forth. "Why do you give a shit?"

"Because I want to make things right."

"You can't."

"The treaty was a bit much. But I can help."

Shawn didn't know what to make of Gordon.

Gordon said, "Will you at least talk if I can get him to—"

"Yeah," said Shawn. "I'm all for peace. But this is it. If that asshole pulls anything else, I'm done trying to offer an olive branch."

Later that evening, shortly after Shawn departed for work, Cedric came home in a rare, good mood.

Gordon took advantage of his high spirits and asked if he would sit down with Shawn to talk about their problems. Cedric shrugged and said sure. It was that easy. No mention was made of the failed treaty or Cedric's written response.

A time was scheduled for the following night.

The meeting was set.

Chapter 28

"SOMETIMES AN ORGANIZATION doesn't appreciate effective leadership," said Dean.

He was upbeat, considering the circumstances.

Dean, Naomi, and Gordon sat in the glow of the setting sun at an outdoor café in Pasadena, draining their second bottle of wine.

"How's that possible?" asked Naomi.

"Companies get set in their ways," said Dean. "They don't want to improve. So out the door the leader must go." The last two words were slightly slurred.

Dean had hastily organized this impromptu celebration.

Gordon had been writing on his calendar when Dean called and, in a tone indicative of a person delivering great news, announced he got fired from Pure Mountain Pacific.

But since Dean was Dean, he was already spinning it in a positive way, as if losing his job was a gift.

To him, he was being liberated from an oppressive, mismanaged company. A true blessing in disguise. He instructed Gordon to meet him and Naomi at six o'clock to "celebrate a new beginning."

But from the moment they sat down, this was no celebration for Naomi, who wasn't thrilled her fiancé was treating his termination so lightly.

"Have you called other companies yet?" asked Naomi.

"I got feelers out there," said Dean.

"Any leads?"

"Try the flat bread."

"*Dean.*"

"Yes. I have leads."

"You want to stay in the water business?" asked Gordon.

"We'll see," said Dean. "It could be the right time to explore different options."

"Like what?" asked Naomi.

Dean found her anxiety cute. "Everything's going to be okay, baby." He went to touch her hand, but she pulled it away.

"I wish you were more concerned," said Naomi. It was a chilly evening, and she edged her chair closer to the heat lamp.

Dean proposed a toast: "To the future."

It was the third toast of the night.

They clinked glasses as dinner arrived. Dean lit up at the sight of food and joked with the waiter.

Gordon studied him.

How much of this was a show for Naomi? Did Dean really feel zero grief about losing his job?

The loss of a job didn't always mean automatic depression. Some people crave a career change but are too timid to pull the trigger. For them, a pink slip can be just what the doctor ordered.

But Dean's job was everything to him. It's what drove him. Why exactly he was fired wasn't discussed at the table. Dean blamed the ignorant management and left it at that, but Naomi didn't nod along. Not once. Because the reality of the situation was this:

Dean had failed.

Despite his grandstanding, he was now reduced to just another schlub in the ever-growing pool of the unemployed. Naomi knew you didn't knock the legs out from under someone like Dean without negative repercussions, but there was no evidence of that yet. Tonight, his mood was downright chipper. She practically expected him to break into song. So perhaps he'd recover quickly.

But if he didn't...

Naomi pulled her knees to her chest. Her proximity to the heat lamp wasn't curbing her chill.

Chapter 29

GORDON FLATTENED THE SHEET of paper Shawn had crumpled into a ball, having retrieved it from the trash in Shawn's bedroom.

It was items like this that he added to the collages in room 116.

Gordon taped the paper on the wall in the Shawn/Cedric section. The *FUCK OFF FAG* sign was now part of the collection, next to the fern branch that Shawn plowed over and above a rough draft of the rejected treaty—all objects and pictures that supplemented the journal entries.

Maintaining three separate lives wasn't easy, but the collages helped keep things straight. He sometimes stared for long periods in order to gauge his feelings. His various personalities were becoming more distinct by the day.

Which appealed to him? Which felt right?

Gordon opened the drawer and removed the journal.

It was time for an entry.

54

There are things I like about my new lives. There are things I hate.

Life with Ash

I like the fact that if I get a hard-on, I don't have to hide it. Boners happen.

I like the fact she isn't predictable. She lives life as it comes to her. I like how I am around her. I don't overthink stuff. No planning, no worrying, none of the bullshit people have heart attacks over.

I like her anger. I like feeling angry. People hide emotions because the place or timing isn't right. Those rules are gone with her. If you love something, love it. If you hate something, hate it.

I hate how life feels sloppy with her. I hate how she won't make decisions until she has to. I hate it because it feels like she's scared of what's coming. So she doesn't deal with it.

I hate the loft. There are no boundaries. Every room bleeds into every other room.

It's a mess. This is like life for me there. When I don't hold things back, everything comes out. It's like dumping all your belongings onto the floor instead of arranging them on a shelf. It's a fucking pile of everything.

Life with Dean

I like the planning. I like the goals. I like having a plan of attack. I like charging into the future and not waiting for it to come.

I like Naomi. I hate Naomi. I can't have her, but she's there. Dean is better for her than I am. I'm diet Dean. She sees me trying to be him. But I'm not the real thing. He got fired, and even that didn't faze him.

His walls are up. She's on the outside. She can kick and scream or love and sing. It wouldn't affect what's going on inside him. I hate that. I hate that he won't let her affect him.

Having goals is good, but what if they're the wrong goals? What if your plan is the wrong plan?

Life with Shawn and Cedric

I like making a difference. I hate not making a difference.

We're going to have a meeting because I wanted to have a meeting. I like that power. I like that this meeting is going to happen because I thought of it.

If I can fix Shawn and Cedric, what else can I do? Can I make a difference in the lives of groups of people? Types of people? Races of people? Should I try?

I want this meeting to work. If I can fix them, I'll move on to fixing other things. What if everyone felt this way? I hate that they don't.

I don't know Cedric. He's hard to know. Most people are hard to know. Is this the problem? People protecting themselves. People not wanting to be fixed. I hate that they resist help. How can I help someone that doesn't want to be helped? Sounds like a fucking pamphlet for addicts.

Chapter 30

Then

OVER THE NEXT FOUR days after visiting Southland Rentals, Gordon's schedule remained consistent.

Wake up, shower, breakfast at McDonald's, shit at McDonald's, eight or nine stops at listed vacancies, chicken-fried steak at Denny's, eleven or so more stops, pick up foot-long meatball sub at Subway, return to the Starlight Inn, staple info together, add to wall. (A wall which was now completely full. He had pushed aside the chest of drawers to make more room.)

To an outsider, the collection would appear to be a mad collage of eclectic images and notes, but there was a system in play, however crude.

Houses over here. Apartments over there.

Cheap rent on the left. Costly rent on the right.

Valley spots up high. Hollywood spots down low.

The vacancies were a lot to think about, but he knew this much—he was done looking. No more. In front of him were ninety-two pieces of paper. Over two hundred photos.

It was time to start narrowing down the selection. He wanted to make a decision by the next morning. He wanted to begin his new life and get the hell out of the hotel.

Gordon extended his arms and opened his palms to the wall, circling them slowly over the pictures as if he was trying to channel some otherworldly force to help him. But it was simply a matter of focusing; ghosts need not apply. He had to go with his gut.

Furnished garage, North Hollywood. *Out.*

Third floor unit, Culver City. *History.*

Brick tenement, Encino. *Adios.*

One by one, they fluttered to the floor.

An hour went by before the process worked its way down to three final profiles.

He looked at each one, the taped-up paperwork forming an odd triangle now that the rest of the wall was clean. He had to rid himself of two more, and his job was done. Just two more to toss into the reject pile.

This wasn't easy.

Gordon ate the last cold chunk of the sub and rearranged the pictures and their attached papers into a neat row, making them easier to look at.

He sat wearily on the carpet, knees pulled up, back against the mattress, and studied the remaining choices. His gut wasn't helping anymore.

All three places felt right, as did the people he'd be living with…

There was Ash, the cute, red headed artist who dwelled in a loft off Venice Beach.

He liked the unconventional flavor of her and the coastal surroundings. From what he saw strewn about during his visit, Ash did everything from drawing to painting to sculpting to God knows what.

Then there was Dean, the full time water salesman who lived in a vaulted ceiling, adobe apartment in Pasadena.

If there was a guy who had his shit together, it was Dean. In his twenties and on the rise, he was a natural, charismatic leader. Maybe this was what Gordon needed. Someone to whip him into shape. Dean kind of reminded him of his high school football coach, and he liked that. When Dean interviewed Gordon for the apartment, it was more of a mini-lecture. While most people discussed rent, utilities, and parking, Dean discussed goal-setting, efficiency, and nutrition. He seemed to *want* a roommate more than *need* one. If only to have someone to bestow his wisdom upon.

And finally there was Shawn and Cedric, roommates in the Pacific Palisades.

Shawn had given the tour by himself, mentioning that Cedric was okay with whomever he chose. The house had the best living conditions by far. The place was sprawling and tricked out. If Best Buy sold it, this place flaunted it. It had style, too. All the variables tapped into a seductive lifestyle Gordon had never tasted. The rent was steep, but he had the cash. Throughout the interview, Gordon had exuded a sense that he could roll with anything. This met with Shawn's approval, as if such a quality was an unspoken prerequisite to begin with.

Ash. Dean. Shawn and Cedric.

The finalists.

All pulled him equally, but he couldn't wait much longer to decide. Although they liked him, he knew they wouldn't wait around for long. Fill the space, get the rent.

So it was down to Ash, Dean, Shawn and Cedric.

Fuck.

He didn't know who to go with, and he was tired of thinking about it. He glanced at the clock. 1:37 am.

Ok, then. He'd sleep on it. He'd make the call in the morning, check out of the hotel, and move into his new home. His first step in figuring out his new life.

Gordon crunched up the Subway wrapper and tossed it in the trash.

Chapter 31

WATER POURED DOWN the beige tile.

Gordon wasn't soaping-up, wasn't shampooing, wasn't doing anything except standing under the shower head.

Night had come and gone, and he still didn't know which roommate to live with.

He was hoping a dream would assist him in making a decision. It's said that dreams are your subconscious at work, so maybe his subconscious could get off its lazy ass and lend a helping hand. Maybe show him an image of Dean combing his hair or Ash washing plaster from her fingers or Shawn programming the buttons on the all-in-one remote control.

But nothing.

He hadn't dreamed at all. He didn't even wake up to piss. The sleep was sound. The sleep was death. And it had yielded nothing.

Dressed and ready for a run to the Golden Arches, Gordon popped open a can of Coke, praying that the jolt of corn syrup and caffeine would kick-start his brain. He took his spot on the carpet in front of the profiles.

He had narrowed it down to three.

All seemed right. All seemed—

He stood, letting the soda can drop to the floor. He could feel the answer boiling to the surface. He could feel the solution coming into focus. Just a few more seconds and—

He had it.

He was fighting the answer all along. He was resisting it, and it was right in front of him.

They were right in front of him.

Chapter 32

Now

JALAPEÑO PORK RINDS and caramel fudge brownies.

Not the healthiest snack in the world, but Gordon and Ash were devouring it for its taste, not its nutritional value. Taste was the reason you ate stuff like that. Kids grab what stimulates their taste buds. They yank beef jerky from the rack for their parents to buy. The yank is instinctual, natural, and will no doubt repeat itself in the future until the brain is taught to override this urge.

Too much fat, the head tells the stomach. *Too much grease, too much salt, too much sugar*. Education becomes the master to instinct.

But not in the loft.

In here, the brain is reverted to its natural state. *Its proper state*, Ash would argue. Free of the bullshit of what others deemed correct.

So Ash and Gordon munched on jalapeño pork rinds and caramel fudge brownies. And why shouldn't they? Was it a crime to enjoy fried fat? Baked fat? Glazed fat? (Not to mention the potent screwdrivers they were drinking to wash it all down.)

Ash shook a bottle of ketchup over her plate.

"Ketchup?" asked Gordon.

She dipped a pork rind into the puddle of red and held it between her lips before drawing it in with her tongue.

"You're burying the taste of pork," said Gordon, crumbs on his chin.

"I'm enhancing it," said Ash.

"It's not supposed to be enhanced."

"The rinds would thank me if they could."

"Some things are fine the way they are."

She held up a pork rind and moved it like a puppet as she spoke in a tiny, seductive voice, "*Oh, Ash. I love that ketchup. Soak me, baby.*"

She drenched the rind in red then tilted her head back and placed it on her tongue, letting out a moan of ecstasy as she sucked it in and chewed.

"Close to cumming?" asked Gordon.

"Sshh, sshh… you'll ruin it."

"I doubt it."

"Sshh…"

"You could cum on a float in the middle of the Rose Bowl Parade."

"That an offer?"

"Point is, some things should be left alone."

Ash lit a cigarette, considering his words. "Like pork rinds?"

"That's right."

"You got another example?"

Gordon searched for one, then said, "The suit of armor at that guy's house."

Ash took a second to figure out what the hell he was talking about. "The one with the strap-on dildo?"

"That's the one."

She burst into laughter. "I totally forgot about that."

"How could you?"

"That guy is *such* a freak."

"A shameless freak."

"Best kind, though. Gotta admire him for that."

"But a strap-on?"

"Maybe knights were partial to black rubber cocks," said Ash. "He could be striving for historical accuracy."

"Except the armor wasn't the only thing he screwed with."

"There were *other* dildos? And you didn't point 'em out?"

"No… not dildos, but…" Gordon leaned back. "… other things."

"Like?"

"A painting. Of an eagle. It had bars drawn on it."

"Maybe they were part of the picture."

"No, you could see where the paint dripped onto the frame."

"But no dildo?"

"No."

"What else?"

"Little things," said Gordon. "A snow globe of a clown. With clouds painted on top."

"Clouds?"

"Stuff like that was everywhere. Stuff that got changed."

The thought didn't sit right with Gordon. He shifted in his seat, like his clothes had shrank two sizes.

Ash shrugged. "Guy's a freak."

Gordon stared at the almost empty bag of pork rinds.

"… but kinda cool," said Ash. "Too bad I gotta kick his son's ass."

"I don't think you have to," said Gordon.

"My payback isn't up for debate."

"I mean, I don't think it was his son that destroyed your exhibit. It was *him*."

She squinted; blew out a stream of smoke. "The dad?"

"I think so."

"Your proof?"

"What've we been talking about?"

"Ketchup."

"After that."

"Things that were changed in his house."

"Things that he *added* to. Each time, he took someone's work and changed it."

Ash wasn't so sure. "The suit of armor isn't someone's—"

"It's an exhibit, right?" said Gordon. "Art to put on display. Doesn't that fit with the type of things that were vandalized?"

Ash finished her screwdriver. "It's a stretch."

"Is it?"

"My exhibit didn't have something added to it. It was destroyed."

"But that's still changing it. Like the angel with the broken wings. Like the globe. The painting. The armor. He didn't even ask what his son did that made us so pissed. That's because he *already knew*."

Ash stubbed out the cigarette, her doubt replaced by indignation.

"Fuck it then," said Ash. "Let's go to his house and find out. I'll accuse him to his face, see what he says."

"In the morning," said Gordon.

"Why wait?"

"I gotta work."

"Now?"

"Soon, yeah. We'll go in the morning."

"It doesn't matter anyway. He'll just deny it."

"Let him. We'll know by his reaction."

Ash sighed at having to wait, but if Gordon's theory was true, then she'd get to deal with it sooner than she had planned. It could've taken months. Who knew how long that prick of a son was going to stay in Europe?

"Okay…" said Ash. "Morning it is."

Chapter 33

OF COURSE, THE *real* reason Gordon couldn't hop in the car with Ash and race over to Myron's house is that he had to be at the meeting with Cedric and Shawn.

The agreed-upon time was seven. Cedric, naturally, was forty minutes late, but at least he showed up. (Shawn had bet Gordon twenty dollars he wouldn't.) The location was the dining room. Its long table had a conference-feel to it, and Gordon liked the fact there was no TV, no stereo, no distractions.

Shawn was waiting on the far end, back to the wall, when Cedric came in, headphones around his neck. He smirked at the sight of Shawn. Cedric had, in a way, forced this meeting, and he was pleased at himself for causing such a ruckus. He sat sideways and unwrapped a gyro.

"So?" said Cedric.

Gordon sat in the middle of the table, feeling very much like a mediator in a debate. He decided to jump right in.

"We don't have to live like this," said Gordon.

"Like what?" asked Cedric.

"You against Shawn. Shawn against you."

"Who're *you* against?"

"I'm neutral."

"No one's neutral."

"Let him speak," said Shawn.

"I am, *Shawny*."

"I'm doing my best to be objective," said Gordon.

"Who'd you get to sign that agreement first? Me or him?"

"Shawn came home when I was working on it."

"Did you ask if I wanted anything added to it? No, you didn't."

"This isn't about—"

"Who interviewed you? Shawny. Who let you move in without

checkin' with me? Shawny. Way I see it, you're anything but neutral."

"That's your opinion," said Gordon. "But we're here to work out what's wrong with you and Shawn."

"What's wrong?"

Shawn sighed. "Did you even read the thing he taped to your door? It listed everything."

"Did it?"

"Let's forget about that," said Gordon. "Let's say what we feel."

"So say it," said Cedric.

"I want respect," said Shawn. "I know you don't like who I am."

"Move the fuck out then," said Cedric. "'Cause I know you don't like who *I* am."

"But I'm willing to endure you."

"*Endure me?* "said Cedric. "That a come-on?"

Shawn gave him the finger.

"Be specific in what you resent," Gordon said to Shawn.

"I resent his disrespect," said Shawn. "The way he treats me like a house guest who's overstayed his welcome. I *live* here, Cedric. That means you not only have to respect me, you have to respect my possessions."

Cedric wiped his hands. "You don't know what disrespect is."

"Whatever."

"Why d'you *really* hate me, Shawny?"

It was an unexpected question. Shawn just looked at him.

"No answer?" asked Cedric. He leaned forward. "Then let me tell you. It's 'cause you're a fag, and you think I don't approve. That's why you hate me. That's why you hate *yourself*."

"Now I hate myself?"

"'Cause you *suck dick*."

"You're just an intolerant asshole. What about you?" Shawn asked Cedric.

"Uh-oh. You gonna hurt me now?" said Cedric.

"Hey. C'mon," said Gordon.

"Shut the fuck up," Cedric said to Gordon. "This is why you wanted us here." He turned back to Shawn. "What about me?" He folded his arms and gave a twisted grin, trying to act impervious, but the act of folding his arms was a defensive posture. He was protecting himself. He just didn't know it.

"How's the family these days?" asked Shawn.

The smile faded from Cedric's face. Shawn had touched a nerve.

"Think I don't hear you talking to your parents on the phone?"

"You don't know shit about my family."

"I know they didn't want their son to become a wedding DJ."

"I'm a recordin' artist, bitch. I got an album."

"Who doesn't? Any nine year old with a computer can make his own album. That doesn't make him Prince."

Cedric grunted. "This all you got? I say you suck dick, you say I'm not on MTV? That it?"

"No," said Shawn. "*This* is it. *Your family's ashamed of you.* They thought you were going be the one that would hoist the family out of the lowest of the lower class and actually do something with your life. But you let them down. You play "Mambo No. 5" at Bar Mitzvahs. You live above your means. You drive your family further into debt because you gotta borrow money. Money they worked their whole life saving, only to piss it away on their son."

Cedric stared at Shawn.

"Mam-bo No. 5!" Shawn overemphasized.

"And what're you doin' with your life?" asked Cedric. "You ain't even got a job. Think your mama brags about that?"

"She doesn't care. See, my family's *rich*. They made something of their lives."

Cedric jumped to his feet. Before Gordon knew it, Cedric had traversed the length of the table and was towering over Shawn.

"Say somethin' about my family again," said Cedric.

"What're you so worked up about?" asked Shawn, surprisingly brazen considering Cedric was within striking distance. "I thought I was full of shit."

"Okay," said Gordon. "Take it easy…"

"I'm done," said Cedric, backing away.

"Yeah, Gordon. He's too successful to talk to us. He's got an album."

Cedric gathered up the gyro wrapper.

"Maybe you could start your own label. Ghetto Records."

Gordon grimaced at what he perceived to be the final straw for Cedric.

It took less than a second to be proved right.

Cedric lunged at Shawn, punching him square in the jaw, then again near the eye.

In the time it took for Gordon to pull them apart, Cedric had landed six strikes. Shawn was on his back, knees tucked into his chest, arms raised to shield himself.

Cedric let himself be torn away, but shoved Gordon back just as quickly.

"Pussy bitch," said Cedric.

"Fuck you…" said Shawn in a voice that sounded like he was speaking through snot and tears.

"What?" said Cedric. "You wanna do *what?*" He unzipped his pants and pulled out his dick. "You wanna suck on this?" He shook his penis and kicked Shawn in the legs. "You'd choke." He tucked his dick away. "Lil' pussy bitch."

Cedric glared at Gordon and marched out.

Shawn rolled onto his side, remaining in the fetal position, his face hidden behind his forearms.

It was safe to say, the meeting was over.

"You okay?" asked Gordon.

"Leave me alone."

Gordon nodded, then slowly left the dining room, leaving Shawn in a bundle.

This was supposed to make things better.

The animosity between Cedric and Shawn was worse than ever.

And it was Gordon's fault.

Chapter 34

THE BOARD IN THE KITCHEN was white.

It used to appear almost solid black from the overwhelming presence of ink. Dean's scribbling once consumed the board like a fungus.

But that was *before* Dean got fired.

Now the white portion of the board was reclaiming ground as the fungus of ink retreated. There simply wasn't anything for Dean to write. Since he was out of work, he didn't have a whole lot to do.

Dean was aware of the obvious lack of entries, and at first he worked at adding content at his previous pace, but found himself jotting down the most mundane activities to fill space:

empty garbage
pay phone bill
replace air filter
organize files

Small time stuff that would've never found its way onto the board before.

Gordon had just returned from the meeting with Cedric and Shawn (fucking disaster that it was) and wanted an energy bar from the kitchen cabinet.

Dean was at the sink, mindlessly loading the dishwasher.

"Where's Naomi?" asked Gordon.

Dean looked at him. "Why?"

"She's usually over at this time."

"Guess she couldn't make it today."

Gordon noticed a half empty bottle of Jim Beam on the counter. Not an earth-shattering sight, but this was Dean's apartment, and though he drank from time to time, he never kept alcohol at home.

His mood was sour, and Gordon was curious as to why, but he just wanted to sleep. That's why he came over. He had nowhere else to go.

Staying the night at Cedric and Shawn's wasn't a good idea. The tension there was at an all-time high.

He couldn't go to Venice since he already lied to Ash about working, plus she'd probably find some way of keeping him up, and he was exhausted.

He could spend the night at the hotel. That made sense. The room was there, paid for, with a bed ready to be slept in. But staying the night at the hotel was something he never did. It was against the rules.

So here he was.

Gordon grabbed an energy bar and exited without saying anything else. There would be another time for that. But he made a mental note of Dean's mood. And the bottle of Jim Beam. And the white that had overtaken the board.

49

It's about seven in the morning. I don't have much time. I promised Ash we'd see Myron. But there are things I want to write before we go, so I drove to the hotel.

Bear with me. I need to bitch. Everything sucks. I have three directions I'm pushing in, and they're all pushing back.

I tried to get Shawn and Cedric to cool it, but Cedric flipped out. I shouldn't give a fuck, but the point of that life is to give a fuck. The only solution is for one of them to leave. Cedric won't, but Shawn might. He says he won't, but he can't be that stubborn. Hopefully, he's packing as I write this.

And Dean. Fucking Dean. He was my guru. I'd even call him my role model. Not to his face, of course. Since he got fired, he's been sliding and treating Naomi like shit. Before he was just neglecting her. Now he's taking shit out on her. I need to say something. Life over there is about achievement. I thought this meant keeping my nose out of their relationship. But maybe it means the opposite.

And Ash. Sweet, fucked up Ash. In less than an hour, I'm picking her up, and we're going to see The Crazy Fuck with the Dildo Knight. When I'm with Ash, I let myself go. She knows this and tests me. I know this and test her. It's a twisted game of chicken.

Chapter 35

"IF I DON'T HOSE 'EM, they'll die," said Myron.

He moved the garden hose in a wide arc, soaking what he referred to as his flowerbed, but to Gordon looked more like a backyard conquered by weeds.

Ash had already accused Myron twice of destroying her exhibit. Once in the driveway and once in the living room. He denied any wrongdoing both times. Now she was launching into her third accusation.

"You snuck onto the warehouse roof, and you trashed my graveyard," said Ash.

"Doesn't rain much," said Myron. "No water, no life."

"We know it was you," said Gordon.

"This hose gives me power. Like I'm God," said Myron. "God of the Yard."

"You don't fuck with someone's work," said Ash.

"You're assuming I did."

"You're not convincing me otherwise, Yard God."

Myron lifted the hose to his lips, took a sip, and wiped his mouth with the sleeve of his robe. "Let's say I *did* pay a visit to your graveyard…"

"Oh, you mother—"

"What took place wasn't vandalism," said Myron, shutting off the flow of water.

"Bullshit!" said Ash.

"I bet you didn't even think about what was in front of you when you first saw it."

"I saw a trashed exhibit," said Gordon.

"*My* trashed exhibit," said Ash.

Myron seemed disappointed. "When I first met you two, I thought there was potential."

"Fuck this guy," said Gordon to Ash. "Call the cops."

"Feel free," said Myron. "I'll deny it." He coiled the hose.

"Even if your son goes to jail too?" asked Gordon.

"My boy's got nothing to do with this," said Myron. "It was my idea."

"But you signed an E," said Ash.

"I did," said Myron.

"For Earnest," said Ash.

Myron laughed. "The E's for *expansion*."

"Should've been a B for bullshit," said Gordon.

Myron looked at him. "I didn't trash anything. I *expanded* it."

"You're insane," said Ash.

"And you're *simple*," said Myron. It was the first time anger entered his voice, and it caught Ash's attention. "You created fancy tombstones. Whoop-dee-doo. You took the most obvious symbol of death—a tombstone—and painted it all nice and pretty. How groundbreaking."

"And what'd you do?" asked Ash.

"What I did, sweetheart, is expand its meaning. I took your tombstones and broke them into a pile to illustrate something greater."

"Like what?"

"A mass grave."

Ash flinched. "Why?"

"Public displays of death are only condoned if they're presented in good taste. People drive by sprawling cemeteries without paying them any attention. They cruise by *thousands of buried corpses* without giving it a second thought. *But the mass grave*—if only they could drive their SUVs by a steaming pile of rotting bodies. I want to see them not spill their Starbucks when the rancid stench hits their nostrils. Mass graves are the reality of this world. So if you ask me if I'm the one that climbed on that warehouse roof, I say yes. I used *your* art as the foundation for *my* art. I expanded it."

Ash was oddly spellbound. "You... had no right."

"Why do I need a right?" asked Myron.

This stumped Ash. She wanted to argue, but if she lived for anything, it was rebellion. How could she argue against herself?

"An artist builds on the work that came before him," said Myron. "Expansion is art."

"And that stuff inside your house?" asked Gordon. "That's expansion too?"

"It certainly is," said Myron, pleased Gordon made the connection.

"What's inside is shit," said Ash. "A knight with a dildo?"

Myron considered her, almost with pity. "Follow me."

He tracked soil through the house as he led them into the den where the suit of armor wearing a strap-on dildo was on display. Ash and Gordon stood in front of the armor, much like tourists standing in front of a museum piece listening to a tour guide.

Myron put his hand on the armor's shoulder.

"Expansion," said Myron.

"We're listening," said Ash.

"Body armor. The trait of a man going into battle," said Myron. "That's what this *was*. Here's how I expanded its meaning. I attached a strap-on dildo. Why? To show how the fighting man not only kills in combat. He literally *fucks* and fucks *with* the opposing society. On every level. Combat is just one facet of the act," said Myron.

"Why black?" asked Ash.

"Hmm?"

"Why a black dildo?"

"Oh." He scratched his beard. "The, uh, color holds no meaning in and of itself. It was the biggest the store sold. Plus, it looked real, and that was important."

"Why?" asked Gordon.

"For the sake of clarity. I thought about using a shiny, metal vibrator to comment on technology, but I stuck with the organic, evolutionary approach so as not to obfuscate what I was trying to say. Which is simple. War fucks."

"War fucks?" asked Ash.

"That's it."

"And you said *my* exhibit wasn't original?" said Ash.

"Hey, sweetheart, this was a conventional suit of armor. I made it into a political statement. I *expanded* its meaning."

Gordon wasn't convinced. "And the rest of this stuff?" He pointed to various items. Myron explained why they were altered.

The Snow Globe of the Juggling Clown:

"I painted storm clouds on top to show that impending doom always lurks for those who frolic in ignorance, which is what the clown is clearly doing."

The Painting of the Eagle:

"Jail bars were added to imprison the bird to illustrate how the government continuously cages our freedoms."

The Park Bench:

"Ah, you like that one? I made it orange, the standard color of jumpsuits prisoners are issued by the state."

"I don't get it," said Gordon.

"It's a bench from a public park. Usually green. You're outdoors, sucking in the smog, thinking *freedom*. Meanwhile you got six surveillance cameras zeroed in on you, transmitting your face into a federal identification database to see if you're a potential threat. You're treated like a prisoner. That's why it's orange. 'Cause you're in jail."

"And the angel statue?" asked Ash. "The one in front of Target?"

"You want an explanation for everything?"

"You wanna talk to the cops?" asked Ash.

Myron smirked at the threat. "The angel is a symbol of Heaven. So I clipped its wings, 'cause we ain't goin' nowhere. *Our time is now.* Stop thinking about Paradise and deal with the world we live in."

The man was parrying the questions with ease, ready for more.

"Why leave an E?" asked Gordon.

"Don't all artists sign their work?" asked Myron.

"You make it easier for the cops to draw a connection," said Ash.

"That's the idea. The E shows them it isn't random. Raises awareness. Leads to more exposure."

Ash glanced at the collection of altered objects. She seemed to be reaching a judgment. "You *really* endorse using art as a foundation for art?"

"All art is art built upon art built upon art," said Myron.

"Hmm..." said Ash.

There was a pregnant pause as Myron and Gordon waited for her to follow up the *hhmm* with actual words.

When she finally spoke, it wasn't with her tongue, but with the thrust of her sandaled foot. She walked to the suit of armor and kicked it right in the gut. When that only resulted in a shuddering of metal, she grabbed it by the helmet and yanked it over.

The armor toppled with a loud *clang*.

Myron did nothing to stop her. He merely watched, partly amused, as

Ash struggled to rip off the dildo. It was attached with a buckled leather strap, and Ash had to calm for a moment to unlatch it from behind. Then she flung it free.

The dildo bounced off the wall, knocking over a potted fern.

"Interpret *that*, asshole," said Ash. "You *ever* touch my shit again, I'll kill you."

"Such passion."

"I mean it."

"I don't doubt your veracity."

She booted the armor again, separating the helmet. It spun across the floor. She turned on her heel, exiting without waiting for Gordon.

"Why don't you do something constructive?" asked Gordon.

Myron turned to him. "What're *you* doing that's so helpful to society?"

Gordon almost answered, then realized he was doing jack shit for society. So he shook his head and left. Myron laughed, waved goodbye.

With Ash in the lead, Gordon made his way down the steep driveway. When Ash got to the bottom, she spit.

The saliva dripped into a crack.

Gordon thought their next stop would be a police station, but Ash dismissed the idea of turning Myron in. The more they discussed Myron's cultural pontifications, the more Gordon realized what Ash was experiencing. There was more confusion than anger. More curiosity than indignation.

She was feeding from a trough of raw emotions and, deep down, relishing every bite.

Chapter 36

THE BRUISING AROUND the eye was severe.

Shawn sat in a reclined patio chair by the pool, although not tanning by a long shot. He wore jeans, a long sleeve shirt, and sneakers, with only his face and hands exposed to the afternoon sun.

It was the first black-eye Gordon had seen since Mike showed up at work sporting a shiner four years ago. According to Mike, a Packers fan was spewing a few too many insults at the offensive line, so naturally a tussle resulted in which the Packer-Backer got in a cheap shot before Soldier Field security intervened.

Shawn's was worse, though. It stretched from above his brow line to below his cheek bone, a pool of dark purple that had swollen his left eye almost shut.

"Why do you take this?" asked Gordon as he sat next to him.

Shawn stared at a dead spider floating on the surface of the pool.

"Because I'm not going to give in," said Shawn.

"Give in to *what?*"

The spider swirled, two legs missing.

"Three years ago, I was scheduled to fly to Boston to visit my family," said Shawn. "We did it every year. Got together at Thanksgiving. So every year I flew out there. Only thing is, I'm scared shitless of flying. I mean, terrified." He grinned. "So what do people do who are scared of flying? One of two things. Avoid flying or dope up. Well, I flew. So I doped up. At first, I thought drinks would do the trick. I figured rum would calm the nerves. But here's the mistake of that philosophy, Gordon Lake. Unless you're in first class, they don't serve drinks 'til you're up in the air. What the fuck, right? For a guy scared of flying, that kinda defeats the purpose. The take-off makes me wanna puke."

Shawn leaned back, closed his eyes.

"So I switched to pills," said Shawn. "Pretty easy to get when you tell a doctor you need something for a flight. They hand 'em out, relieved your problem can be fixed by a pill. Ever take prescription sedatives?"

"No."

"I highly recommend it. They dull life's blade. I took some a half-hour before boarding. Before long, I was in my seat, watching the flight attendant review the procedure for exiting the plane after it's crashed."

Shawn opened his eyes. He seemed to be looking into the sun, inviting the rays to burn his corneas to a crisp.

"And there I am. Sedated like a fool. Using chemicals to numb me. And I watch her review the safety procedures. And somewhere deep down, below the levels of chemicals I've ingested, I can still feel the fear. It's still there. Inside me. Then we land. My family greets me. And I have to explain my sedated state. I say I was up all night or tired from the flight."

Shawn looked to Gordon.

"But last Thanksgiving, that all changed. I popped the lid off the bottle. Tapped out two pills. But I couldn't bring myself to swallow them. I was disgusted for having to succumb to drugs to deal with fear. So I didn't take them. I made the decision right then. Standing there with those pills in my palm, I made the decision to never again back down from fear. I may feel it. It may come for me. But I will never again duck from it. Ever. So I dumped the pills, all of 'em, in the trash. And I went to the airport. Unmedicated. My heart raced, my stomach felt nauseous, but I faced it. I faced the fear. Straight the fuck on. 'Cause I was *sick* of living in fear. And I swore I'd never again let it dictate how I live." Shawn nodded to the house. "That fuck in there? He's not going to set the rules. I won't be intimidated. I won't move out. I picked my path last November. Cedric can go fuck himself. He hit me. Fine. So the fuck what?"

They sat there. The air feeling more dry than Gordon had ever felt it.

"You're fighting the wrong battle, Shawn."

Shawn smiled, as if he could no longer keep a straight face at Gordon's ignorance. "I'm fighting fear. The only battle I've ever known."

Chapter 37

IT WAS THE SMELL that hit him first.

Before he saw the bed made, the vacuumed carpet, the arranged towels. It was the smell of pine disinfectant.

Son of a bitch.

Gordon remained in the doorway of room 116 at the Starlight Inn, shocked at how clean everything was.

The maid. The fucking maid. The fucking maid had been in there. The room had been cleaned, been touched, been... violated. It wasn't a disaster; the walls were still fraught with the collages. But still. He left instructions. He'd made it clear to the manager.

Gordon left the room, slammed the door, locked it (not that locking it made a fucking difference apparently), and went to the registration office, a place he had not stepped foot in since the day he arrived in LA. A Hispanic woman in her thirties smiled as he reached the counter.

Gordon said, "A maid cleaned 116."

She squinted.

"I said *no maids.*"

The woman spoke politely, and apparently oblivious to the extent of his indignation. "All rooms are serviced on a daily—"

"Where's the older gentleman?" asked Gordon.

"Who?"

"The guy that runs this place."

"He's in Italy."

"Italy?"

"On vacation. Due back in a week. Is there something I can help you with?"

"I said no maids in 116. No maids."

"I didn't know, sir."

"The *maids* should know."

"Can I have your name?"

"Lake. Gordon. I'm a long term resident. I paid up front. No one enters. The old guy knows that."

"He's in—"

"I know he's in Italy. He could be on the dark side of the moon for all I care. The *maids* should know. I have research material. It's sensitive."

"Okay, sir."

"Can you make sure they don't go in 116? Can you promise me that?"

"I'll speak with the staff."

"Thank you," said Gordon.

Gordon left the registration office, fighting the urge to put his fist through the glass door.

Chapter 38

"FIRST TIME IN RECORDED history he's been late," said Naomi.

"He's never been late?" asked Gordon.

"Not from day one. Boy was a preemie. Popped out a full month before his due date."

Naomi had come home from her shift, showered, dressed, and was waiting on the balcony. More worried than angry.

"Times like these, I wish I smoked," she said. "What else are you supposed to do while killing time on a balcony? There's no birds to feed. Nothing."

It was almost nine. Dean was supposed to pick her up two hours earlier. He wasn't answering his cell and hadn't spoken of any plans that could have tied him up. This was a guy who lived and died by the clock, who took pride in his punctuality.

She tried his cell again. The voicemail picked up. She left a brief message. Her third.

"Maybe the battery's dead," said Gordon.

"He keeps an extra one in the glove compartment."

"Traffic?"

"It's Saturday."

"Accident?"

"Don't say that."

"Maybe he just forgot."

"Maybe." She didn't believe that for a second.

The moment was awkward. Now Gordon wished *he* had a cigarette.

"You guys ever settle the church debate?" he asked.

"No. Ever since Dean lost his job, I didn't want to bring it up again. It's not an easy time for him."

"He really liked that company?"

"He wanted to climb the ladder. The top circle of executives go on retreats to Maui ever year. He wanted to be in that circle *so bad*."

"And you?"

She looked at him.

"There's no ladder you wanna climb?" asked Gordon.

She thought about this. "Not anymore. I was gonna get a business degree way back when. International Corporate Relations. Be the American Rep for some big company."

"What happened?"

"I met Dean," she said, as if the answer should've been obvious. "Fell in love. He wanted to provide for me."

"You're waiting tables."

"I got bored. He doesn't like me working."

"Go back to school. Get the degree."

"I gave up on that."

"Why?"

"It was a stupid idea. Something spun from a meeting with a guidance counselor." They laughed. "Seriously, when my high school counselor, Ms. Preston, asked what I wanted to do, I had to say something, so I said 'international businesswoman.' But the more we talked, the more it seemed like something I could do. I liked the idea of traveling the world. Being greeted by foreign executives. Meetings in exotic places. I was going to blog about the whole thing. Keep an online journal."

The word *journal* caused Gordon to unconsciously sit up.

"I'd write about my adventures and post photos. Pass along what I was learning about other cultures, business practices, people. I'd answer questions and offer encouragement through email and have chat sessions. I was going to share the whole experience."

There was an energy in her words… *a sense of hope*… that he hadn't heard before.

"But here I am on a balcony with nothing to smoke," she said, the energy depleting as fast as it spiked. "Think he's okay?" She dialed again, then hung up when Dean's recorded message came on.

"You don't want to do that anymore?" asked Gordon. "Be a company rep, travel the world, write?"

Naomi shrugged. "I'm with Dean now. He has plans for us."

Plans for *himself*, thought Gordon.

"Naomi, you gotta be careful," said Gordon, not knowing exactly where he was going with the thought and not sure if he should find out.

"Of what?"

"If you let things keep going like this… if you keep letting Dean make all the decisions…"

She waited for him to finish.

"Your life could get lost in his."

Naomi's eyes widened ever so slightly, and she appeared uncomfortable, as if she had been awakened from a dream.

The front door opened.

"Let's go," called Dean.

His voice was flat, far from the enthused rallying cry of a man about to spend an evening with his fiancée. Naomi rose and left Gordon alone on the balcony. He could hear her ask Dean to explain his tardiness. Dean mumbled something back.

The door shut, and they were gone.

Gordon was supposed to be pragmatic when dealing with Dean and Naomi, and the reality was this: Naomi had given up her life plans for Dean.

Gordon no longer knew how he should conduct himself with her.

Well, for one, you can stop hitting on her. She's engaged.

Yeah, but engaged isn't married.

She's taken. What part of that don't you understand?

All of it.

Gordon wished to fucking hell he had a cigarette.

Chapter 39

THERE ARE PEOPLE you want out of your life.

You meet them, interact for the short term, then move on. Not everyone you meet can come along for the grand ride, rambling down the path of your days. So you tell the person to cease contact with you, or you flat-out neglect them. The person you wish to jettison will usually get the message.

Myron didn't get the message.

And strange that he didn't. After all, Ash had made a spectacle of her exit during their last encounter. She had mocked his intentions, insulted him, and ripped apart the suit of armor. A few days had passed since then, and Ash had figured the series of odd events starting with the destruction of her exhibit and finishing with the armor dismantling was finally over.

Then she came home from buying hot sauce at Vons and checked her home voicemail.

"What the fuck is he doing on my voicemail?" asked Ash.

Gordon shrugged.

"You give him my number?" asked Ash.

"Why would I do that?"

Ash sighed and played the message on speaker.

Myron's scratchy voice came out of the small, heart-shaped phone, sounding distant as if he was talking into a speaker phone.

"I'm, uh... hey. This is Myron. Hope you don't mind me calling you..."

"Fuck yeah, I mind," said Ash.

"I wanted to say I enjoyed our little get together the other night. There was a shared passion, one I'm sure you felt. Our means of harnessing our inner energy seem different. But are they? You're a vibrant, young lady, Ashley. I think we should chat again. Why not stop by Wednesday evening? I'll supply the merlot. You have a fire, sweetheart. But is the world seeing it? If passion isn't expressed, it's wasted. Think about that. I look forward to seeing you again."

There was a pause as if Myron needed to walk to the speaker phone to hang up, then the message ended.

Something in the voicemail dug at Ash. Something that went beyond being bothered by the fact he had somehow gotten her number.

She played the message again, and her anger waned, replaced by the same mixture of confusion and curiosity Gordon had detected the last time they saw Myron.

"Something wrong?" asked Gordon.

"Everything's wrong."

She walked to the living room and sat cross-legged on the floor. She used a thin brush to add a coat of gloss to a tiny, wooden figurine she had shaped with sandpaper. She set the brush down and blew lightly on the piece, twirling it between her fingers. She stared at the piece, considering it with an air of dissatisfaction.

47

She fucking went to see him. I can't believe it.

I don't know what went down. Ash did the smart thing and left a note telling me. She knew I'd be pissed. I guarantee Myron mind-fucked her. Blew his brain-load right into her skull.

Did I mention Dean is a prick? Naomi sees happiness if she stays with him. How? He's a product he sold to her. A cool-looking car with a shitty engine.

There's no saving Shawn and Cedric. I'm giving it one last shot. This is the first true sign of failure for me.

Fucking Ash. I can't believe she went to see him.

Chapter 40

"HE DIDN'T MIND-FUCK ME," said Ash.

She was finally back at the loft, and Gordon was waiting. Tonight was supposed to be spent with Shawn and Cedric, but Gordon threw out that plan. He had to know what transpired between Ash and Myron.

"All the guy does is mind-fuck," said Gordon.

"Not me," said Ash.

"Then what happened?"

"We talked."

"I don't know why you'd go—"

"He said some things, okay? Things I'd been thinking about."

"On the message?"

"Yes."

"Such as?"

"It doesn't matter."

"Ash…"

"He just… things like, I've been wasting who I am."

"That's a load of shit," said Gordon.

"No, he's right," said Ash.

"That you're wasting your life?"

"How many people know I'm even alive?"

"You wanna be famous?" asked Gordon. "Is that it?"

"It's not about fame," said Ash. "It's about *exposure*."

"For your work?"

"Yes."

"I don't—what more can you do? You do what you do."

"But no one *sees* what I do. It all goes to waste."

"Not true. Your stuff shows in exhibits."

"Please, the same fifty LA snobs go to those things," said Ash. "I wanna go beyond that."

"You want a bigger audience?" asked Gordon.

"In so few words."

"And lemme guess, Myron has a remedy for this?"

Ash leaned against the wall. "He does."

Despite his frustration, Gordon could see that something was stirring inside Ash. It was making her excited, and Ash's excitement was always contagious.

"Care to share?" asked Gordon.

"Our friend Myron was affected by our visit."

"Sure…"

"I'm serious. He said he'd been 'expanding' the work of fellow artists, but now realized it was wrong to do that. Apparently, we're capable of a little mind-fucking ourselves, 'cause he sounded like a different guy."

"I'm sure he did."

"Exposure, Gordon. It's all about exposure. He offered me the opportunity to create something that would be seen by thousands. Tens of thousands. Maybe more."

"By doing what?"

"I may need help."

"By doing what?"

"First answer me this," said Ash. She bent her chin down, looking up at him with a devilish stare. "You want in?"

"To what?"

"No answer, no admittance."

"It's illegal, isn't it?"

Ash whistled, looked at her nails.

Don't deny.

He took a breath. "Okay."

She applauded the decision. "We're gonna have some fun," she said. "You and me."

***

It was everywhere.

Thick, powdery lines of chalk wound their way through the house like a swarm of hungry snakes.

Chalk lines on the floor, the walls, the furniture. Orange chalk, white, red, black. The lines bordered everything they wandered near:

A circle traced around the hallway clock.

A rectangle drawn around the coffee table in the den.

A square etched on the kitchen counter around the microwave.

In the bathroom, tiny circles were present around a bottle of mouthwash, around a floor mat, around the air freshener perched on the toilet lid.

The whole place reeked of chalk. The scent hung in the air, reminding Gordon of elementary school. He checked his bedroom. Inside was unmarked, but a thick, neon-blue line was drawn before the doorway, designating the entrance.

Gordon made his way through the rest of the house. Through a window, he saw Shawn in the backyard, on his hands and knees by the edge of the pool, carefully tracing a line around a patio chair with a stub of red chalk.

Just what the fuck was this guy doing?

Gordon swung open the back door, trying to act casual.

"Heya Shawn."

"Hey."

"What'cha doin'?"

"Making things clear."

"How?"

Shawn finished encircling the chair and leaned back on his knees. "I'm defining boundaries."

Gordon looked at the red circle. "Little extreme, don't you think?"

"No."

"There's chalk everywhere, man."

"There's *boundaries* everywhere."

"Cedric's gonna shit."

"He's the one that defined the limits," said Shawn. "I'm just making 'em visible. Making it clear who owns what, who can go where."

"You should consider cleaning up."

"Can't do that."

"You're asking for trouble."

"These limits need to be set," said Shawn. "This is *my* chair, see?" He held up the chalk. "Red. My color. Cedric's is white, and you're blue... but uh, there's not a lot around since you don't own much."

The color-coding made Gordon think of Dean (who would probably get an erection if he saw this), but even Dean wouldn't go this far. Dean was about efficiency. Shawn was trying to impose order.

Shawn said, "I think he'll like it." He turned his head to study the backyard, searching for his next target to trace. The black eye on Shawn's face was more evident at this angle, though it looked like make-up had been applied to conceal it.

He pocketed the red chalk, exchanging it for a stick of white, climbed to his feet, and headed to the barbecue grill by the Jacuzzi.

"Shawn."

Shawn ignored him, got on his knees, and begun tracing.

***

Dean's eyes had a glaze to them that Gordon had always attributed to the effects of a grueling day at work. Except it was two in the afternoon, and Dean was unemployed. Standing in the kitchen wearing sweats, he was twitchy; anxious.

"What're these?" asked Dean, holding up a handful of white sheets of paper.

"Don't know," said Gordon.

Gordon noticed Dean's gaze drift to his pants. Smears of chalk were visible just above Gordon's knees where he had wiped his hands clean after his visit with Shawn.

"Naomi says it was *your* idea," said Dean, tossing the papers to Gordon's chest. A few escaped, floating to the ground.

Gordon looked at the papers. They were print-outs of web pages devoted to universities, programs, and other information on the study of international business.

Good for her.

"What the fuck, Lake?"

"What?"

"I thought we had this talk."

"What talk?"

"The 'you-undermining-me' talk."

"What Naomi does is outta my control."

"She said it was *your* idea she rekindle this notion of being some… international representative."

"She's twenty-two."

"Lake…" Dean said with the uneasy laugh of someone trying to control their temper. "Get outta my business."

Dean swiped the papers from Gordon and jammed them into the trash, using his foot to stomp-stomp-stomp them to the bottom. The container tilted over.

"I don't know if you want to counsel her or fuck her or what…" said Dean. "But *leave her alone.*"

It was in that instant that Gordon thought they would fight. Right then and there. In the kitchen. At two in the afternoon.

Dean walked out.

Gordon looked at the tipped-over trash can. It felt like everything in his life was tipping at the moment.

Tilting.

Falling.

About to hit the ground.

Chapter 41

FUNNY ENOUGH, Cedric handled the deluge of chalk in stride.

"Fag's cleanin' it up," Cedric said, scraping the bottom of a tub of cream cheese. "It's his little game. Tryin' to needle me and shit."

"You don't care?" asked Gordon.

"Ain't my house. Maybe I'll call the management company, let 'em take a little look-see. But me? Fuck it." He wolfed down half an onion bagel.

Gordon watched as Cedric tossed the knife in the sink. It landed inches away from the coffee maker that had a thick circle of red chalk traced around it.

"Fag's lucky I ain't allergic to this shit," said Cedric. He'd taken to calling Shawn "fag" full-time now.

Gordon said, "I've spent the last seven weeks watching you two go at it. Both of you refuse to move. Both of you hate each other. And for what?"

"Sure you ain't guzzlin' his gizz?"

"Look at this place."

"You seen this yet?" Cedric dug in his pocket and handed him a postcard, the type people stuck under your windshield wiper when you weren't around. It was an advertisement promoting the upcoming release of *Blast Your Bone*, Cedric's new album. "Sweet, huh?"

So this was why Cedric was in a good mood. His album was finally due to see the light of day.

"Havin' *two* release parties," said Cedric. "One at the The Ditch on Pico and one here."

"Here?"

"Few weeks from now. Two hundred people. Tons of bleach-blonde, fake titty pussy." Cedric shuddered like he was having an orgasm. "It's gonna be sweeeeeeet. You're invited."

Thanks. I only live here.

"And Shawn?" asked Gordon.

"Shit no," said Cedric. "Told him this mornin'. Well in advance."

Gordon could only imagine how that conversation went down (if it was a conversation at all). Cedric probably shouted something at Shawn.

"And the chalk?" asked Gordon.

"Fuck the chalk. I got a party to plan." Cedric shuddered. "It's gonna be sweeeeeeet."

Chapter 42

UP ON THE WALL went Naomi's university research.

Gordon had thought about returning it to her after he removed it from the trash Dean tipped over. But they were print-outs of web pages. She could print more. Plus, if the same info reappeared in her possession, crinkles and all, Dean would have a coronary.

So, up they went in Dean's section in room 116.

Gordon sat on the carpet and took in the collage, letting his brain soak in the imagery. The pictures, the mementos, the fragments of his days spent in that life, all adding up to... *what?*

He looked to the other collages.

All three were engulfing the wall, masking the pattern of sea shells that lay beneath. (Gordon had long since removed the landscape paintings). The cumulative effect of the images was usually exhilarating in the opening minutes, then numbing. Then melancholy. Gordon would often take a nap right there on the carpet, head on a pillow, sheets dragged down to cover him.

He recharged here.

Never turned on a radio or TV. Never used the phone. Never spoke aloud. The silence was crucial. It gave him the foundation to think. That's what room 116 was for. Thinking. Reflecting. Letting the experiences churn in his head, one after the other. He let any and all thoughts flood through his brain, freely opening the mental dam that usually remained shut.

The purpose was simple: to guide Gordon to a single, new life.

The time when this would happen, when he would suddenly break from all three residences at once to forge a new direction, was only six weeks away.

So he let the thoughts come.

And come they did...

Of the power he felt negotiating the peace between Cedric and Shawn. Then the subsequent failure.

Of the gratitude he felt when Shawn opened up to him by the pool. People never opened up to him before. This was a good sign.

Of the urgency he felt with Ash at Myron's house. How every second at her side was a powder keg set to explode. She had a way of making you consume life in the moment. It was a rush. Ash was upping the stakes as the days passed, as if she was in a race with herself.

Of the love he felt for Naomi. There was no way around this anymore. It was love. Unrequited, but love just the same. Gordon had spent less and less time at Dean's almost unconsciously because of this. Dean was right. Gordon *was* undermining the relationship. But what the fuck happened to "All's fair in love and war?" Fair to whom? Gordon had put restraints on his feelings for Naomi almost immediately after meeting her. Restraints that were born in the reality that she was taken. But reality changes from day to day. From mind to mind.

If Gordon had learned anything since his father stopped breathing, it was that reality can change the instant you define it.

… his father…

Gordon didn't stop thoughts of his father, but he didn't welcome them either. It was the past. It was behind him. The thoughts usually came when the unexpected would set off a memory…

The smell of coffee mixed with the scent of car vinyl.

The feel of a wooden counter.

Any Frank Sinatra song (especially the early stuff).

The Chicago Bears logo.

The sound of a truck's horn.

All touchstones to Gordon's memory. Touchstones he didn't want. (No Sinatra tune lasted more than four notes before being turned off.) Those days were gone for good. He was here to start anew.

It was time for a journal entry.

Gordon rose from the carpet and opened the drawer where the journal was stashed. He dug it out and sat at the table to write.

He made it a point to never review the other entries. Not yet. He was only six weeks away from finishing, so time was precious. When the journal was out, he wrote without looking back.

He uncapped the pen with his teeth and flipped to the next blank page.

Each entry began with the day's number. He had started with 93 and was already down to 45.

As he lowered the pen to write 44, the clothes he set out on the bed caught his eye: black pants, black long sleeve shirt, black socks.

Tonight was the night he and Ash were going to expand... something. Ash hadn't filled him in on the details yet, details that had come from Myron. She only told him to wear all black (which never was a good sign if you thought about it).

He glanced at the bedside clock. He was running late. Ash was expecting him.

The blank page of the journal stared up at him, yearning for ink. But he didn't have time.

Shit.

He should've done this first, before he taped up Naomi's print-outs, before he planted himself on the ground to lazily soak in the collages. Time had gotten away from him, as it often did in this space. He needed to change and leave.

It was getting harder and harder to find time to drive to the Starlight Inn. It was his neutral place, a sacred spot, so Gordon thought he needed it. But maybe the journal entries didn't have to be written in room 116. He could come here to think, to reflect. That would remain the same, but maybe he could write the entries elsewhere. On the go. It would certainly save time.

Gordon capped the pen and closed the journal. He'd add an entry later, after his outing with Ash. In the morning, maybe.

***

Gordon stepped out of room 116 clad in black with the journal tucked under his arm. Two parking spaces from where he stood, a family of four was unloading luggage from a minivan. The mother considered Gordon with an air of suspicion and took the youngest daughter by the hand, drawing her close.

Gordon averted his eyes and crossed to the rental car he parked in the spot farthest from the street lamp. Climbing in, he looked for a place to hide the journal. He ended up sticking the book in the glove compartment, sliding it under the rental paperwork. He locked the small door. It wasn't the best hiding place, but it'd do for now.

Gordon drove past the family of four, the mother watching him, and headed to the loft.

Chapter 43

"HE CHOSE THIS?" asked Gordon.

"Yep," said Ash.

"Man's got issues."

A twenty foot billboard of a supermodel smiled at them from the side of a four story, brick building. High cheekbones, crystal blue eyes, perfect skin. The grand prize winner of the DNA lottery.

"Probably pukes her breakfast," said Ash.

Next to the model's lips (the entire picture was only of her face. An extreme, smacking close-up) were the words:

youth

will

rule

Next to that proclamation was the logo for a sneaker.

"That make you wanna buy shoes?" asked Ash.

"Twice over," said Gordon.

Ash smirked, slinging her backpack over her shoulder. Like Gordon, she was dressed head-to-toe in black.

"C'mon," she said.

They moved to the base of the building and got to work. It was late, and the traffic on the adjacent freeway was minimal. Access to the billboard wasn't a problem, but being seen was a concern.

Ash removed a rifle from her backpack.

"What the fuck's that?" asked Gordon.

"BBs," said Ash. "Don't piss yourself."

"If someone sees you…"

"I'll shoot 'em."

Ash winked, then pumped the rifle and aimed at the mural's overhead lights. She pulled the trigger. A bulb shattered.

"Good shot," said Gordon.

"Thanks."

She pumped again, shot. A second bulb went dark.

"Wanna try?" asked Ash, handing the rifle to Gordon. "Six pumps."

A grocery store truck rumbled by on the freeway, casting its headlights briefly on Gordon. He hid the rifle lengthwise next to his leg.

"Whenever you're ready," said Ash.

"Mind if we don't go to jail?" asked Gordon.

Gordon pumped the rifle and shot, missing. He handed the weapon back to Ash.

"We'll be here all night," he said.

She shot out the last remaining bulb. The mural was cast into darkness save for the occasional stray headlights of a passing car.

"Where'd you learn to shoot?" asked Gordon.

"Brother had one as a kid. Used to shoot lizards off fences."

"You got a brother?"

Ash shot him a sideways glance. "Think you know everything about me?"

Gordon's role that night was twofold: to act as lookout in case a cop or security guard or random passerby suddenly became interested, and to hold the extension ladder steady while Ash worked. (Myron had let Ash borrow the ladder, even saying it was good luck. Gordon had never heard of a good luck ladder, but then again, he hadn't heard of a lot of things before coming to LA.) Once Ash was up the ladder, she could shimmy across the frame of the billboard and get down to business.

***

They had estimated that the "expansion" would take twenty minutes. It took sixteen.

Ash climbed down, exhilarated, specks of beige paint on her face.

"Masterful job," said Gordon.

"Does the trick," said Ash.

They returned to Ash's car at a brisk pace. The ladder downsized nicely and slid into the backseat where she covered it with a sheet to shield it from curious eyes. Ash noticed Gordon leaning against the car, his gaze once again on the billboard.

"Even better from back here," said Gordon.

Ash looked back at how she had altered—how she had *expanded* —

the billboard, and found the ensuing adrenaline rush arousing.

"Every second we stay here is another second someone will see us," said Ash, speaking not so much in a tone of warning, but rather in the way a woman speaks during foreplay, her words flowing in a playful, teasing rhythm.

"We better go," said Gordon.

"Yeah, we should…" said Ash, her hand finding Gordon's leg, sliding to his crotch. He was already hard. That turned her on even more.

"This sorta stuff excite you?" asked Ash, rubbing him.

"Guess so," said Gordon, surprised the words came out in the right order. "Should get outta here, though."

"Yeah," she said.

A passing car illuminated them for a moment.

"Someone's gonna see us," said Gordon.

"Yeah…"

Ash lowered to her knees and unzipped his pants.

Gordon looked around, but there was no one in sight. He watched as Ash took him in her mouth, the muscles in his legs tightening. The mixture of wanting to flee and wanting Ash to continue was an overwhelming concoction of fear and lust that made him light-headed.

Gordon let his sight return to the billboard.

The paint that Ash had added to the visage of the supermodel was almost a perfect match.

Over the mouth, chin, forehead, nose, and cheeks, Ash had painted wrinkles, convincingly aging the model a good forty years. The face overlooking the freeway now belonged to a woman in her sixties. Worn, pensive, sad.

Next to the image was the slogan. That alteration was more obvious, but still a decent job. Ash had copied the exact style of the words with impressive skill considering the speed with which she'd painted.

In the bottom corner of the billboard was the last thing she added before climbing down. It was the letter E, brushed in orange paint, the signature Myron insisted they include. The one he marked every expansion with. He wanted the letter to appear in the identical style he had drawn it on previous occasions. Myron had demonstrated to Ash the correct brush strokes to form the E and even made her practice in front of him.

The vandalism would be discovered, a report would be filed, and the incident would inevitably be connected with the others, increasing the press the rest of the expansion strikes received, Myron had told them. The strikes would be debated, written about, studied, argued over. It was all he talked about.

Leaning against the car, Gordon exhaled, only then realizing he'd been holding his breath.

As he drew closer to orgasm, his eyes remaining fixed on the billboard. With only the final word of the slogan replaced, the sentence next to the woman now read:

youth
will
rot

28

It's getting hard to think. I'm in my car. In a Ralph's parking lot. It's raining.

I'm tired. It's not easy living these lives. Fuck, it's hard enough to live one of them. I'm four weeks from the end.

Separating the lives was easy at first. I just had to keep the beat. Fast beat with Ash. Steady beat with Cedric and Shawn. Slow beat with Dean. But the beats are fucked now. The rhythm is off.

In order to concentrate on who I'm supposed to be from one life to the next, I've tried to concentrate on how I look. It helps to keep me focused. That way, when I'm at Shawn's, I can look in the mirror and see my clean, casual appearance and refocus on making things better.

If I'm with Ash, I can look at my reflection and see my messy, stained style and know I need to let her do what she wants.

If I'm with Naomi, I can look in the mirror and see my carefully groomed appearance and remember I have self-control.

The clothes are a reminder. And believe me, I need them, because it's hard to think.

It's raining like a motherfucker in LA.

What the fuck?

Sometimes I want to make a move on Naomi. There are moments when I think she'd let me. I don't know what I am to her. I want to know. I want to know a lot of things.

It's so fucking hard to fucking think.

Chapter 44

RAIN BROKE THE LIGHT into fragments as Gordon shut the journal.

He set it on the passenger seat and closed his eyes, taking a breath. He wanted it to be a deep breath, but it was shallow.

Water tapped the glass with a relentless fervor, as if trying to provoke him. He turned on the radio to drown out the noise. The familiar hook of a White Stripes song pumped through the car, and that was enough to push him into action.

He opened his eyes, shifted the car in gear, and navigated out of the parking lot, his thoughts straining to coalesce.

Where to now... where to now...

He glanced to the passenger's side view mirror. He noticed the journal sitting on the seat.

He almost hit a woman pushing a shopping cart as he leaned to swoop up the book. The car swerved, the woman cursed, and Gordon's heart raced—not at the near collision, but at the fact that he'd forgotten to hide the journal.

It was risky enough keeping the book in the car without him growing careless. Clutching it to his chest, he steered with one hand. The moment he found an open parking spot, he pulled in so he could hide the journal.

Gordon popped the trunk.

Braving the rain, he exited the car, shielded the book under his shirt, and opened the trunk. The new hiding spot was under the spare tire which was concealed under a flap of rug.

Water soaked his back as he took his time positioning the journal in an indentation near the jack. He slid the tire back into place and repositioned the rug, pausing a moment to make sure everything matched.

At the rear of the trunk were three trash bags, each holding different style clothes for each of the lives. He often had to change in the car before heading to a new location. Inconvenient, but alternating the way he looked really helped keep his thoughts straight, however difficult that was becoming lately.

Satisfied the trunk was in order, he slammed it shut.

Chapter 45

THE CHALK HAD NEVER been removed.

The colorful lines that bordered just about everything were slowly fading due to objects being moved, foot traffic, the wind, but there was no deliberate effort to remove the chalk boundaries that Shawn had meticulously outlined a few weeks earlier. After a while, they weren't acknowledged at all.

Shawn wasn't going to remove the chalk, Cedric was too proud to let it bother him, and Gordon's pleas to erase the obvious symbol of a stewing problem had been ignored.

It was difficult for Gordon to care about two people who didn't seem fazed by the decaying sense of normality. But maybe the normality was an illusion to begin with.

The boundaries, however, were always there. Shawn had just taken the time to trace them. Is that why the chalk lines seemed to belong?

"Forget your umbrella?" asked Cedric.

"Don't own one," said Gordon as he tore sheets of paper towel from a mounted rack and patted his face and hair. He was still wet from hiding the journal.

"Get one," said Cedric.

"It's LA."

"So?"

"It hardly rains."

"Yeah…" Cedric laughed. "Go ahead and do that."

"Do what?"

"Think it's all sunshine."

The cardboard roll spun as Gordon whipped off the last sheet. "Is that what I'm doing?"

"That's when this place gets you, man, when you drop your guard. That's when it eats you. One gulp." He made a slurping sound and nodded at his own wisdom.

***

Office Supplies.

That's what Gordon actually wrote on the goal board in black marker inside the Wednesday box.

Even though his communication with Dean, the advocator of maintaining a schedule, had become nearly nonexistent, Gordon still added his daily tasks to the board, so he wrote *Office Supplies* to remind himself to pick up pens and a letter tray.

Fucking office supplies. Who gives a shit?

Dean was no longer encouraging him. He was Gordon's life coach for a few months, but now that was over. Dean had since been downgraded to just another roommate, albeit one with increasingly erratic behavior (and Gordon should know, being somewhat of an expert on erratic behavior).

Gordon heard the TV playing at 4 a.m. the night before. When he went out to look, Dean was there. Not just awake. Not just wide awake. *Wired.*

Dean had glanced at him as if he was being bothered, then returned his attention to the movie (*Rounders*). This late night schedule was a new feature in the apartment, one that the former Dean would've never condoned.

Gordon wondered if Dean was taking drugs. Ephedra? Cocaine? Meth? He wasn't showing any obvious symptoms, but Gordon always maintained a private theory as to why Dean was fired. He failed a company issued drug test. It made sense. Why terminate a guy who was producing? Dean never mentioned any payroll cutbacks. No one else was let go. Maybe he was a speed freak. Take the fuel, get the results.

Either way, the guy who used to run his days down to the minute was now freewheeling the hours. Naomi still came over, but it seemed to be more out of habit. She slept while Dean watched TV. In the morning, she'd leave while he was going to bed.

Fucking office supplies.

Gordon wiped his hand through the ink, smearing it across the Wednesday box, well into Thursday and Friday.

***

When Gordon asked Shawn if he was going to be around for Cedric's party, he shrugged and said, "What do you think?"

***

"The beef was bad," said Ash.

She was on her mattress, laying her on side, forearm under her head, not sleeping, but not exactly awake either. Just sort of staring. Zoned out. Drained.

She'd been vomiting for the last six hours. Fortunately, she'd finally reached the stomach-straining, dry-heaving stage of food poisoning where the body continues to try to expel any dangerous bacteria, even if there's nothing left to expel, the point where every muscle contracts, and you're left hanging over the toilet with your mouth locked open... waiting... waiting... pleading... but nothing comes. Then the moment passes and you spit, your hands clasped on porcelain.

"Which beef?" asked Gordon. He didn't want to accidentally cook anything from the same batch.

"From the Chinese place. Near the bike shop."

"Thought they had an 'A' rating."

All restaurants in LA were given a letter grade by the health department. Gordon had seen mostly A's since moving here, but there were a handful of B's around, even one or two C's, which were somehow still full with patrons. Go figure.

"It was an 'A'," said Ash.

"And they had bad beef?"

"Guess the grades mean shit."

"What'd you eat?"

"Don't really feel like engaging in conversation."

"All right," said Gordon. "You want anything?"

She shook her head, content with staring at the wall.

***

Naomi was wearing a shoulder-length, 1920s flapper-style, platinum blonde wig that accentuated her natural beauty.

This girl would be gorgeous with *any* hairstyle. Honest to God. Pluck her into any time period from prehistoric man until now, and she'd turn heads. Some women need a long cut to complement their features or a short cut so they won't look so fat. But not Naomi. The girl could sport a purple Mohawk, and Gordon would still be proud to have her on his arm.

"Found it in my closet," said Naomi, running a hand through the blonde hair. "My friends and I used to dress up and go shopping."

"This your way of reminiscing?" asked Gordon.

She shrugged. "I miss the old me."

"How so?" asked Gordon.

She twirled the hair of the wig with one finger. "Things were easier back then."

"Dean see you in that?"

"Nope."

"You want him to?"

Naomi looked at him with those eyes. His attention had never been so rapt.

"I don't know what I want," she said.

Gordon considered making a suggestion, but held off.

"I like the look," said Gordon. *Loved* the look, actually.

"It's stupid," said Naomi, dragging off the wig.

Her real hair was a mess underneath, but it didn't matter. He'd marry her that instant even if she decided to wear a rainbow clown wig for the rest of her days.

***

Ash read the label on the can of Ensure. "Whatever happened to chicken soup?"

"This is better for you," said Gordon.

"Says who?"

"The pharmacist."

"Are pharmacists real doctors?"

"They wear white coats."

"So do valet drivers."

"They dispense drugs."

"So do half my friends."

She was still recovering from food poisoning and solid food wasn't something she was ready for, so Gordon had picked up a six-pack of Ensure.

"It's a meal replacement," said Gordon.

"I can read that."

"It's got vitamins, minerals, all the stuff meals have."

"Except taste. Why does everyone recommend chicken soup?"

"That's what they learned from their grandmas, I guess."

"Serrick said Whole Foods Market sells it fresh."

"You want soup? I'll get you soup. Is that what you want?"

The key question, as usual. The only question, it could be argued. At least in the loft.

Ash sighed. "This is fine."

"It's chocolate, doesn't taste like medicine or anything."

She popped open the can. "Or anything?"

"Anything you wouldn't want to taste."

"That list is short."

She winked.

He got hard.

Chapter 46

IT WAS PRINTED in gold ink on black, plastic cups:

~ blast your bone bacchanal ~

Gordon wondered if all Hollywood parties had names, and if they did, were they always imprinted on cups?

He filled his cup with a healthy shot of Patron Silver and tossed in a few ice cubes. Gordon didn't want to feel much of anything tonight, and this was a good way to start.

Cedric's album release party was in full swing.

There were a lot of hip people in the house. At least, Gordon assumed they were hip via their basketball jerseys and baggy clothing. The thought of someone concealing a weapon came to him, and suddenly he was envisioning a full-blown, John Woo-style shoot-out. There had to be guns in the house. At least a few. But this wasn't South Central. This was Pacific Palisades, an upscale neighborhood. Then again, what did that matter? People were shot and killed all the time in upscale neighborhoods. Especially people in baggy clothes.

Gordon finished his drink quicker than he intended, poured another, then ventured into the living room. He looked around for the one person he was curious about at the moment. Shawn. But Shawn wasn't in attendance. It wasn't a snub exactly, since you can't really snub an event unless you've been invited. Good for Shawn anyway. Gordon toasted his drink to this thought, then lowered his cup just as fast. Seems the tequila was already becoming cozy with his brain.

The ubiquitous chalk lines were still visible. They looked like they were added for the party, as if Cedric hired someone to trace the furniture just for tonight. Gordon had heard someone comment about how they liked the "postmodern border look" and how they might use it for a party of their own. The lines did look cool in an avant-garde kinda way, but not *that* cool. Or maybe Gordon was having a hard time embracing the work of a roommate who had a meltdown.

Gordon made his way to the backyard which was illuminated with bone-shaped string lights. The Jacuzzi was filled with people he didn't know, mostly women in bras, laughing loudly (people he'd like to know). Out here, Cedric's album was playing, an eclectic mix of beats similar to all the other eclectic mixes of beats Gordon had been exposed to, but apparently this album was *the shit*. At least, that's what everyone kept telling Cedric.

"Yo man, this music's the shit," said a guy.

"Thanks, bro," said Cedric, a resounding failure at feigning humility.

"It's off the hook," said another.

"Yeah?" said Cedric with a salesman's smile. "You like?"

"Fuck yeah, I like. It's the shit."

They all liked the shit, as far as Gordon could tell. But it's easy to say you like something in this town. Everyone seemed to like everything.

A tall woman with enormous breasts strolled by with a tight t-shirt that read "blast your bone" across her chest, her erect nipples poking at the cotton. Cedric's admirers high-fived at the sight.

"I'll blast my bone over dem titties," said one.

"*All* over 'em," said the other.

"Blast it all night long."

"*All* night long."

Another high-five.

"Get on that shit," said Cedric, nodding to the woman.

"Huh?"

"She's single, yo. Go fetch."

The two guys looked at each other, then in the direction the woman walked.

"High maintenance bitch," said one.

"Big titty ho," said the other.

And that was all they needed to convince each other to not pursue the woman in the tight t-shirt. Cedric waved them off and took Gordon by the shoulder, walking him away.

"See?" said Cedric. "Put food in front of the starvin', yet they don't eat."

"She really single?"

"Husband's a bodyguard for Will Smith."

"But you said—"

"I knew they wouldn't chase that ass. Lookie here…" said Cedric, pointing to someone standing at the edge of the pool. "See that guy? That's Davenport, an exec from the label that's gonna sign me."

Davenport was a bald man in his forties with an earring and goatee. No one knew his first name. He was talking to a girl that looked eighteen.

"I *pray* he hooks up with that bitch," said Cedric. "Can only help. Know what I'm sayin'?"

"Yeah," said Gordon, glancing at the rest of the crowd. "Good turnout."

"Half these fools I don't know. They just follow the party trail. Like a pack of dogs."

Gordon started to say something, but Cedric was already off, greeting a group of girls with open arms. Gordon stood there for a while, soaking in the atmosphere. No one was over forty except for Davenport the Exec, and he was trying hard as hell to look *under* forty. The bass of the music pounded in Gordon's chest. He took a sip of his drink and heard a voice nearby say, "Gold's the color of power and wealth."

"Yeah, but the album's red," said another voice.

Gordon's blood chilled. He didn't want to look.

"But gold's subliminal," said the first voice. "You hold the cup and see gold on black, right?"

"Right…"

"Your mind senses money and fame without even knowing it."

Gordon recognized the voice. It didn't seem possible. He turned and looked.

Dean was standing ten feet away.

Gordon averted his glance.

Holy shit. What the fuck was Dean doing here?

Options, options. Gordon needed a plan. Run, leave, flee, escape. That was a good plan. Dean was blocking the way into the house, so he had to exit through the yard. He could slip out the side gate. That wouldn't seem too peculiar. His heart raced as his eyes found the easiest path to the gate—around the keg, by the pool, pass Davenport the Exec, around the table of hor d'oeuvres, right through the—

"Lake!"

Fuuuuuck.

Gordon turned, and Dean was right in front of him.

"Fuck you doing here, Lake?"

"Drinking," said Gordon, raising his cup.

"I didn't know you partied."

"Every now and then."

Gordon's eyes found Cedric mingling on the other side of the yard. A safe enough distance. He just had to bullshit with Dean for a few moments, then leave.

"Here with Naomi?" asked Dean.

"No…" said Gordon. A strange question that didn't help the situation.

"I don't know where the fuck she is," said Dean. "She turned off her cell." He looked around at the guests, bobbed his head slightly to the music. "So how'd you find out about this?"

"Actually," said Gordon, fumbling for a reason, "a girl told me."

"Which one?"

"One inside. She's inside."

"You banging her?"

"Trying to."

"Choose success, Lake," said Dean. His eyes were bloodshot.

This moment was something Gordon wasn't prepared for. Seeing Dean tugged at Gordon's current persona. He didn't know how to act.

Was he the Gordon of Cedric's life talking to Dean? Or the Gordon of Dean's life who happened to be at Cedric's party?

He felt nauseous and caught sight of Cedric. The socializing shuffle was carrying him in their direction.

"You haven't asked me," said Dean.

"Asked you what?" asked Gordon.

"What *I'm* doing here."

"What're you doing here?"

"Glad you asked. I'm a manager now."

"For water?"

"Not for fucking water. For talent."

"Really?"

"Got no clients yet, but people are interested. Thing is, I know people. It's my gift. Fuck Pacific Water for not seeing that, corporate cocksuckers. But this is good for me. I mean, look at the town I'm in…

fucking Hollywood."

Cedric was getting closer. Gordon couldn't risk interaction with Dean *and* Cedric at the same time. He tried to wrap up the chit-chat with Dean.

"Good seein' you."

"So I'm thinking I dip my toe in the music business, the acting business, the directing business. Got wind of this party from a friend. You know if he's got representation?"

"Who?"

"Guy who made the album."

Gordon wasn't about to start discussing Cedric with Dean.

"I don't know," said Gordon.

Dean nodded, looked around. He was fidgety, anxious. "Where's your woman?"

"Inside."

"Go get her, before she starts sucking cock in the bathroom."

Gordon felt like he should take offense to that, but since the girl didn't exist, he didn't bother. Still, he didn't like the thought of his imaginary date giving head to a stranger. Even more disturbing, there was an anger in all of Dean's jokes that was never there before. It had to be because of Naomi. Gordon would kill to know what was going on between them, if she had cut off sex from him, where exactly she was at the moment, what she thought of.

"Lookie here…"

Gordon felt Cedric's arm drape his shoulder.

"Pussy's everywhere, yo," said Cedric to no one in particular.

"This your party?" asked Dean to Cedric.

Gordon wanted to die.

"That it is," said Cedric.

"Dean Monroe," said Dean, hand extended. "Manager."

Cedric shook the hundredth palm of the evening, enjoying the attention. "Cool. Which firm?"

"My own."

"All right."

"You repped?"

"Not yet."

"I could work with you."

"Yeah?" said Cedric. He looked him over, nodding to the pulsating music. "Like what you hear?"

"It's tight," said Dean.

Everyone liked everything.

"Got a card?" asked Cedric. He was playing it cool, but some excitement bled through.

Dean actually produced a card from his wallet. Gordon craned his neck to catch a glimpse. Yep. It said talent manager. Looked like the water business was behind Dean after all. But this was good. Dean and Cedric were ignoring Gordon who tried to be perfectly still.

"You two know each other?" asked Dean.

"Who?" asked Cedric. "Me and Gordon?"

"Yeah."

"You kiddin'?" asked Cedric, laughing. "He's like family, man."

Gordon would gladly swallow a cyanide pill.

"I can see that," said Dean, lying for the sake of agreement. "Couldn't ask for a better roommate."

"Yeah," said Cedric. "When it comes to roommates, he's the shit."

"The total shit."

Gordon prayed for instant death. Right there. Under the string lights.

"So you rep anyone I'd know?" asked Cedric.

"Not really," said Dean. "Got a stable of up-and-comers. Like yourself."

"I hear ya."

Gordon exhaled. They'd forgotten about him again. Good.

"So how'd you two meet?" asked Dean.

Not good.

"In my kitchen," said Cedric.

"Tonight?"

"Months ago."

"Small world," said Gordon.

It was the first words he'd spoken since Cedric joined them.

"Months?" asked Dean.

"I didn't even know his ass was movin' in," said Cedric.

"To LA?" Dean looked at Gordon. Something felt wrong to him. Dean knew people. Said so himself. It was his gift. And right now, his gift was about to crucify Gordon. "You knew Lake *before* he moved here?" asked Dean.

"What?" said Cedric.

"You said you didn't know he was moving here."

"How could I?"

"I don't know."

"Met the fucker in my house."

Dean nodded, trying to fit the pieces together. He was moments away from asking the right question.

A shriek shot through the crowd, grabbing their attention, then tailed off into laughter. It only lasted a second and was quickly replaced by more laughter, then loud bursts of cheering.

It mercifully arrested Dean's informal interrogation of Cedric. Gordon was thankful at first, then saw the reason for the crowd's reaction.

It was Shawn. He decided to show after all.

And he wasn't alone.

Holding his hand was another man in his twenties with frizzy hair and a look of fearful cooperation.

Shawn and his companion were both completely nude.

They walked at a purposeful pace, as if they expected to be publicly executed, but didn't mind. It was their sentence, however unjust, and they were going to serve it out.

To the end.

For a few moments, Gordon heard nothing. He could only see. Shawn and this man. Hand in hand. Not saying a word. Not acknowledging the people around them.

Nude. Exposed.

Then, as if a stereo was cranked, noise flooded back into Gordon's head.

Cackling. Whistling. Taunting.

And yet Shawn and the man kept walking. Guests cleared their path voluntarily and quickly, no one wishing to collide with naked homosexuals. If someone wasn't careful, they could inadvertently brush against a penis. So the crowd backed away (pushed away in some spots) as if a pair of brain-sucking zombies had invaded.

"Fag strippers, C.?" asked a girl smoking a clove cigarette.

"Ain't mine," said Cedric, enraged, but in control.

Dean laughed the loudest as the crowd took note of the men's obliviousness.

As if to test the level at which they were shutting everyone out, a guy, no older than nineteen, took a single, lengthy stride toward the nude men and emptied his cup of beer on them. The foamy liquid splashed against their skin.

They stopped walking.

A cheer erupted as the crowd waited for the reaction from Shawn and the man.

The man with the frizzy hair raised his left hand to wipe beer from his eyes, but kept his other hand clasped with Shawn's. Both their forearm muscles were taught, evidence they were holding on tight.

But they did nothing.

This bizarre twosome apparently had no intention of retaliating. This wasn't the type of crowd you wanted to know that. Their odd indifference to being soaked with beer was the green light to what happened next.

Shawn and his companion resumed walking. It dawned on Gordon where they were headed.

The pool.

"Look at 'em," said Dean with a detached bemusement. "Fag robots. Fagbots."

Another drink was launched at the men in a high arc. Red liquid splattered on them, dripping down their bare chests like blood.

Gordon turned to see who threw it. It was a pale, heavy-set girl. She applauded the direct hit.

Another drink landed on them. Then another.

The more that were thrown, the more acceptable it was deemed to join in. If enough people did something, no matter how aggressive, it cleared the way for the timid to fall in line. Mob mentality. Hitting the nude men with your drink became the instant game. People stepped forward to take their shot, jockeying for position. A shower of tumbling black cups with gold ink pelted the walking targets.

And all along, Shawn and the man were resigned to their fate.

All along, they kept walking toward the pool.

Drenched with a dozen brands of alcohol, they carried on.

Cedric glared at Shawn as he passed, unsure of whether to ride this incident out or confront him. The guests were mostly strangers. They didn't know who Shawn was. But if Cedric said something to Shawn, who the fuck knows what Shawn might spew out. It'd certainly be revealed they're roommates. No need for that information to come out.

Hand-in-hand, Shawn and his companion took the first steps into the illuminated water. They descended, dipping down to let the water rise to their necks.

It was there that Shawn whispered something in the other man's ear. The man turned away, hesitant, giving his first true look to the crowd. The mocking was intense, more than he had expected. Shawn whispered again, and the man nodded in a way that suggested he was summoning courage.

He turned back to Shawn, and they kissed.

The crowd roared with laughter and cheers.

Cedric was incredulous. He had told Shawn not to come. *Told him.* He gauged the reaction of the crowd. Most were amused. Some were indifferent. (This was LA, not Arkansas. A display of homosexuality wasn't exactly akin to a U.F.O. sighting.) A few were repulsed.

But then his eyes fell upon Davenport the Exec, the one he wanted to impress— *needed* to impress—the one who was his ticket to a deal with a label.

And Davenport was shaking his head. Cedric suddenly had the feeling that Shawn's stunt could somehow jeopardize his future. The whole fucking purpose of this party.

Gordon didn't notice that Cedric had left his side until it was too late. Until Cedric was already *in the pool*, waist-deep in water, approaching Shawn.

"Deserve what they get," said Dean.

For a moment, Dean's voice froze Gordon. But with Dean, it was about achievement. About taking action.

In the pool, Cedric grabbed Shawn by the shoulder, ending the kiss, and clutched his neck.

"Told you not to come," said Cedric.

The other man said, "It's his house too."

Cedric kept his attention on Shawn. "I told you."

"Let go of me," said Shawn.

Cedric slapped Shawn across the face with an open palm to the delight of the crowd.

"Act like a bitch, get slapped like one," said Cedric. He drew his hand back for another slap, but found himself being pulled back.

Gordon had him in a half-nelson head-lock, one arm wrapped under his armpit and behind his neck.

"Enough!" said Gordon.

Cedric jerked free and threw an off-balance punch. Gordon dodged it and moved back in, wrapping his arm around Cedric's head. Gordon wanted to restrain Cedric, not fight him.

Cedric shifted his weight and pulled down, and Gordon found himself underwater.

The voices from above were muffled. Loud. Adamant.

Gordon managed to swallow a mouthful of water. He heard splashes as others plunged in. Cedric's body lifted off him.

Gordon burst above the surface and started coughing. He could see they were now joined by a half-dozen people in the pool; three pushing back Cedric, two making sure Gordon didn't retaliate, and one just watching as if the excitement had caused him to jump in, but now that he was all wet, he didn't want to get involved.

A lot of people were shouting a lot of things, but it all blended into an incomprehensible mix, and Gordon didn't give a shit anyway. He looked to Shawn who was rather motionless considering the circumstances. This *had* to have been how he expected things to unfold, but Shawn didn't seem content by any means. Surely, his plan had been to disrupt the party, and he had done so exquisitely. So why was Gordon sensing gloom?

Shawn whispered something in the other man's ear, and they slipped out of the pool.

Their exit was much quicker than their arrival with Cedric shouting a stream of obscenities. Within moments, they disappeared from view.

Still waist-deep in water, Cedric was curious to know the crowd's response to his assault on Shawn. He scanned the faces and spotted the person who had unknowingly pushed him to take action. Davenport the Exec. The bald man nodded his approval with a wide grin. Cedric smiled back, though he didn't mean to. He wanted to stay angry—he *was* angry—but he couldn't help being pleased.

What could've been a disaster for Cedric may have worked to his benefit. Imagine the story Davenport could tell. A hot, new artist slapped around a fag at his own release party. Cedric smiled again and this time didn't care if the world saw it. He was happy Shawny and his ass-lickin' friend paraded in the buff.

Cedric climbed from the pool, saying to Gordon, "Lucky I didn't drown *your* ass."

The crowd was still buzzing at the fight. It wasn't just Davenport that had a new story to tell.

"Jesus, Lake…" said Dean.

He couldn't understand why Gordon had bothered to get involved. Gordon didn't expect him to. But he *had* to get involved with Cedric and Shawn. That was the whole point.

Gordon got out of the pool, ignoring the insults and jeers. He was clearly one of the villains in this mess.

Gordon made his way to the side gate.

Fuck these people. Hollywood ass-kissers.

He paused for a moment at the fence and pondered the significance of him leaving through the yard. Should he march back through the house, head held high? Were they making him crawl away? He almost turned around, then shrugged it off. He didn't care how they interpreted it.

Fuck these people.

The gate creaked as he left the backyard and cut through the grass on the side of the house. As he made his way toward the street, he heard a rustling from below. Scurrying along the bottom of the wall, a plump rat was moving in the same direction.

Gordon and the rat proceeded toward the street at the same pace, leaving the party behind.

23

The days are going by fast. I feel time slipping away.

Twenty-three days left of this shit, then I'm out. Good news is, I feel like it's a blurry picture that's sloooooowly coming into focus. But I still can't make out the picture. Too much blur still. But it's focusing.

Do other people put a clock on stuff like this? Might as well. Sitting around won't make it happen. Sometimes a time frame is all that gets people off their ass. Some sports teams don't turn it on until they realize the end of the game is near. But the end of the game is ALWAYS near. People know they're going to die, but they wait around like they have all the time in the world. Is this because they think life carries on in Heaven? Like the clock never stops?

Fuck that. You got to put a time frame on life. I waited too long to put one on mine.

23 days.

Ash is worrying me. She's always been up and down, but her moods have been weird. I need to spend more time with her.

I haven't seen Shawn since the party. Cedric talked to me through his car window the next morning. He said I shouldn't stick up for that fag. He was in a good mood when he said it, big smile and everything.

Naomi has stopped coming over to see Dean. I'm not sure if they broke up. I wonder if she knows he's a talent manager. I hope she's given up on him, but my gut tells me she hasn't. It takes a lot for a girl to give up on a guy sometimes. She won't give up hoping he'll change.

Hope isn't always a good thing.

Chapter 47

"HAVEN'T SEEN HER since last week," said Toby, leaning against the rack that supported the buckets of bath salt.

Gordon was standing on the Venice Beach Boardwalk in front of the spot where Ash sold her figurines. It was now occupied by a woman selling elaborately painted spoons.

"She move to a different spot?" asked Gordon.

"Don't think so," said Toby. "One day she left early, said she might do somethin' else with her time. Next day, she didn't show. Then came the spoon lady." Toby leaned in and whispered, "She complains about the smell of the lotion."

Toby offered free samples of the lotion he sold, squirting out liberal portions on the hands and wrists of women from around the world.

"Gives me dirty looks all day," said Toby. "You believe that?"

"Ash ever do this before?" asked Gordon. "Take a break?"

"Nah, man. Who can afford to take a break?"

Gordon thanked Toby, then left, keeping his eyes open for Ash.

She had agreed to get together with him and check out the next target Myron wanted them to hit. It was the middle of the day, so he assumed she'd be selling her stuff by the beach. Instead, he found Ash waiting in front of the loft, smoking a cigarette on the hood of her car.

"Thought you'd be on the boardwalk," said Gordon.

Ash flicked the cigarette into the road and hopped down. "You drive."

***

"Why does he get to choose?" asked Gordon.

"'Cause he does," said Ash.

"That's not an answer."

Gordon was behind the wheel of the rental car with Ash in the passenger seat. Sunglasses on, she kept her sight out the window, though there was nothing to see except other cars crawling along at the same numbing pace, heading east on the 10 freeway.

"So?" said Gordon.

"Whole thing was his idea, remember?" said Ash.

"But we're the ones taking the risk."

They were currently on their way to scout their next target located in Hollywood, the most visible address yet, thereby the most dangerous, which had Gordon concerned.

"Can't believe you're being a pussy," said Ash.

Neither could he.

But this was the first time he was convinced they were getting in too deep. The other missions were different in a way. Since vandalizing the billboard of the supermodel, they had struck two other locations:

1. They painted a series of limousines that were scheduled to carry state legislators to a self-congratulatory banquet funded with tax dollars. When the politicians exited their hotel, they were greeted with limos awash with a dull gray to make them appear like prisoner transports. "State Penitentiary" was written in official, bold letters on the hoods, a not-too-subtle hint on where they *should* be going.

2. Following the announcement of the construction of an oil rig within sight of a beach popular with surfers, Ash and Gordon had drenched an office building owned by the oil company with a custom mix of red paint that looked just like blood. This made the AP Wire and the local news, pleasing Myron to no end.

Both strikes were signed with an orange painted E (a mark becoming equally familiar and frustrating to the police, but offering no substantial help in tracking down the vandals), and both were the brainchildren of Myron.

Yet it was Ash and Gordon who were putting their necks on the line. They were the faithful foot soldiers carrying out the missions. Gordon had been going along with the expansion strikes in the spirit of chaos and rebellion, but he was starting to see things differently.

"It's not about being a pussy," said Gordon. "It's about questioning the purpose behind it all."

"Behind *it all*?" asked Ash.

"Yeah."

"As in the meaning of life?"

"'It all' as it applies to *this*."

"I think your job's working you dead."

She was right. Kind of. He was being worked into the ground, but it wasn't by his fictitious job. It was from living all these fucking lives.

"We should get to choose the targets," said Gordon. "That's all."

"Mini-Coops are everywhere," said Ash.

Gordon glanced out the window and saw two Mini-Coopers next to each other.

"Little British roaches," said Ash.

"Why don't you—" said Gordon, suddenly remembering it was a Mini-Coop that caused his father to swerve and flip the furniture truck. He could still picture the female driver standing on the hill, talking on her cell as his father lay in the snow dying.

"Why don't I what?" asked Ash.

Gordon shook off the memory. He didn't want to think about that day.

"I don't know," he said.

"Why're you being difficult?" asked Ash.

"It feels like we're his servants."

"That's bullshit."

Gordon glanced to her. "You really consider this art?"

"Yeah," said Ash.

"*Your* art?"

"I'm the one doing it, aren't I?"

"But *he's* telling you what to do."

"I end up doing it my way. You know that."

"It's not the same," said Gordon. "You used to work on your own stuff. Toby said you haven't been on the boardwalk since last week."

"I've retired," said Ash.

"How can you? You need the money."

Ash shrugged.

"Are you taking cash from Myron?" asked Gordon.

She glanced away, considered avoiding the answer. "Just until I figure things out."

"He offer or did you ask?"

"It's a loan. Don't sweat it."

"Money changes things, Ash. You shouldn't have taken it. You had a job."

"Selling junk to tourists. Wasting my life making things for people who'd rather own a Venice Beach t-shirt. What we did on Monday—that oil company bloodbath—was national news."

"For fifteen seconds," said Gordon.

"So? I'm sure most people brushed off the image of the oil company office covered in blood, but who knows? Mass exposure equals maximum effect."

"Those are Myron's words," said Gordon.

"And he's right."

"And that makes it better than your personal stuff?"

"Isn't it better to reach a thousand people than a hundred? A million people than a thousand? A billion people than a million?"

"I'm not sure."

She looked at him like he was high.

They drove in silence for a few moments.

"What exit?" asked Gordon.

"La Brea," said Ash.

"Your figurines could mean something to someone," said Gordon. "A little girl could've bought one on the beach and took it home. It could be sitting on her nightstand right now. Right next to her bed. Could be the last thing she sees before clicking off the light. And it could mean something to her."

"It's not like I'm gonna stop doing my stuff."

"You have."

Ash considered the truth of that as they exited the freeway. They drove up La Brea, passing strip malls and the occasional vagrant.

"This is important to me," said Ash.

She said it with such conviction, Gordon didn't respond. He knew she'd placed a growing importance on these expansion strikes, but he didn't share her feelings. At least she knew that.

"Don't deny" was still the guiding principle with Ash, and that meant Gordon shouldn't swallow his dissent. He had to voice his objections. He could've done it more smoothly, but he had a bad feeling about the next target. He didn't even know what it was. She was feeding him directions piecemeal. Exit here. Turn there. Ash didn't want to give him the street address and have him guess at what they were going to do. She wanted him to see it first.

Nineteen minutes later, he saw it.

Gordon parked in a loading zone so they could take it in. He and Ash looked up at the target.

"What you were expecting?" asked Ash.

"I learned not to expect anything," said Gordon.

Ash liked his answer. He had a feeling this was the exact condition she preferred everyone around her to be in. A state of no expectations.

"So?" he said. "What's the plan?"

After Ash told him what they'd be doing the following night, Gordon felt dizzy, like he'd stumbled off a carnival ride during a heat wave.

Chapter 48

GORDON TOOK A MENU from the hostess, but he wasn't at Gilroy's Chophouse for their fine selection of steak. He was there to see Naomi.

He waited an extra half hour to be seated in her section, but that was beneficial. He was still recovering from the trip with Ash to see the next target. Since Naomi had stopped coming to the apartment, he had to come to the restaurant to lay eyes on her and find out the skinny on her relationship with Dean.

If life was simple (which by now, Gordon had discovered, it wasn't, not by a fucking long shot), and Naomi had decided to leave Dean, Gordon could swoop in. But Naomi was emotionally entwined with Dean. She was like a person you rescued from a cult after years of brainwashing. The victim just doesn't snap out of it and return to a normal life. There's psychological residue that has to be dealt with.

And that's *if* Naomi had actually broken up with Dean. If she had, that didn't mean it was over for good. Couples often endure a string of false endings before they find themselves at the real end. Sometimes it never comes.

"Hey," said Naomi, sliding the pad and pen from her apron.

Gordon was seated at the original table where he first set eyes on her.

The intensity of that first moment had yet to fade, but he didn't like the way she just greeted him. Her tone said she didn't want to see him. Did she think he was there spying on Dean's behalf? Being associated with her boyfriend (ex or not) wasn't something he wanted, because if the day came when she finally washed her hands of the relationship, Gordon would roll down the same drain.

"I'm here on my own," said Gordon.

"You're always on your own," said Naomi, pen over pad, waiting for the order.

"I mean, for my own sake. Not because of Dean."

She pursed her lips in a *yeah whatever* kind of way.

"Gonna eat?" asked Naomi.

"What's the soup?"

"Cheese and potato."

"Bowl of that, then."

"And to drink?"

"Iced tea. Dean didn't put me up to this."

"I didn't think he did. If he wants to know something, he asks."

"I haven't seen you lately."

"Bread's on its way."

She walked off.

Was she planning on reconciling with Dean? That was the question he'd ask when she brought out the basket of bread. But when she returned, what came out was, "You know Dean is a talent manager?"

"No." She set down the bread.

"He's got a card." As if having a card made you something.

There was a pause. Naomi stood there. Another person would've thought she was waiting for Gordon to continue, but he knew her better than that. She was about to say something. He let the silence linger.

Naomi said, "I'm moving."

"When?"

"Next month."

"Why?"

"Going back to school."

Gordon nodded, taking time to measure his response.

"Why the look?"

"There's no look."

"Think I'm making a mistake?"

"Does Dean know?"

"Not yet. I want you to tell him for me."

"Yeah," said Gordon, laughing.

"To soften the blow."

"Ever hear of the messenger getting his head cut off?"

"Please?"

"If you want to soften the blow, call him. That's what phones are for. Delivering bad news from a distance."

"Fine," said Naomi, heading to another table to take the order of an elderly couple.

This was tricky. Gordon would do anything for Naomi, but his gut told him to side-step this request.

Naomi brought the cheese and potato soup without saying a word. Gordon ate quietly. The cheese was a little hard. A little cold. He wondered if this was culinary retaliation for his refusal to help. She could've let the soup sit a few minutes to congeal. Hell hath no fury like a waitress scorned.

"Dessert?" she asked as she placed the billfold before him.

"I support you," said Gordon, laying out cash. "You do the right thing 'cause it's right, not 'cause it's easy." It's what his father had always said, but he was surprised to hear himself say it. He didn't think there was much of his father left in him, but tiny moments like this proved him wrong.

"I'll tell him," said Naomi.

"I think you need to be the one," said Gordon.

"Yeah…"

"Which college?"

"Stanford."

"Nice. Not too far."

"Not far enough, but I like it."

"When are you gonna tell him?"

"After work. Might as well get it over with."

"Want me to be with you?"

Naomi looked at him, taken aback. She seemed honestly touched. "No, I can handle it. It's no biggie." She picked up the money. "I'll tell him tonight."

***

"Most people don't breathe properly," said Shawn. "They rush around with their triple espresso trying to do everything at once without learning the simplest, most natural thing." He took a slow, controlled breath. "How to breathe."

"Everyone breathes," said Gordon, as if he was letting him in on a secret.

"Not in the most efficient way. And lemme tell you somethin', improper breathing hinders you, my friend. Hinders you in ways you'd never realize."

This was the happiest he'd ever seen Shawn.

They were standing in Shawn's bedroom where Shawn was busy rearranging his furniture. Gordon helped reposition a dresser that had little circular moving pads under its legs to let it slide without damaging the wooden floor. It was the first piece of furniture Gordon had lifted in months. He couldn't believe he used to do this for a living. It seemed like another life. It *was* another life. Thank fucking God.

"Better," said Shawn. "You think it's better?"

"Yeah," said Gordon.

"You must think I'm crazy," said Shawn.

"'Cause you moved your dresser?"

"At the party. Me showing up with Alan. Must've thought I flipped out."

"It wasn't the most normal thing."

"But it was the *greatest* thing I've ever done."

"Yeah?"

"The greatest."

"If you were coming outta the closet, it would've been more of a statement, but everyone knows your preference."

"That wasn't the purpose."

"So why do it? Cedric almost killed you."

"Almost." Shawn actually smiled at this.

"And after the fight in the pool, you still looked depressed."

"I was worried about Alan. Whole thing was my idea. I wanted him outta there at that point."

Everything Shawn said was underlined by an emotional state that bordered on giddy. As a matter of fact, the only other person Gordon had seen *this* happy lately was Cedric. What the fuck?

Somehow, both roommates had emerged from the party happier.

Cedric had joyfully claimed the incident and his violent response had boosted his image and brought him closer to signing a deal.

Now Shawn was proclaiming the stunt was the greatest thing he'd ever done. Either he'd done a scant amount of great things since birth, or he really was evaluating the party as an earth-shattering turning point.

It couldn't be that simple.

All he did was walk around in the nude, and yes, although the move was extraordinarily bold and risky, and although his lover happened to be of the same sex, the act itself wasn't groundbreaking. The world must be littered with nude couples strolling about, genitals waving in the wind. Nude beaches boast a generous share. Environment had to play a critical role. You had to show your bare ass in a place that wasn't receptive to bare asses. Hence Cedric's party (the "blast your bone bacchanal," a name that, in retrospect, certainly invited penis-based trouble).

"Best decision ever," said Shawn.

Naked Couple Walking had to be a one-of-a-kind elixir to life's problems. Otherwise, Gordon would have foregone the multi-life experiment, grabbed the nearest girl, shed his clothes (and hers), and started walking around.

But this was Shawn's personal, liberating solution. Although he was already out of the closet, he had to come out again.

Run out. Rage out. Burst out. Explode out.

This is who I am. Declaring that once and for all had freed Shawn.

"I can give you a book on breathing," said Shawn. "This woman instructs you how to breathe. Walks you through it."

"Nah."

"Gotta have oxygen."

"I get my fair share."

"But are you breathing? Are you *really* breathing?"

"I got other problems."

"Like?"

Shawn's voice was inviting and sincere, and for an instant, Gordon felt like spilling the beans. Just for an instant. His silence made it clear he didn't want to get into it.

"Y'know, "said Shawn. "I appreciate your help."

"I don't know how much help I've been. Everything I did blew up in my face. *The treaty?* C'mon. Holy fucking shit."

"That *was* a nightmare," said Shawn.

Gordon waited for Shawn to laugh, but he didn't. Shawn thought the treaty was a disaster. He pulled a book from a shelf.

"Give it a try," said Shawn, offering the book.

"I don't—"

"For me."

Gordon took the book. He wasn't going to argue.

"If you're not breathing right, you're not *living* right."

Living right. That would be nice.

20

Shawn said I helped him. He seems happy, talks happy, acts happy, and he's crediting me with helping make him that way. It's about time someone's happy.

Fuck it. I'll take whatever thanks I can get. No one said I helped in Chicago, not including customers saying, "Thanks for helping with the sofa." I'm talking about real thanks for real help. Shawn's better. Cedric's better. With the magic I'm working, I'll have Shawn walking naked with Cedric by the time I'm done.

Tonight's the night with Ash. We're going to do it. Balls to the wall. She's fucking nuts. I tried to talk her out of it. She said no, then undressed me. She knows how to shut me up. We had sex next to an open window. She hoped we were being watched.

If tonight's the night for Ash, then today's the day for Naomi. She's supposed to be breaking the moving-out-of-town news to Dean. I told her to tell him in the morning because I thought he wouldn't be high from whatever shit he seems to be on, though I didn't tell her that part. Being sober might make Dean easier to deal with. But what if he has some killer hangover?

Fuck. No one wants to hear bad news with a hangover.

Chapter 49

GORDON CREPT UP THE STAIRS to Dean's apartment like the first cop to arrive at a crime scene.

Dean's car was outside, but Naomi's wasn't. She'd told Gordon to give her until noon to break the news that she was moving away, then Gordon could drop in for damage control. She knew that Dean would flip out and want to argue, but she'd leave quickly without giving him the chance.

A classic hit-and-run.

Gordon opened the door, and there was Dean. Standing in the kitchen. Staring at him. It was creepy as fuck, like Dean knew he was coming. Gordon was prepared for the worst as he stepped inside. But Dean just stood there. Waiting.

Ding-ding-ding, beeped the microwave.

Dean turned away from Gordon and opened the microwave. He touched a burrito with his finger, deemed it warm enough, and set it on the counter.

"Can't believe it," said Dean. "Those fags walking out like that. Dicks hanging free. Then you jumping in. I'm surprised you didn't get shot."

"I wasn't thinking about it at the time."

Gordon didn't know what else to say. He watched Dean take a heaping bite from the burrito. A glob of cheese and salsa dripped to the ground. For a second, Gordon forgot why he was there, then it came to him. "Naomi."

Chewing, Dean looked at him, suspicious. "What about her?"

Naomi didn't tell him, Gordon thought. She chickened out.

"She stopped by," said Dean. "Looked upset. You say something to piss her off?"

"Like what?"

"You tell me. You go to Gilroy's to talk to her."

Gordon didn't want to deal with this until she told him. It wasn't worth it. He'd wait for the real storm. He decided to change the subject. "How's the managing going?"

"I was gonna go after your friend. Try to sign him."

"Who?"

"Cedric."

Gordon stepped right into that one. Conversational land mine. He didn't want to talk about the party.

"I'm not gonna represent him until he gets his shit straightened out," said Dean.

"What shit?"

"His homosexuality."

"What?" asked Gordon with an incredulous laugh.

Dean took another monstrous bite, causing another glob to drip. With a full mouth, he mumbled, "Guy's a fag."

"Cedric?"

"Yeah."

"You think he's gay?"

Dean let out a belch. "I called around to gauge interest in his album. Story is, he's a butt pirate. Story is, his gay lover marched out in the middle of his party with the guy he was cheating on him with. Know what they're calling him?"

"What?"

"See-dick. Ce-dric. See-dick. Funny shit, huh?"

"Jesus…"

"So I'm not gonna represent him. No worries."

No worries for Dean maybe.

Gordon felt like picking up the phone in front of Dean and calling Shawn to scream *Get outta the house!* Like some ax murderer was on the way.

Shawn had no reason to spread the rumors. He had carried out the greatest thing he'd ever done. Except his greatest thing was turning into Cedric's worst.

"Gotta call someone?" asked Dean.

Gordon realized he'd been staring at the phone. "No, just…"

He walked out without finishing. He'd come here to handle the repercussions of Naomi's decision to skip town, but now his mind was back on Shawn and Cedric.

It wasn't supposed to be like this. The lives were supposed to be *separate*. Now they were bleeding together like burning candles mixing their wax into a single pool, creating a new, muddy color.

Isn't that what he wanted? To be the byproduct of three burning lives?

Chapter 50

THE BAG WAS IN the trunk.

Ash was dead sober, which was unusual considering the circumstances. She'd had a few drinks before the other missions to build up her nerve. But not this time. This time, she was dead fucking sober, which was bizarre to Gordon since the task that lay ahead trumped every other stunt they'd carried out.

Maybe she didn't need to drink anymore. Hell, come to think of it, he was dead sober too. Downing a few shots didn't even cross his mind back at the loft. They were too busy loading the bag, although that alone warranted a cocktail. But Ash had kept busy without needing to take the edge off, so Gordon had followed suit. At least they were focused.

She drove her car with Gordon next to her, both dressed in black. They were ten minutes away from their destination.

"Gotta be quick once we get up there," said Gordon.

They had done a fair amount of prepping, but it would still take time to arrange what they had to arrange.

"You tired?" asked Gordon.

"Why?" asked Ash.

"You're not saying much."

"I usually do?"

"Usually."

She shifted lanes. "I feel like shit, is all."

"Then why do it tonight?"

"Gotta."

"'Cause he said so?"

"Don't start."

Gordon didn't want to argue the point again. They were already on their way. He thought about bailing, but Ash needed him. This had to be the last one, though. Had to be. Shouldn't he tell her that?

Don't deny.

"This has to be the last one," said Gordon. "You can do what you want, but I'm done."

"Damn it, Gordon. You're puttin' a shit vibe in the air."

"So?"

"Shit vibes don't mesh with risk."

"I'm saying what I feel."

"You've said it. Now stop." She grimaced slightly.

"What is it?"

"Nothing."

"We should turn around."

"Gordo n."

The way she said his name meant stop.

He stopped. It was no use at this point anyway. She was already parking on a back street. Three blocks away. It meant they'd have to walk there and back, barely visible, but still visible, but they couldn't take the chance of the car being seen.

Ash popped the trunk.

"One question," said Gordon.

She couldn't believe he was still at it.

"Is it worth it?" asked Gordon.

"Expression is always worth it."

"And you consider this *your* expression?"

"That's two questions."

"Do you?"

Without looking at him, she said, "The message is more important than the messenger." She got out of the car.

Gordon let a few seconds pass, then exited. He took the bag out of the trunk and slung it over his shoulder.

They walked at a quick clip toward the location that Myron had picked himself.

The Column of Light Cathedral.

It was an eighty-year-old landmark church with a towering steeple. Adjacent to it was a two-floor recreational facility containing classrooms, offices, a dining room, and a gym.

Though it was past eleven o'clock, a Gamblers Anonymous meeting was still in progress. Myron had told Ash and Gordon, via information culled from a poker addict friend who found himself at GA meetings whenever he went bust, that a side door near the dumpster would be unlocked. The gamblers used it to get outside to smoke during session breaks and never bothered to lock it until the end of the night.

Ash and Gordon made their way in quite easily, though Gordon wondered how they would explain their presence and cat-burglar-like appearance if caught. Ash had concocted a story about location scouting for a film, saying there's so much filmmaking around, no one would question the excuse. Did location scouts check out properties late at night dressed in black?

Ash and Gordon traversed a thin hallway, slipped through a stairwell door, and climbed two flights of concrete steps to the roof. Cool air touched their skin. They walked a short distance, crouching low, careful to make their footfalls light, and jumped four feet to the back side of the church's steeple.

This is where it got a bit more complicated. With a nod from Ash, Gordon balanced himself on the sloping surface and opened the bag.

Inside were twenty-two life-sized baby dolls.

It was Myron's idea. It was all Myron's idea. That's what pissed Gordon off.

Why the fuck wasn't he up here?

They worked in silence.

Ash took the babies, two at a time, and attached them together with thick rubber bands that almost perfectly matched the dolls' skin tone. Each doll was attached to another at the hips with rubber bands.

Ash reached in the bag and took out a large Tupperware bowl filled with fake blood, the sticky leftovers of the concoction they brewed for the strike on the oil company office. Using her fingers, Ash started dabbing the babies with blood.

That motherfucker Myron.

Lights dotted the Hollywood Hills, shining from the hundreds of homes nestled along the canyon roads. With some bad luck, Gordon thought, anyone could peer over a balcony at them, perhaps through a telescope, and watch babies get smeared with blood. They were completely exposed. Even worse, from a distance, the dolls would look real.

What if someone called the cops? Within minutes, police cars would arrive. The church would be surrounded. Gordon forced himself to push aside the thought, but the lights were there, scattered across hills like the glowing eyes of wolves.

Ash finished with the dolls and nodded to Gordon. It was time to arrange the blood-soaked babies.

The unveiling would coincide with an outdoor ceremony announcing the forming of a pro-life community outreach program. Big celebrities would be present when the speeches were made on the cathedral's steps. News crews were scheduled to be there.

Exposure. It's all about exposure. Myron had an engorged cock for exposure.

Attention seeking prick.

When *Entertainment Tonight*, *Access Hollywood*, and whoever the fuck else showed up, the unveiling would happen, and the bloody babies would be revealed.

How much of this would actually be broadcast was anyone's guess, but in the age of the internet, video and pictures would circulate far and wide, so it'd be seen by the masses one way or the other.

Myron had explained the significance of the babies to Ash, who had passed along the basic theory to Gordon. It went something like this: The church may be reaching out to the community, but meanwhile, they pour money into the coffers of the Republican party which wages war where it sees fit. So ultimately, the pro-life stance was a load of shit. Babies were dying all over the world in the name of combating evil and so on and so forth. Ash couldn't remember the finer points.

The message boiled down to one word, and it was the word that Myron wanted under the babies.

"Sometimes, you gotta spell it out for them," Myron had said.

So they did. In a single word on a thirty foot, vertical, white banner that would hang next to a string of bloody babies.

It was crude. It was extreme. It was Myron.

The customary signature of E was drawn in orange paint at the bottom of the banner. Myron drew it himself back at the house, taking extra relish in the process, making sure it looked just right. After the last stroke of the brush, Myron had scratched his beard, leaving a generous smear of orange below his chin. He started talking about perception and the medium of television, but all Gordon could do was stare at the paint on his beard. It made him look like a mad wizard. Wild eyes, flowing robe, orange beard. The Sorcerer of Silver Lake. The wooden brush was his wand, and he gestured with it in sweeping arcs. Gordon was sure he'd be transformed into a goat at any instant.

Ash removed the rolled-up banner from the bag. It would be high and out-of-reach on the cathedral's roof.

The unveiling, of course, was the tricky part. If they set it up now, it'd almost certainly be seen before morning and worse, removed. So they needed to ready it, but hold off exposing it until the speeches.

Gordon credited Myron for the solution to this problem. It was well planned, and even tested. The banner, with the babies tucked inside, would be rolled up with strings attached to small charges, like firecrackers, which would be activated via remote. Myron would wait with the remote in the crowd of onlookers as the celebrities prepared to speak about the sanctity of life. (He wanted to set off the tiny explosives himself to get the timing right. Whatever. As long as Gordon didn't have to be there). Then, when the moment was right, Myron would set off the charges.

Working swiftly and in silence, Ash and Gordon attached the babies, held together by rubber bands and fishing line, to the banner, then they—

Ash doubled over, arms folded on her stomach.

"Ash…" whispered Gordon.

The pain subsided for a moment, and Ash steadied herself. Gordon heard her suck in a lungful of air.

"What is it?" asked Gordon.

"I'm okay," said Ash.

"Are you—"

She grunted as the pain returned, snapping into a fetal position.

Gordon touched her shoulder as she rolled onto her knees and vomited. Puke dripped down the roof. She flattened her palms on the tile, eyes wide. Frightened. She spit, breathed, then tightened as she threw up again.

Gordon waited for her to relax. "You take anything?" It'd explain why she avoided alcohol. Maybe she didn't want to mix her poisons. "Pills or…"

"No."

"You sure?"

"Fuck I just say?"

She spit. Vomit and saliva pooled around the bag. Ash sat up, summoned enough strength, and finished positioning the banner.

***

The walk back was slow and unsteady.

Ash didn't say a word as they crossed the roof, nor when they descended the stairs.

When they reached the first floor door leading to the hallway, they heard voices talking on the other side. Gambling addicts, no doubt. Maybe taking a break, maybe wrapping up for the night. They had to wait for them to go away.

Ash sat on the floor. She was sweating. Gordon sat next to her. If she puked again, people would hear for sure. He felt Ash knew this. He could see her concentrating, trying to relax.

The chatter in the hall continued, echoing off tile.

What the fuck? Meeting's over. Go home.

Gordon heard someone say, "See ya." Then footsteps. But he didn't hear a door close. Someone could be lingering.

Ash put her face in her hands. There was no doubt a countdown was on until the next time her stomach contracted and emptied. It was only a matter of minutes, maybe less. They had to get the fuck out of the building.

Gordon listened, heard nothing. He opened the door a crack, peeked out. The hall was empty. They had to make a break.

"All right," said Gordon.

He helped Ash to her feet, then opened the door.

They headed down the thin hall which seemed to have simultaneously lengthened and shrunk from the first time they saw it, as if it was trying to prevent their escape. They reached the side door and exited. Then froze.

Two men were smoking by the dumpster. They looked at Ash and Gordon.

"Hiya," said one of the men.

"Hey," said Gordon, trying to mask his surprise.

"She okay?" asked the other, pointing to Ash with his lit cigarette.

"Fine," said Ash, managing a smile.

The man didn't think so. He saw the sweat, saw her pallor, but more alarming, saw her blood-covered shirt and hands.

"You're hurt," said the older of the men, taking out his cell.

"No," said Gordon.

"She's hurt," the man said to Gordon as if he was mentally deficient.

"I'm okay…" said Ash.

The conversation had already gone on too long, and Gordon was wishing they had just ignored them, but fake blood was on Ash, and it *did* look like she was stabbed or shot or—

"Should call an ambulance," said the man.

"That's alright," said Ash.

"Bleedin' awful bad, miss…"

"Cut my leg puttin' together a sign for the church picnic," said Ash.

"Yeah?"

"Yeah."

"Should have it looked at," said the younger of the men. "Could need stitches."

The older guy was no longer talking. He wasn't buying the story. His cell phone remained flipped open in his hand like a drawn revolver. Gordon could see the guy looking at their black clothes, sizing them up. Shit, he was a gambler which meant he could be a poker player. Couldn't poker players tell when you were lying?

"We'll get it looked at," said Gordon. "You guys have a good night."

"Night," said the younger man, stubbing out his cigarette.

Gordon and Ash walked away. They were about thirty feet from the door when the older man said, "No limp."

Ash looked back.

"Ya got no limp. Couldn't've hurt your leg *too* bad."

"Hurts like a motherfucker though."

"I bet."

Yeah, we know you bet, Gordon thought. You bet all the fucking time 'til you're flat broke, you fucking degenerate.

Ash and Gordon headed into the shadows. The moment they were out of sight, Ash let her agony show. When they reached the car, she knelt by the bumper and puked.

"… shit…" she said. Gordon saw what she was reacting to.

There was blood in the vomit. *Real* blood.

Ash climbed in the passenger side and rested her head against the window. Whether or not the old guy by the dumpster was using his phone to call the police, Gordon suddenly didn't care anymore.

"We're going to the hospital," said Gordon.

"No."

"It wasn't a question."

"I just need to lie down."

"You're puking blood."

She squeezed her eyes shut, fighting back the pain.

"What's hurting you?" asked Gordon.

She didn't answer.

"Ash…"

She kept quiet. Kept her eyes closed. Kept fighting it back.

Chapter 51

AFTER ARRIVING AT the emergency room of Cedars-Sinai Medical Center, it took two hours for Ash to be admitted.

At first, the triage nurse had seen the fake blood, and like the gambling addicts by the dumpster, assumed it was real. Once the nurse found out otherwise, she relaxed. She took Ash's blood pressure (normal), temperature (normal), and asked a few questions. She didn't inquire about the reason for the fake blood. It was Hollywood. The stuff was pretty much everywhere.

Gordon did make it clear that real blood *had* been in Ash's vomit. Despite this, the nurse had Ash return to the waiting room. During that stretch, Ash had vomited three more times in the restroom.

Gordon learned quickly that in a hospital vomiting wasn't exactly unusual, and it wasn't viewed as a life or death situation. Gordon wished he'd lied about the fake blood. If he had let the nurse believe it was real, maybe she would've rushed Ash back to see a doctor. Instead, Gordon had flipped through six issues of *People* magazine with Ash curled in a chair next to him. When her name was finally called, she had to go alone.

Gordon thought about calling Myron, but he didn't have Myron's number, and it was probably good that he didn't. He might want to come down, and Gordon didn't want to see him. They'd talk again soon, though. Gordon would make sure of that.

After another hour, Gordon was asked by a nurse if he wanted to see Ash. He was led through automatic doors, past a series of curtains until he reached Ash who was in bed, dressed in a hospital gown, IV in her arm. Her eyes were closed, and he thought she was sleeping until she said, "Steal whatever pills you see." She opened her eyes.

"What'd the doctor say?" asked Gordon.

"Not much. Had the nurse give me some Dilaudid for the pain. Good shit."

"They take any tests?"

"Yeah."

"And?"

"He's not sure what's wrong," said Ash.

"How can he not be sure?" asked Gordon.

"Doctors don't know everything."

"You tell him it happened before?"

"Yep."

"What about the blood?"

"I hate hospitals," said Ash, shifting on the bed. "It's like you're a prisoner."

Gordon felt like she was holding back information. The doctor had to have *some* idea, but she obviously didn't want to talk about it.

"Hey," said Ash. "Do me a favor?"

"Anything."

"After we get home, I'm probably gonna crash."

"Okay…"

"Can you record the news for me?"

"Why?"

Ash smiled. "I wanna see those fuckers' faces when the babies drop."

Gordon had almost forgotten about why he was dressed in black to begin with. The banner with the babies was still positioned in a concealed spot on top of the church's roof, poised to drop the moment Myron triggered the small explosives that would sever the strings and unravel the whole thing.

Gordon agreed to record the news. If anything was important to Ash at this moment, it was important to him. He glanced at the wall clock. The celebrity speech in front of the cathedral was six hours away.

"Can't wait to see their faces," said Ash, gazing up at the fluorescents. "Wish I could see the faces of all the people watching it on TV. Wouldn't that be great? To see all those mouths hangin' open, all those eyes goin' wide. Thousands and thousands of faces reacting. Wish I could see 'em all."

Chapter 52

"BECAUSE," SAID NAOMI.

"Because isn't an answer," said Gordon.

He was sitting in a booth at Gilroy's Chophouse, nursing a glass of Stoli. He almost never ate when visiting Naomi, preferring to stick to vodka and free bread.

"Timing's important," said Naomi, pretending to take his order. "I can't just blurt it out over drinks, not that we *have* drinks anymore."

"That's why we both agreed morning was the best time. It's why I've been to see him twice on the days you said you were gonna tell him."

"I said I was sorry."

"Why're you holding off?"

"Because."

Gordon sighed.

"I asked you to tell him for me," said Naomi as if the whole thing was his fault.

Naomi brought this up from time to time, but no way in soul-encrusted hell was he going to tell Dean she was moving away. He really cared about Naomi, but she'd have to have the conversation herself. Unless—

"You could just leave," said Gordon.

"Leave?"

"Pack up and hit the road without saying a word."

"Do I get to leave a note?"

"If you want."

A customer at another table was waving, trying to get Naomi's attention, but she ignored him.

"I can't run away like that," said Naomi.

"Why not?"

"He deserves more."

"Why?"

"Because."

Gordon gave her a look.

"Okay," said Naomi. "I'll tell him."

"Yeah, yeah..." said Gordon.

"I promise. I'll tell him tonight." She turned toward the customer seeking service, acting as though she just noticed him.

Gordon *so* relished the turn of events, he wanted Dean to lose his precious girlfriend sooner rather than later. Gordon was becoming the architect of their demise, subconsciously or not. He was the one that reintroduced the idea of college to her. That's what Dean would say, and he was right.

Truth is, other than the topic of Dean the Asshole, Gordon didn't have much to talk to Naomi about. There were always dry topics like what classes she'd take at Stanford, where she'd live, the traffic, the weather... but when it came to the good stuff, the private stuff, there was only the subject of Dean.

But for Gordon, there was *so much* more to talk about—other than the freeways being jammed or the smog being bad—like why he couldn't go a single hour without thinking about her.

Should he tell her? She wasn't going to be around for much longer. Should a woman know if a man loves her even if the man knows she doesn't love him?

"What're you thinking about?" asked Naomi, once again standing at his table. She set down a fresh basket of bread.

"Oh... I dunno... things."

"Me and Dean?"

You and me.

"I said, I promise, okay? I'll tell him. But I like that you care. It's sweet."

Naomi thought he was sweet. Nice, but far from great. Actually, she didn't say *he* was sweet, she said "it" was sweet. *It's* sweet. The trait of caring was sweet, not him. He wasn't sweet enough to be labeled sweet in a sweeping, general sort of way, only the single fact that he cared.

Come to think of it, in the game that was Naomi and Dean, in the area of his life where he wanted so much more, being the possessor of a sweet trait was a rather lame consolation prize. But that's not what he told her. What he said was—

"Thanks."

For nothing.

***

"I never thought there'd be so much paperwork between a pair of roommates," said Shawn. "The treaty, the notes, the signs… now he wants me to write a letter."

"A letter?" asked Gordon.

"Yes, indeed."

"Saying what?"

"That I'm not sucking his cock… or that he's not sucking mine."

"He wants you to write *that*?"

"I guess some are starting to think I'm actually his spurned lover."

They were standing in the living room where Shawn was cleaning— yes, cleaning—the faint remainder of the chalk lines. He was on his knees, wiping in circular motions with a damp sponge, a bucket of water next to him.

"You gonna write it?" asked Gordon.

"A part of me says to let the guy off the hook. That's the mature part of me. But the other side—which has a way of being more dominant— says to let him stew in a boiling pot of perceived homosexuality. Let him cook in his own hatred, so to speak." He scrubbed blue chalk from the floor. "Soooo much paperwork. You'd think I'd be allowed to send an email and be done with it, but he wants a handwritten letter."

"One that says he's not gay?"

"Precisely."

"When does he want it?"

"Today."

Things had been looking up for Shawn. One would think he'd take the path of least resistance and be done with it. (Then again, the path of least resistance was moving out, and he'd rejected that months ago.) So even though Shawn was currently sailing toward smoother seas, despite the odd request from Cedric, deep down he seemed to crave the nauseating dip of a monster swell.

"You gonna write it?" asked Gordon.

"I guess so." Shawn scrubbed. "I guess I'll let the fucker off the hook." He wrung the sponge over the bucket. "Paperwork sucks."

Chapter 53

ASH HAD BEEN HOME from the hospital for two days and her mood had yet to improve. She was already cranky when Gordon picked her up, but when she found out the church strike had failed, her mood had soured even more.

She dropped a handful of plastic bags she'd saved from the grocery store in front of the shelves near Gordon's room. She was still wearing the hospital gown and plastic I.D. bracelet with the minor addition of shorts and sandals, and she showed no sign of changing clothes. She went everywhere in her escaped mental patient look. To the beach, the liquor store, the gas station. Even to the bank, where a security guard kept a close eye on her.

"You've been discharged, y'know," said Gordon.

"Have I?" said Ash.

"Weren't you going on about patients being like prisoners?"

"So?"

"So prisoners don't lounge in their jumpsuits after they're paroled."

Ash opened a bag and started to load in the collection of small figurines that were perched on the shelves. Figurines she created on the boardwalk, but had decided, for whatever reason, not to sell.

Her art was designed impulsively, with no preconception, as if she channeled its form and features from a cosmic source. Despite the purity of the process, she felt no attachment to most of the pieces and could easily part with them in exchange for a few dollars. The figurines were born, placed on the Indian rug in random order, then sold to strangers. Carried off to new homes, never to be seen again.

But occasionally—after the wood was carved, the wire twisted, the parts glued—Ash found herself holding a figurine that felt significant, that roused emotions. A piece she couldn't let go. These found their way back to the loft and onto the shelf.

And now here she was, dressed in a hospital gown, tossing them into a bag.

"What're you doing?" asked Gordon.

"Taking out the trash."

"Since when is your art trash?"

"Since I realized it's useless."

Gordon joined her by the shelves, watched her for a moment. He picked a figurine off a shelf as she reached for it. The figurine was in the shape of a little girl clutching a white flag cut from a piece of shredded bedsheet.

"Give it," said Ash.

"Can't I look?"

"You've had months to look."

Gordon studied the piece. "What's she surrendering from?"

"It doesn't matter."

"Don't you know?"

She snatched the little girl out of Gordon's hand.

"I know," she said. "But no one else does. That's the point."

"Then tell them," said Gordon. "Put it in a—"

"Show? Is that what you were gonna say?" She dropped the figurine into a bag. It clacked on top of the others.

"What's your problem?" asked Gordon.

Ash started to answer, then bagged the remaining figurines.

"Now I get it," said Gordon. "The old art ain't big enough for the new Ash. Since when were you obsessed with the size of your audience?"

"It doesn't matter."

"Ash…"

"I want to change things."

"Then do it. One person at a time."

"No, no, it's different now. It's gotta be bigger, louder, brighter. Myron says—"

"*Myron?*"

"Yeah, he says—"

"Don't you ever think for yourself anymore?"

"Fuck you," said Ash.

"Yeah. Fuck me," said Gordon. "The guy that dragged your ass to the hospital."

"If you don't like who I'm becoming, you can leave."

It was the first time Ash mentioned the notion of him moving out.

"Maybe I will," said Gordon.

"Fine." Ash picked up the bags. "You came, you had a few laughs, you fucked, you left. Not a bad legacy." She headed to the door.

"Now I'm trash too?" Gordon said. "Time to bag me up and throw me out?"

Ash slammed the door.

Talking to her had become futile. It was time for Gordon to turn his attention to someone else. The only other person that mattered in this mess.

***

"Moisture," said Myron. "Only thing I can point to that could've naturally disabled the explosives. Handset was fine. Checked it when I got home. But god damn, you should've seen me standing there in the crowd. Hand in my pocket. Pressing that thing so damn much I looked like I was going into an epileptic seizure. Pressing and pressing. Nothing." He looked to Gordon. "Sure you rigged it right?"

"Yes."

"'Cause if the connection wasn't made properly..."

"It was rigged right."

"You sure?"

"Look, I'm not here to talk about that."

Myron was sitting in his unruly garden, the green hose rolled up at his feet like a charmed snake. He adjusted his robe and tilted his head slightly as if to say: Okay, I'm listening.

"It's about Ash," said Gordon.

Myron waited, head tilted.

"I want you to release her," said Gordon.

"Come again?"

"From your service."

"I'm not the mafia, son. She's under no contract. She can do what she pleases."

"But she does what *you* please."

"Does she?"

"The strikes, the straining for exposure..."

"Don't you join her on the outings?" asked Myron with the style of a seasoned prosecutor.

"Yeah, but—"

"Don't you help her execute the plans?"

"Yeah, but that's not—"

"I'm failing to understand what you want from me."

"I want you to stop influencing her. That's what I want."

"And how shall I accomplish this?"

"Stop calling her. Stop giving her ideas. Stop giving her goals, notions, thoughts… higher, bullshit ambitions."

Myron considered the request. He let his hand drop. His fingertips brushed the coiled hose.

"Are you in love with our Ash?" asked Myron.

"I care about her."

"I see," said Myron. "What are you anyway?"

"Excuse me?"

"In life, son. She's an artist. What are *you*?"

There was no answer for this. It was the one question Gordon asked himself every morning, and he still had no answer. Clues, hints, suggestions maybe. But no answer. Suddenly, the smell of dirt was overwhelming.

"Since you're having trouble answering," said Myron, "let's discard the question and concentrate on the statement that preceded it. 'She's an artist.' Understand? And an artist does what her gut tells her to do."

"Not Ash," said Gordon. "Not anymore."

"You don't know that," said Myron.

"I know who she was before you entered her life."

"And who was she?"

"A person who thought about art, not audience."

"It's always about the audience."

"How can you say that?"

"Because it's what I do with my days, son."

"That's, that's…" Gordon stuttered, frustrated, "… bullshit. I know I'm not an artist like you, sitting around in a dead garden all day thinking about life and death and angels and strapping dildos to suits of armor. But saying it's all about the audience? Even I know that's bullshit. There's change *within* the artist. That's what I do with *my* days. I'm trying to change *me*."

Myron considered his words. "You think that's enough?"

"Yeah, I do."

"And the audience? The potential for changing them?"

"That's not up to me or you. Or *her*."

Myron shrugged, brushed the hose. He snorted to clear his nose and glanced out at the garden. "Maybe it is, maybe it isn't." He rose from the chair.

"What about Ash?"

Myron shrugged again, bent over with a slight grunt, twisted the faucet handle. Water sputtered then poured from the hose. "Tell her I hope she feels better." He picked up the hose and sent a stream of water arcing over the yard.

Chapter 54

IT WAS THE THIRD MORNING in which Naomi promised she'd break the news to Dean that she was splitting town, and Gordon was on his way to handle the damage control.

Though he wanted to exit the 134 early and not bother with it, Gordon pressed on, reminding himself he was doing this for Naomi, though he wasn't really sure why. He had a crush on her, sure. That was one reason. (He had decided to downgrade his feelings from "love" to "crush.") He was weaning himself off Naomi like a recovering addict. But why else was he getting involved?

It is what it is. And what Naomi is/was/will be is just a friend. An acquaintance. A girl that dated his roommate. A soon-to-be memory.

And here he was, preparing to clean up her mess. Or at least sweep it into a manageable pile. It was starting to feel like a chore.

And being stuck in traffic didn't help.

Brake lights were popping up all over the place, as if waking from a collective slumber. Gordon slowed, cursed, glanced at the car clock.

The rental car crawled the last half-mile to where Gordon finally exited, only to find out that the accident that was responsible for the slow-down was at the bottom of the ramp. Cars merged onto the shoulder.

"C'mon," said Gordon.

He was driving to Dean's straight from Myron's and was still aggravated.

Stubborn fucker watering the fucking garden with his fucking hose.

If Myron ever decided to kill himself, Gordon was sure he'd choose the method of hanging. A curious neighbor would find the man swaying from a tree, the hose tied in a noose around his neck, his unwashed robe billowing in the breeze, exposing a nude, lifeless body.

Gordon reached the point of the accident, and there were no ambulances or fire trucks or bodies laying grotesquely in the middle of the road. Just a BMW Roadster turned sideways, its rear smashed into a light pole, its shattered glass creating a glimmering puddle of light. A patrol car was parked nearby with two officers huddled around the driver.

Gordon knew a thing or two about accidents far worse than this, about the smell of smoldering plastic, about the color of blood mixed with snow. About trucks and worlds turned upside down.

Traffic sped up, and Gordon was relieved.

Then he saw her walking on the side of the road.

Naomi.

Gordon tapped the brakes and lowered the passenger window.

"Hey..." said Gordon.

She didn't look.

"Naomi."

She glanced at him without breaking stride. A teenager laid on the horn of an SUV. Gordon pulled over, cut the engine, and jogged to catch up to Naomi.

Now they were both walking alongside the road.

"Afternoon stroll?" asked Gordon.

She didn't answer.

"Least tell me where you're going," said Gordon.

"Out of this fucking city."

"On foot?"

She glared at him, and that's when he saw the other side of her face.

A bloody laceration ran from her forehead to her cheekbone. A line of drying blood ran even lower, down to her neck.

"Holy shit," said Gordon.

"Could've been worse," said Naomi.

"What happened?"

"Didn't you see the accident?"

"That was Dean's car?!"

"He wanted to run some errands..."

"Naomi..."

"... said he was too busy to talk."

"What?"

"I came over like I promised," said Naomi. "I was gonna bail, but it was the third time. So I did it. I told him I was leaving. He said I was bluffing. That I was trying to scare him. I said I wasn't. I said we were over. He laughed, then realized I was serious. He said I was betraying him."

Gordon kept pace with Naomi as she walked along in an almost trance-like state.

"He told me to take it back," said Naomi. "Like a kid says, y'know? 'Take it back.' I told him I wish I could… I wish I could take back all the years I spent with him. I wish I could take *that* back."

"How'd you two get from that to slamming into a pole?"

"He grabbed my arm. I twisted his fingers so he'd let go. He went to…" Naomi measured her words. "He lost control of the car."

"Did he hit you?"

"No."

"Don't cover for him," said Gordon.

"He didn't," said Naomi. "He *wanted* to… *tried* to…"

"He tried to hit you?"

"He took his eyes off the road when he grabbed me. It was… we hit the pole before anything happened."

"Has he hit you before?"

She kept walking, not wanting to answer.

"Has he?" pressed Gordon.

She glanced at Gordon. "A long time ago," she said, figuring that was all Gordon needed to know. "He was drunk."

Picking a spot for no particular reason other than physical weariness or mental weariness or both, Naomi sat down on a curb outside a shopping center and leaned her back against a newspaper dispenser. Gordon sat next to her.

The way Naomi gazed at the road with blood twisting down from the rip in her skin made her look like pictures Gordon had seen of civilians involved in bombings. Fresh, bleeding wounds on vacant, dazed faces.

Cars passed in front of them with only five feet to spare.

"You shouldn't stay at your place tonight," said Gordon. "You should never see him again."

"I've wasted so much time…" said Naomi.

"You listening?"

"Years…"

"He's gonna try to find you."

"I wanna keep walking."

"Naomi."

"Maybe I will leave this place on foot. Leave it behind forever."

14

I'm writing this looking out the window of Dean's apartment.

The lights are off. I parked around the corner. I don't want him to know I'm here. I've been waiting for five hours. I don't know where he is. Last I know, he was talking to the cops where he crashed his car. Naomi is at her friend's house, some waitress that works with her. Dean is probably out looking for her. I keep staring at his parking spot, willing him to come home.

I don't know what I'm going to do to that fucker.

What I think I'll do is lay down the fucking law. He better stay THE FUCK away from Naomi. Don't call her, don't see her, don't fucking dream about her. Leave her the fuck alone.

I'll take a chair to his head, I swear. If he opens his mouth, I'll whack his fucking teeth out with the chair I'm sitting on now. He's going to say he didn't hit her, that the glass cut her up, but he tried to hit her. That's why they fucking crashed.

I'm supposed to be at the loft. I promised Ash I'd be there, but I'm not going anywhere until Dean shows up.

Funny thing is, what I felt for Naomi, the love and all that, I didn't really feel it today. It's not like blood running down her face made her unattractive or anything, it's just that, I get nothing from her. I'm just a guy that plopped into her life. Someone to talk to.

She won't be sitting up at Stanford longing to see me, to serve me steak, to refill my water, to talk to me about her problems. She won't be writing me, asking me to come visit. She's going to put LA behind her, and I'm part of it, which means she doesn't feel anything, which means the mix of romantic bullshit I've been entertaining is just that—bullshit. There has to be a saying that says someone has to love you in return or the love will die. Fuck, this is depressing. Sitting in the dark doesn't help. I can barely see what the fuck I'm writing.

I saw headlights coming. It's the woman across the street. She has like nine dogs. I don't know if they're hers or if she's a dogsitter or what. When he comes up those stairs, I'm not going to make a sound. I'm going to hide in the corner or maybe his room. Give him a jolt, then lay down the fucking law.

Chapter 55

THE JOURNAL SAT on the kitchen table.

It'd been over two hours since Gordon wrote anything. He was leaning back in the chair, gazing out the window with the blinds half-closed.

The anticipation that Dean was going to be home anytime soon had dissipated. Now Gordon doubted he was coming home at all. It had been a long day, and Gordon wanted to sleep. But not here. He'd come back tomorrow to see if Dean had returned. He'd call Naomi to see if she knew where Dean was.

He'd be patient, but persistent.

Perhaps it was for the best that Dean didn't come home tonight. Gordon was being given the opportunity to cool down. Exactly how much his anger would lower remained to be seen. He kept telling himself not to get *too* involved. Not to care *too* much. And the way to do that, the only way for him, was to convince himself that his feelings for Naomi were fading. It was an infatuation. Something light and meaningless that was floating away.

It was true, when Naomi was sitting on the curb, blood caked to her perfect skin, she'd given him nothing that indicated he was more than a warm body for her to vent to. If a homeless guy had been squatting there, her emotional output would've been identical.

Naomi had never given him much of anything to work with.

That was a joke all its own. All this time he'd been daydreaming about Naomi while spending more than a few nights (and mornings and early afternoons) having sex with Ash.

Separating sex from love wasn't a problem for Gordon, that was evident. This thought gave him another: maybe *that* was the cause of Ash's recent bitchiness. Yeah, she'd been sick, but what if she had developed feelings for him? Ash could be going through a similar situation. She could be sitting by *her* window waiting for *him* to come home, which he promised to do but didn't.

Was he breaking Ash's heart while Naomi was breaking his? Maybe it was a fucked-up circle of unrequited love.

Gordon rose from the chair, stretched, and headed to his bedroom. Only when he was making his way down the dark hall did he remember he left the journal on the kitchen table. The realization scared him. He quickly retrieved it. Getting careless this late in the game was not an option.

He flipped the light on in his bedroom to retrieve a few clean shirts and boxers before he departed. Juggling three lives was a hard task. Juggling three lives while keeping up with laundry was downright impossible.

Gordon walked to the water cooler and filled a paper cone. A large bubble rose in the five gallon bottle and burst at the surface.

He drank, crumpled the cone, tossed it in the trash, and opened a drawer. As he ruffled through clothes, the goal board mounted on the wall caught his eye.

Dean had convinced him to create order in his life. Order would bring stability, stability would bring progress, progress would bring happiness. An appealing chain of results, but one that never manifested. Gordon hadn't written jack shit in days. Though he sincerely wanted to get his shit together and explore the disciplined side of himself, half the reason Gordon filled the board was to please Dean.

At the beginning, Dean would peek in to inspect what was being written. He'd question Gordon about his success in following through with the planned tasks. Gordon liked the attention. It was like having a personal coach, but things had changed since then. Dean wasn't even keeping up with *his* goal board anymore.

When the teacher falls, the student stumbles.

Gordon stood before the board, its scribbled lies staring back, its fictitious events, its imaginary tasks. He'd been keeping track of a life that, for the most part, didn't exist. He'd been trying to make order out of something that wasn't there.

The utter futility of the schedule didn't dawn on Gordon until that moment. The true order, if there was any, was being maintained in his journal.

The goal board was shit.

A show for Dean. A lie for me.

Gordon reached up and grabbed the corner of the board...

He tried to hit her.

... yanked it back, peeled it off the wall...

Crashed the car. Cut her face.

... ripped it down, put his foot in the middle...

Fucking undeserving asshole.

... grabbed the sides, snapped the board in two...

UNGRATEFUL.

... snapped it again...

UNDESERVING.

... snapped it again...

CUT HER FACE.

... snapped it again.

Gordon took a step back, breathing loudly, and took stock of the damage.

Pieces of board were everywhere.

Blood was smeared on a section leaning against the mattress. Gordon raised his hand. There was a cut on his palm. He squeezed his hand into a fist, causing the wound to sting. It felt good.

Gordon grabbed the framed motivational poster, the one of the rock-climber hanging next to the mountain, and brought it down on his knee, smashing the glass. He yanked the poster free and tore it apart.

As the pieces fell around him, Gordon turned to the water cooler and kicked it over. The bottle dislodged, spilling water across the floor. He watched the water reach his feet and mix with the small pool of blood that was dripping from his hand.

He wiped his palm on his shirt. As for the wet mess, he'd leave it alone. He'd let the pieces of board and poster and glass stay right where they lay. He'd let the water sit. Dean needed to see. He needed to understand that this was over. He was done.

Dean and Naomi were a fucked up couple in a fucked up city. Period. Let them deal with it. Gordon had his own life to figure out.

He started emptying the drawer, using only his left hand to keep blood off the clothes.

Chapter 56

THE SILHOUETTE STOOD in the frame of the door.

All Gordon wanted to do was sleep. He was supposed to crash at the loft, but at the last moment, had decided against it. He had a vision of Ash confronting him. An argument was brewing within her, and he didn't want to get into it. Not tonight. All he wanted to do was let his skull sink into the pillow and drift into blackness.

But here was this silhouette.

Gordon caught enough of a glimpse to know who it was, so he closed his eyes and tried to act like he was asleep.

"I finished it," said the figure.

Gordon didn't move.

"Gordon." The silhouette stepped forward. "It's done."

Gordon opened his eyes.

"The letter," said Shawn from the darkness. "I finished it."

Gordon heard the rustling of paper.

"I need your advice," said Shawn. "On the content."

Gordon's head pounded with a headache. Finding Naomi on the side of the road in a daze, seeing her wince in pain, waiting for Dean for hours to return, it had all taken its toll. His mental stamina was at an all-time low, and he wasn't in any mood to deal with Shawn. He should've went to the hotel to sleep. It was his rule to always sleep at one of the three residences, but surely, he could've made an exception tonight.

"Can I turn on the light?" said Shawn.

"Sure."

The room was illuminated, and there was Shawn, standing in front of him holding a piece of paper. Gordon squinted as his eyes adjusted.

"I'm done, but..." said Shawn. "You weren't sleeping-sleeping, were you?"

"Not really. Not yet."

"This is the letter Cedric wanted me to write."

Gordon sat up on his elbows. "Has he read it?"

"Not yet."

"When's he gonna?"

"When everyone else does. I'm sending it to the record company tomorrow, the one he signed with. I'm also sending it to his friends. And his lawyer. And his parents."

"Don't you think he should read it first?"

"He wanted me to write a letter, so I did, and I'm sending it out tomorrow. But I need your advice."

Gordon's headache suddenly felt worse.

"I'll read it." Shawn's voice was quiet, but Gordon's headache made the words arrive like rows of spikes tapping lightly against his brain. "Due to the string of misconstrued events at Cedric's recent party at his house, a.k.a. the 'blast your bone bacchanal,' I was asked by Cedric to compose a letter to clarify my presence during that evening. I hope the following does just that and thereby washes away any and all misunderstanding of my place in Cedric's life."

Gordon could hear Shawn take a breath.

"I am Cedric's roommate," read Shawn. "I am also his friend, his companion, and his lover. I apologize for my shameless and selfish public exhibition of nudity. It was an inappropriate, immature, petty act. The gentleman that accompanied me also expresses the same regret. But what transpired, though unfortunate, doesn't change how I feel about Cedric nor how he feels about me."

Shawn took another breath, paused for a moment, then continued.

"His love couldn't be stronger, his touch couldn't be softer, his kiss couldn't be warmer, his semen couldn't be sweeter. For this, I am eternally grateful. Cedric and I have nothing to hide, and I pray this letter paves the way for a smoother road in both his career and his personal life. Sincerely and truly, Shawn Ellis."

Silence as Shawn waited for a reaction.

"Well?" said Shawn.

"It's a lie," said Gordon.

"I know."

"Might as well be a suicide letter."

"I know."

"Rip it up. That's my advice."

"I can't do that. I promised myself I'd put this behind me. That I'd move out. This whole, little war with Cedric," said Shawn. "It's childish."

"I agree."

"Good."

"So why send the letter?"

"For the same reason I do a lot of things in my life. To say *fuck you*. Fuck you for making me write a letter. Fuck you for making me feel ashamed. Fuck you for making me feel small, weird, unworthy."

"You're doing this to yourself, man. It's like you crave self-punishment."

"I swear this is it. This and no more."

"You can't send that thing."

"I have to."

"Rip it up."

"No."

"Seems like your mind is made up," said Gordon. "Why ask for my advice? You know what'll happen if you send it. He'll go ballistic."

"Probably."

"Can't you at least... re-word it?"

"I don't want to. When I sat down to write, that's what came out."

"Then fuck it. Do what you want," said Gordon. "Don't deny."

13

There are no walls anymore. That's the problem. Everything's bleeding into everything else. I try to keep things separate, but the second I shut the door on a life to deal with the next, the other life comes seeping in like a sickness. I can smell it before I see it.

There are parts of me only certain people should be seeing.

The impulsive-me belongs to Ash.

The disciplined-me belongs to Dean.

The parental-me belongs to Shawn and Cedric.

That was the point of it all. To see how I am. To find out who I am. Now they're all dripping through the cracks.

How am I supposed to find myself if I can't control myself?

I need separation for 13 more days. That's all. Then I'm done. Then I can peel back the bandages and look at the new me. I want the new me. I need the new me. Who I am now? I'm everyone and no one. That's not how it's supposed to be.

I'm not done cooking. I shouldn't peek in the oven until I'm done. This is all adding up to something. I have to keep it together for a little bit longer.

I need to go to the hotel and update the walls. I need to study them like I used to. That could be why things are falling apart. I used to go there every day and keep careful track of the lives. I used to measure them. I need to go back.

I'll go tonight.

Chapter 57

"YOU BROKE OUR TRUST," said Ash.

Gordon didn't respond.

He was riding in the passenger seat of the rent-a-car which was inching forward on the 405 in the standard, nightmarish, morning traffic. Ash had wanted to drive but didn't want to take her car, which was having its usual engine problems, so Gordon agreed to let her drive the rental car. She wanted to take him to a café she dubbed, "The Eatery for the Unwanted." Greasy food priced to move.

Gordon had shown up at the loft right at daybreak to speak with Ash, thinking she'd be too groggy to argue. It was a trick in a way. She was usually lethargic before noon, content on wandering around the loft, stopping to unleash a protracted yawn at least four times an hour. He wanted to take advantage of that. No energy, no anger.

But Ash had delayed the discussion, insisting they get something to eat. Now she was waking up, and Gordon was stuck in the car like a caged mouse watching a python stir, knowing the first thing on its to-do list was eat.

Sure enough, with each passing minute, Ash was becoming more vocal, more combative, though Gordon made sure he didn't feed into her rising anger. Keeping his mouth shut, he leaned against the window and closed his eyes to feign a nap. Not only was she not buying the "can't hear you, I'm napping" act, she had no problem jabbing him in his side to get his attention.

So they drove and she talked on their way to the eatery on Melrose.

"Broke our trust," said Ash.

Gordon said nothing.

"You listening?" She jabbed him.

Gordon straightened. Didn't anyone respect a person sleeping anymore?

"I thought we had a trust," said Ash.

"We do," said Gordon.

"Then why go to Myron behind my back?"

Gordon had figured Myron would tell her and had readied his response well in advance. "I was concerned."

"He won't return my calls," said Ash. "What'd you tell him?"

"What'd he tell you I told him?"

"Fuck off."

Gordon shut up. Ash allowed a few moments to go by until she couldn't take it anymore. "Just tell me."

"I asked him to leave you alone," said Gordon.

"Why?"

"'Cause I was concerned."

"I need this," said Ash.

"Need what?"

"His guidance."

"Bullshit."

"It's not bullshit," said Ash. "I was drifting. He's given me direction."

"You're wrong," said Gordon.

"I'm not. Fuck off."

"Saying 'fuck off' over and over isn't the best way to carry on a conversation."

"You're a fucking dick, and I can't trust you. Better?"

Gordon looked out the window.

"Answer me," said Ash.

"Yes," said Gordon. "That's better."

"Asshole."

Gordon rubbed his eyes.

"Don't think you can stall for time," said Ash. "I'll drive in circles 'til we run outta gas or 'til you explain to me to my satisfaction why *you* broke *our* trust."

"I made a decision to help you," said Gordon.

"Help me?" said Ash.

"You're a mess."

"You ain't exactly Mr. Got-It-Together."

"Thanks for the bulletin."

"Myron wants to shake things up," said Ash.

"No," said Gordon. "He wants *you* to do what *he* wants to shake things up."

"So?"

"You really wanna live your life that way?"

"As opposed to what?"

"Doing your own thing."

"I churn out shit no one sees," said Ash.

"It's not shit," said Gordon.

"No one."

"I don't know what happened to you. You've become…"

"What? What have I become?"

"Nothing."

"I've become what?" said Ash.

"Forget it," said Gordon.

"Too much a pussy to say it?"

"Where's this place?"

"Say it."

"We even close to it?"

"I've become *what*, Gordon?"

"Let it go."

"No."

"You're being a bitch."

"And you're being a pussy," said Ash. "I know you *want* to say it, and what do we say about want? Don't deny. That's our rule. Don't deny."

Gordon sighed.

"You're a pathetic bag of denial," Ash said, looking to the road, then to him. The road, then to him. "Well?"

"Wanna drive in circles all day?" said Gordon. "Fine."

"Don't deny. What have I become? Say it. *What the fuck have I become?* Don't deny."

"All I'm denying right now is my stomach which is demanding a stack of buttermilk pancakes with strawberry syrup and whip cream."

"Pussy," said Ash.

"Whole strawberries buried in cream," said Gordon.

Gordon was doing a fair job of burying his frustration. Concentrating on breakfast was working better than he had anticipated.

"You're containing emotion," said Ash. "You may think you're being mature, but all you're doing is being a pussy."

"Whatever," said Gordon.

"Release your emotion. What're you feeling right now?"

"Give it a rest, okay?"

"No. What're you feeling right now?"

"Hunger."

"What else?"

"Anger."

"But you're not showing it," said Ash.

"No."

"Why?"

"'Cause I don't wanna fucking fight."

"But you're angry."

"Yeah, I am."

"Then let it out."

"Nope."

"Don't deny this moment," said Ash. "Don't push it aside as something to be dealt with later. There is no later. There's only *right now*." Ash smacked the steering wheel. "Don't deny."

Gordon was steaming. Hunger had a way of making him grumpy if left unchecked. But if he was already frustrated, pissed off, and ready to fucking scream, it made him downright homicidal.

"Let it out," said Ash.

"Just drive," said Gordon.

"Why not let it out?"

"Why not let *me* out?"

"Wanna run away?"

"Drive," said Gordon, his emotions boiling. "Just drive."

"Let it out."

"Where the fuck is this place?"

When they finally reached Melrose, Gordon was desperate to find a place to eat. *Any* place. He'd settle for cold coffee and a moldy bagel from a gas station if it meant getting out of the car and away from Ash. He was starting to wonder whether she had concocted this mysterious eatery in order to justify the lengthy trek. Maybe she trapped him so she could lecture him.

"You sure this place exists?" said Gordon.

"What's that supposed to mean?" said Ash.

"Means we've been in this car forever."

"Think I made it up?"

"You've done stranger things."

"'Cause I've become... *something*, right? Something you won't tell me."

Ash was relentless. She wanted Gordon to reach the end of his patience. So she kept pushing and pushing.

"What have I become?" said Ash.

"For fuck sake."

"Don't—"

"I'm not denying."

"Then let it out!"

Gordon couldn't take it anymore. All shreds of composure vanished. "You know what you've become? You've become a puppet. A fucking puppet. A fucking tool. *That's* what you've become. A plaything for Myron. His servant. You used to be a free spirit. Now you're a fucking string-bound puppet. It's fucking pathetic and sad and depressing, and it reeks of someone who's scared."

"I'm not scared," said Ash.

"The fuck you're not," said Gordon. "You're scared shitless of not being noticed. Of not being on the public's almighty radar. Who gives a shit? Fuck the public."

"Every time he sent me out, you went with me."

They stopped at a red light.

"I thought it was... temporary," said Gordon. "A diversion. I don't know."

"You shouldn't have come along."

"Wish I didn't."

Just then, Gordon noticed something on the sidewalk.

"I wanna be more," said Ash.

Noticed *someone* on the sidewalk.

"I wanna be loud."

Noticed *Dean* on the sidewalk.

"I wanna be seen."

Dean.

"I wanna be heard."

Don't deny.

"I wanna—"

By the time Ash heard the passenger door open, Gordon had already left the car.

Dean had just finished feeding change into a meter when Gordon first spotted him. Dean had just flipped open his cell when Gordon opened the car door. Dean would never get the chance to dial.

Gordon tackled Dean to the ground. There's a lot to be said for the element of surprise. Gordon landed three clean shots before Dean knew what hit him.

"Ungrateful!" said Gordon.

"The fuck?" said Dean, managing to grab hold of Gordon's left wrist.

"Ungrateful!"

They became locked in a sloppy wrestling hold.

"Ungrateful!"

Gordon broke free of Dean's grip. He got to his knees and spit in Dean's face.

Then punched him. Then twisted his arm.

Then locked a hand around his throat.

Only now was Ash out of the car, which was left sitting in the street, engine running. *"What the fuck're you doing!"* she screamed.

Dean was trying to pry Gordon's fingers free.

"... ungrateful..." said Gordon.

"Gordon," said Ash.

Dean shoved Gordon away. The two got to their feet and squared off.

Ash was trying to put the pieces together in her head. One second, she was having an argument with Gordon. The next, he was assaulting a stranger.

"You wanna *die*, Lake?" said Dean.

"You cut her face," said Gordon.

"What?"

"You tried to hit her."

"Better back down, man."

"Who the fuck is this?" said Ash.

"An ungrateful asshole," said Gordon.

"And you're a loser who's hung up on *my* woman," said Dean.

"She ain't yours."

"Sure the fuck ain't yours."

"Would someone tell me *what the fuck* is going on?" said Ash.

"Don't deny…" said Gordon, under his breath.

"What's that?" said Dean.

Gordon charged Dean, taking him to the cement.

This time, Gordon truly unleashed. He let it out. He let it all out. He swung and swung.

No form. No control.

No balance.

"Gordon!" screamed Ash.

A bystander shouted something. Another yelled at Gordon to stop. A third *made* him stop, ripping him off Dean.

"Take it easy," said the man, pinning Gordon to the cement, his knee pressed against Gordon's chest. "Take—it—easy." Gordon didn't resist.

Dean rolled to his knees, blood dripping from his nose and mouth.

"I'll kill you…" said Dean.

"Ain't gonna do a damn thing 'cept stay where you are," said the man.

"He's fucking crazy," said Dean.

Gordon stayed flat on his back, gasping, his eyes on Dean.

"It's over," said the man.

Gordon glared at the man. "Get off me."

The man thought about this. "Give me your license."

"What?"

"If I get off you, you're gonna run. So give me your driver's license."

"What the fuck're you? Citizen of the month?"

"Someone who's been mugged twice. That's who I am."

Gordon thought about struggling. He could move this guy by force, but he didn't feel like fighting anymore. Gordon looked to Ash.

"My wallet's under the front seat," said Gordon.

Ash nodded, shaken from the odd turn of events, and hurried to the car.

"We're gonna wait for the cops," said the man.

"The cops?" said Dean. He stood, unsure of his next move.

"That's right."

"I didn't do shit," said Dean. "*He* jumped *me*."

Ash reached under the front seat, but felt nothing. She bent and looked. No wallet. Maybe he left it in the glove compartment. She'd seen him put it there before. She tried to open it, but it was stuck.

"Tell it to the cops," said the man.

"I'm outta here," said Dean.

"They need a statement," said the man, but Dean was already walking away.

Ash pulled the keys from the ignition and inserted the engine key into the glove compartment. The door fell open, and Ash rummaged through the contents, wanting to find the wallet to get this mess over with. Should they wait for the cops? Maybe it'd serve Gordon right for being an asshole.

She dug around. No luck.

Ash crammed the stuff back in, but some of it was unruly and tumbled back out. She caught one item as it tilted and fell.

When she looked down, she saw that she was holding a black composition book.

She was holding Gordon's journal.

Chapter 58

THE STALE ODOR OF HOTEL carpet offered a comfort that Gordon didn't think was possible.

He was back in room 116 at the Starlight Inn. The neutrality of the location served as an instant anesthetic. The last few days had been a sweltering cesspool of emotions, and he needed a break.

Lying flat on the floor with his nose pressed against the carpet, each inhalation sucked in the scent of worn fabric. Each breath dampened his mind.

Gordon had thought he'd crawl right into bed once he got here for a much needed, death-like nap, but the relief of being back in the room led him to simply lie on his stomach right on the floor. The hardness was welcomed. It offered a stability that made him feel things weren't *too* bad.

But they were. And they were only getting worse.

After Dean had declared, "I'm outta here," and walked away following the unexpected fight, the Good Samaritan who was restraining Gordon became frustrated. With Ash unwilling to give a statement to the cops, he reluctantly gave up and let them go. Ash drove Gordon back to the loft, but they didn't speak the entire way. When they arrived, she climbed out without so much as looking at him.

Gordon slid into the driver's seat of the rental car and drove straight to the hotel, his personality sanctuary. His place to be blank. Everyone should have one, he thought. A hole to crawl back into when times got rough, if only for a few hours. The motel business would boom if the idea ever caught on.

The way Gordon was positioned on the floor—face down, one leg on top of the other, one arm out, one arm tucked under his belly, chin angled up—if a maid happened to stroll in, she'd probably scream with the horrifying assumption that she'd stumbled into the scene of a murder.

But although his limb configuration appeared corpse-like,

uncomfortable, even painful, it felt perfect. Numbing. It allowed his mind to focus on the day's events, to study them under the light of silence.

Why'd he go after Dean like that?

Well, he knew *why*, but where was the self-control he possessed when he was around Dean?

But he was also around Ash.

Ash was there, true. He was around Ash around Dean. Around Dean around Ash.

He took a deep breath, inhaling a particularly potent whiff of the carpet's stench. This blending of lives was happening more and more.

It could be that he was simply ahead of schedule. He'd given himself three months to explore the separate aspects of his personality, the plan being to form a new, single personality at the end of that stretch.

A New Gordon. The *Real* Gordon.

His rebirth was supposed to occur like clockwork after ninety-three days.

But it was naïve to think life worked on a schedule. The shell of the egg was cracked whether he wanted it to be or not. Whatever waited inside was already coming free. Making itself known. Stepping into the world.

Gordon couldn't stop the blending of thoughts.

With Shawn and Cedric. *Make it better.*

With Naomi and Dean. *It is what it is.*

With Ash. *Give in to desire.*

They were becoming part of a larger philosophy.

It is what it is. Give in to desire. Make it better.

All part of the same person. The same mind. What were they together?

… give in… desire… make it… better… it is… what it is…

Together. Bring them together.

Give in to what it is, but desire to make it better.

Gordon's eyes opened.

That was it. That was always it. Separating them for months allowed him to see that. He had to purify the ingredients before mixing them.

Or maybe he was just high from inhaling carpet glue.

Either way, he wanted to write these thoughts down. He wanted to write an entry.

Gordon picked himself off the ground, feeling like he weighed three hundred pounds, and went to the rental car to retrieve the journal. He opened the trunk, searched, but the journal wasn't there.

The glove compartment. That's right. He remembered stashing it in the glove compartment right before he left for the loft.

Gordon made his way to the passenger door, glancing around the hotel parking lot. A teenage couple was arguing by a dirty Mustang, but other than that—empty.

Gordon unlocked the glove compartment and dug his hand in, searched, felt, but—

The journal wasn't there.

In one swipe, he emptied the contents onto the seat. No journal. Gordon froze and concentrated. Where did he last see it? He had finished an entry, then stashed the book in the glove compartment. He was sure of it.

He looked again. Dug. Searched. Felt.

The fucking thing was gone.

Gordon returned to the trunk and tore it apart, ripping up the rug that concealed the spare tire (the arguing teenage couple was now staring at him), but the journal was missing.

How? Who?

Ash.

That had to be it. Gordon recalled the moment clearly. The man's knee was pressed against his chest. He was demanding Gordon's license. Ash went to the car to retrieve his wallet (it was lodged under the seat, against the chair rail), but she seemed to be gone for a long time.

She must have looked in the glove compartment. She must have found the journal. But she hadn't said a word riding back.

Why?

'Cause she wants to read it first.

Gordon locked the door to room 116 and drove straight to the loft. As he expected, Ash wasn't there. He searched for the journal, but, also as he expected, found nothing. He sat on her mattress and thought.

If Ash actually had the journal in her possession, she'd come to him soon enough.

If she ever spoke to him again.

Chapter 59

A MOVING TRUCK was parked in front of Cedric and Shawn's house.

Movers were marching in and out of the house, up and down the truck ramp, loading boxes, furniture, and appliances.

Someone was moving out. The war must be over. Someone had finally surrendered.

Hallelujah.

Was it Cedric or Shawn? It didn't really matter to Gordon since he was out himself in a few days, but he was hoping it was Shawn who was saying adios.

Turns out, that's who it was. Gordon recognized the chest of drawers he helped Shawn reposition in his bedroom. It was being carried up the ramp by two men wearing faded blue t-shirts.

Good for Shawn, then. He was finally leaving.

Gordon walked up the pathway, eager to congratulate Shawn in person. When he got to the front door, a pair of men in knit caps and baggy clothes joined at the shoulder to stop him.

"Yeah?" said one of the men, chewing on something.

"Hey," said Gordon. They didn't move. "Excuse me…"

"Where you think you're goin'?"

"Inside."

"No you ain't."

"I live here."

"It's cool," said a voice.

Gordon looked through the window and saw Cedric walking toward the door. The men parted, letting Cedric see Gordon.

"If you gonna come in, come in," said Cedric.

"We have guards now?" said Gordon, not moving from the porch.

"They ain't guards. They're… facilitators."

"What exactly are they facilitating?"

"Shawn's departure."

"Where is he?"

"Shawn?"

"Yeah."

"I don't know where the fuck he is."

"That's his stuff getting loaded, right?"

"Shit yeah."

"So he's moving out?"

"Shit yeah."

Gordon glanced through the window at the men in baggy clothing who were now sitting on the couch playing a video game.

"Why wouldn't Shawn be here?" asked Gordon.

"It's like this," said Cedric. "I know you know about the letter."

Gordon hesitated. "Yeah."

Cedric was talking about the letter Shawn composed in which he inferred Cedric was gay.

"He sent it everywhere," said Cedric. "He tell you that?"

"Yeah," said Gordon. "He told me that." He took a step back to let a mover pass who was carrying a box that wasn't taped and wasn't marked. A rush job.

"Thought I'd flip out, didn't you?" said Cedric.

"Did you?"

"My boys were gonna fuck him up. Stomp his fag ass in the ground. But I said no. I said I was a businessman who didn't jump people like that. I got a future, see?"

A mover slid Shawn's exercise bike into the truck. They were treating the items like junk. Gordon wondered what instructions Cedric had given them.

"That fag's a problem, though," said Cedric. "And businessmen solve problems. He solves them by making them go away."

"He doesn't know about this, does he?"

"Best he didn't."

"Is that what your friends are for?" asked Gordon, not breaking eye contact with Cedric. "'Case he shows up?"

"What d'you care? Problem's been solved. Ain't that what you wanted?"

A lamp was tossed on top of a table. Gordon heard the bulb shatter.

"Where's his stuff going?" said Gordon.

"Away."

"Where's he gonna live?"

"Somewhere else."

"You make it sound easy."

"Is for me."

Cedric went back inside. One of the guys playing the video game glanced to Cedric, then out the window to Gordon. Cedric and the guy spoke, but Gordon couldn't hear what was said. Gordon's attention returned to the truck.

Cedric was probably having all of Shawn's possessions put into storage. After the job was done, hopefully he'd tell Shawn where he could find his belongings, maybe lace the revelation with a few threats, and that would be that.

Emptying the house of Shawn's belongings wasn't a clean solution, but it *was* a solution. Gordon wondered about the reaction Cedric's friends and family had to the letter. No one could've taken it seriously, Gordon thought.

Whatever the reaction, Cedric had to retaliate. That was the only way he could make things right in the eyes of others. To his credit, he'd avoided a violent response, instead choosing to hire a company to clean house. Literally.

It was a forced move, an unapproved relocation, but a solution nonetheless.

Gordon thought about contacting Shawn to tell him that his stuff was getting moved, but he couldn't reach him if he wanted to. He didn't have Shawn's cell number, and he didn't know where he was.

Gordon could call the cops, but by the time they arrived, the truck would probably be long gone, and Gordon didn't need Cedric on his case as well. Let them sort it out on their own. Gordon had wanted to make things better, so maybe the forced move was a blessing in disguise.

Someone had to leave, right?

A mover leaned a monitor against a framed photograph of Shawn and his family, splintering the glass.

Chapter 60

"HEY," SAID NAOMI.

Standing at the entrance of Gilroy's Chophouse, Gordon deflated a bit. It was the most lukewarm greeting he had ever received from her. He tried not to personalize it, instead telling himself she'd just been through a lot of shit lately.

Hovering nearby with a stack of menus in hand, the hostess picked up on the familiar interaction and said, "Wanna sit in Naomi's section?"

"I'm not eating," said Gordon.

The hostess gave them space.

"What is it?" asked Naomi.

"When's your break?"

"Twenty minutes or so."

"Can you talk then?"

Twenty-six minutes later, Naomi was standing next to Gordon under the awning outside the restaurant.

Gordon had made the decision to talk with her for one reason. He felt like he was running out of time and wanted to tell her how he felt.

"Is this about Dean?" asked Naomi.

"No."

"Did you see him?"

He wasn't about to answer *that*. "No… it's… I want to tell you some things."

"So you haven't seen him?"

"No."

She nodded in a way that could have indicated relief or disappointment. He couldn't tell which.

"I wanted to tell you how I see you," said Gordon.

"How you see me?"

"How I think about you."

"I don't have time for a lecture," said Naomi with a sweetness that felt condescending.

"It's not a lecture. This has nothing to do with Dean. Fuck Dean."

"What then?"

"Naomi... when I first saw you... the world stopped. I don't know if you know that."

She shrugged slightly, shook her head no.

"Well, it did," said Gordon. There was no turning back now. "I know you got your future pretty well planned, and I'm... that's good. That's a good thing."

"Why're you telling me this?" asked Naomi, not exactly comfortable with the topic.

Give in to what it is, but desire to make it better.

"'Cause some things need to be said," said Gordon. "And now I'm running out of time. You're moving soon, and I'm gonna move too."

"You're leaving?"

"In a way, yeah."

"To where?"

"Haven't decided yet."

She reacted to his answer, wondering if he was joking.

"Naomi, I've never met anyone like you," said Gordon, grasping for the right phrases like a first-time ice skater struggling to maintain balance. "You're amazing and you deserve the best."

"Gordon," said Naomi. It already sounded like she wanted to stop him before he truly got going. "You know how much I appreciate your friendship."

Here it comes. Naomi was wrapping her fingers around the handle of the dagger...

"And I know you care about me."

... raising the weapon high into the air...

"But I don't feel the same."

... and plunging the blade straight through his heart.

"I'm sorry."

It's funny, but even though Gordon knew a dagger in his heart was an inevitability, like a convict on death row knows his days on Earth will end in the electric chair, the actual moment of the piercing was far more painful than he could have anticipated.

"I gotta get back inside," said Naomi.

"Thanks for letting me say what I had to say."

"Sure."

"I hope you find all the happiness in the world."

"I wish you the same."

It was the exchange of two people who weren't going to see each other again. Naomi grinned with half her mouth, then headed inside. Gordon stood in the same spot for a few minutes, digesting what had just transpired.

Why'd he say those things?

To make things better.

Pfft. Right. If this was making things better, why'd he feel so much worse?

Chapter 61

ASH WASN'T AT THE LOFT. Again.

And the place was a fucking mess. Art supplies were strewn about, ashtrays needed dumping, trashcans needed emptying, floors needed sweeping.

She'd been avoiding Gordon because of the journal, he thought, although he still wasn't one-hundred percent positive it was in her possession. But it would explain her behavior. She had also witnessed him attack Dean, a person she took to be a stranger, and that could also be the cause for her absence. No one wants to be around a raving lunatic. But he blamed it on the journal.

Sunlight leaked through the window. Gordon hated the loft in the daytime. It was a space meant for the night, a location meant to be wrapped in darkness. The sun felt intrusive. He and Ash enjoyed Venice Beach and its assorted daytime freaks, performers, and vendors, but here in the loft, the night was a blanket welcomed for its ability to conceal. The sun was a suspicious parent peeking in a teenage bedroom.

Gordon craved darkness. He wanted to hide in it, get lost in it.

He sat on Ash's mattress and thought about Dean. He leaned against its stained sheets and thought about Shawn. About Cedric. He turned on his side and thought about Naomi. About Ash. About his father.

Gordon sat up.

The memory of his father was something he didn't want to dwell on, not for a minute, not for a second. He had developed a method of getting rid of the thought which had a tendency of popping into his head at odd moments. Gordon put his hands over his ears and hummed. If he did it quick enough and forcefully enough, the thought of his father would shoot from his brain like a fly being swept by the wind out a window.

So he clasped his hands around his ears and hummed. So the thought went.

Strange, but it worked.

Gordon stood and headed for the door. Sooner or later, he'd see Ash again, and when he did, he planned to—

His hand was reaching for the doorknob when he saw it.

It was sitting in a salad bowl in the center of the kitchen table.

His journal.

Gordon stepped closer, noticing that the table was elegantly set for a single person to dine: table cloth, placemat, dish, spoon, fork, knife, folded napkin, glass, candlesticks with new candles.

And the journal. Sitting in the salad bowl.

Gordon pulled out the chair in front of the neatly arranged setting and sat. He picked up the journal, looking at its front and back cover, both unaltered. He opened it, glancing at one of the first entries he made three months prior, the *91* written on top, and its first words:

I thought about calling home to Chicago, but didn't.

He flipped ahead, wondering how much of the journal Ash had read. Probably the whole thing. He had to assume the whole thing. He glanced at entries here and there, not wanting to reread them himself (not yet anyway), but wanting to see if any of the pages had been ripped out. He could imagine Ash getting furious while reading an entry detailing her moods or her participation in the Myron stunts or her voracious sexuality, then tearing the pages out.

But everything seemed intact.

He glanced at another page with *23* scrawled on top and its first sentence:

The days are going by fast.

No pages missing.

He reached his most recent entry, marked with the heading *13* and its initial proclamation:

There are no walls anymore.

Ash must know everything. She'd left the journal out in the open to tell him that. Whatever reality Gordon had established with her had been obliterated. He had embraced this bohemian notion of not denying urges, feelings, or thoughts, yet he had lied to her from the beginning.

His days of freewheeling at the loft were over.

He leaned back, awestruck at his ability to fuck things up. It was a born talent. Some people came into this world with an aptitude to play the piano, to sing, to draw. His inherent ability was to royally fuck things up.

His relationship with Ash may have been far from perfect, but it was good. It was probably the best thing to emerge out of this deranged, multi-life idea, and she deserved better. With all she was going through, she certainly deserved the truth.

Isn't the truth the least a person deserves? Any person? Well, she got it.

As he pondered the shit storm he'd conjured, Gordon's fingers ran along the edge of the journal, along the page of the last entry.

Then, almost subconsciously, as if the paper's subtle crinkles were whispering something they felt he should know…

Gordon turned the page.

And there it was.

Spread over an area that should've been blank, that should've been empty, was the blue ink of a new entry.

An entry Gordon didn't write.

The words were in Ash's handwriting.

Gordon leaned forward in the kitchen chair and read:

Your Number's Up

I didn't need this diary to know you weren't the person I thought you were, I knew the second you jumped out of the car and beat the shit out of that guy, that's when I knew, this book just filled in the gaps, of course I read it, so I know your dad died, I know that's why you came out to LA, to find out who you are, I know about the others, Naomi and Shawn and Dean and Cedric, makes sense now that I think about it, you were always gone at weird times, I knew your job was bullshit, it sounded like bullshit all along, so here we are, Gordon Lake of the Chicago Lakes, here we are, at first I was going to shred this thing, then I was going to burn it and leave you the ashes, but that's not what we've been doing lately is it, I'm not about destroying, what we've, I've, whoever, whatever, what I've been doing is expanding preexisting things, preexisting ideas, and whether you realize it or not, like it or not, this little revealing book of yours is art, my sneaky friend, it's something you're building, so instead of ripping it to pieces, I decided to add to it, to expand it, I'm going to pick up my own bricks and clay and I'm going to build onto what you already created, I was looking for my next target, now I found it.

Seems you love this Naomi, did you ever think about her when we were fucking, did you ever pretend that my pussy was her pussy, did you ever taste my skin and wish it was hers, did you ever cum inside my mouth with your thoughts overflowing with her face, I suspect you did, Mr. Lake, I'm guessing her boyfriend Dean is the same guy you beat the snot out of, that seems to be what you two were yelling about between punches if I recall, does love always push you to violence, Mr. Lake, feel free to think about these questions one at a time, I don't want to overload your head, god knows you're already overcome with shit to remember with all these lives, I wonder what you were going to tell me when the numbers of this diary reached 1, what were you going to tell me when you packed up your shit and moved out, more lies, more bullshit, ah well I let myself be taken in, you seemed so eager to just be in this fucked up world, and I believed you because that's all I wanted to do—just be—but I guess that's a tall order when the shit you think is real isn't, I guess nothing is real, it's something I knew, but ignored I guess.

Here we are then, Mr. Lake, what the fuck am I supposed to do with your lying, deceptive, manipulative, creepy, fucked up, psychologically twisted, confused ass? Tell me, what? I don't know if I even give a shit, if there's no reality, then why would I care if you're a ghost in my world? Why would I care if you're a figment of my imagination? Can't I wipe that clean?

I can and I will, my mind is getting churned like soup, seems appropriate, my guts may spill out my mouth too, feels like I was built with pieces that don't fit, like someone fucked up the instructions when they put me together, nothing about me works as a whole, I'm a puzzle with the wrong pieces, something that's never going to get solved, when things don't match and don't fit, eventually everything breaks down, that's what's happening to me in every little corner and crevice and joint of my life, I'm breaking down, I'm a misfit toy that's better off banished than in the hands of a child, that's all I am, so if you're worried about me, about my reaction to this bullshit, your bullshit, your book of revelations, your answers to questions I didn't know existed, then don't fret, Mr. Lake, I'm already down the path without your help, you just cranked up the speed at which I travel, my parts are failing me, they don't know which, if something doesn't work, it doesn't work, reasons are meaningless once the thing stops once and for all.

So I hope you helped Shawn and Cedric, they sound like they needed it, and I hope the beating you gave Dean keeps him clear of you and Naomi, and I hope Naomi falls madly in love with you and you two marry and have kids and go on vacations in Orlando.

Me, I'm broken and I'm fine with that, falling apart isn't so bad if you accept it, hope I didn't take up too much space in your book of lives, but you only had a few days left anyway, right?

Chapter 62

THE REST OF THE PAGES were blank.

Gordon closed the book and held it to his chest under folded arms, feeling like everybody and nobody at the same time.

In that moment of quiet reflection, he wanted to run away. Just pick up and go. Anywhere. But wasn't it the same urge that led him to LA? A personal crisis had swatted him to the icy ground in Chicago, making him fly west in an effort to start fresh. Now the same feeling was back.

Run away.

But where would he go this time? New York? Kentucky? Florida? Out of the country? To the darkest corner of China? To the most barren stretch of the Antarctic? If he wasn't careful, his life could end up being a series of escapes.

All temporary. All leading to more problems. All leading to more escapes.

So running away wasn't the answer. A novice therapist could tell you that, but that little seed of wisdom didn't make the urge disappear. Of course, there was always the *ultimate* method of running away—suicide. The final, grand escape. But Gordon didn't want to die. Suicide was a solution that solved your problems, sure, but it took everything else with it. Sort of like nuking a city to get rid of the mosquitoes.

He had to forget about leaving LA. Running away was not an option. Not this time.

And why should he flee? Hadn't he found the key to this world of bullshit? What was it again?

Give in to what it is, but desire to make it better.

Wasn't that the answer? Sure as fuck didn't feel like the answer, because everything was turning to shit. And because of that, even though there were three days left to this experiment, it was time to pull the plug.

It was time to leave the lives for good.

He'd pack up his belongings at each locale and spend the remaining days holed up in his room at the Starlight Inn. Not the worst plan, Gordon thought. Returning to the Starlight for the end stretch kind of added a sense of symmetry to the whole thing since his first days were also spent there. He'd just be returning sooner than he thought.

He'd lock himself in, order in food, and incubate. Take in the collages one last time and when the days were up, he'd strip the walls clean, stroll into the sunlight, and check out.

After that... well, he'd probably check into another hotel. It sounded odd to leap from one hotel to another, but he should probably leave the Starlight Inn behind, and he needed a buffer week to find another place to live (properly this time, without roommates, and as a whole person) and begin his life anew.

That's what he would do.

Gordon stood from the kitchen table, tucked the journal under his arm, and reached in the cupboard under the sink. He pulled out two black, double-ply, Hefty trash bags and began loading in everything that belonged to him within the confines of the loft.

Ash deserved the truth, he thought, but not like this. What a shitty way to find out. That barren stretch in the Antarctic was sounding better already. The self-inflicted misery that would be caused by relocating to a frozen wasteland would be his atonement.

But why leave town for *that*, some might argue. LA is the perfect place for self-inflicted misery.

Chapter 63

TWO TRASH BAGS in hand, Gordon crossed the lawn to gather his stuff from Cedric and Shawn's.

The question of whether Shawn had found out that Cedric had moved him out without his knowledge was answered seconds after he stepped in the house.

Shawn's lover, the man Gordon had last seen walking nude, peered around the hall to see who had come in. When he saw it was Gordon (and not Cedric which was probably the fear), he disappeared from sight, returning in the direction of Shawn's room.

Gordon followed.

The door was open, and there was Shawn and the man, sitting on the floor against the wall of the empty bedroom. It was dark, save for the fading sunlight. They were holding hands with the man's head resting on Shawn's shoulder. Gordon immediately picked up on the somber mood, and only an idiot would have to ask what brought it on.

"Came to finish the job?" asked Shawn.

"Hhmm?" said Gordon.

"You're holding two plastic bags, and there are two of us. I can only surmise you plan on chopping us up, sweeping us into separate bags, then burying us somewhere between here and Palmdale. You don't need two bags though. We wouldn't mind being in the same one, would we, Alan? Unless the quantity of bags is due to the volume of expected carnage and not the separation of parts."

"It's for my stuff," said Gordon. "I'm moving out."

"Oooohh," said Shawn. "You're going to move your possessions *yourself*. How yesterday of you. Don't you know personal items in this household vanish for you if you give it enough time? No need for backbreaking labor."

"What he did was really fucked up," said Gordon.

"Looks like we both underestimated our little record spinner, didn't we?" said Shawn. "I expected him to be furious with my letter. I was even bracing myself for a physical assault, and not the kind that I prefer. But this," Shawn nodded to the empty room, "this was creative. I have to give him that."

"He tell you where he put your stuff?" asked Gordon.

"Was he supposed to?" said Shawn.

"I figured—"

"I think that may be the punch line. I have no idea where my stuff is."

"Gonna call the police?"

"Think I should?"

"What other choice do you have?"

Alan lifted his head at this question and looked at Gordon, almost as if he was expecting Gordon to offer alternative choices. When he didn't, Alan rested his head back on Shawn's shoulder.

"Choices aren't really my thing," said Shawn. "I like to toss fate to the wind."

"Aren't you upset?" asked Gordon.

"At losing everything? At coming home to find everything I own gone? Why would that possibly upset me?"

Stupid question.

"Where are you moving to?" asked Shawn.

"I don't know," said Gordon.

"Just want outta the war zone?"

"You could say that."

"Don't blame you. I apologize for bringing you in to begin with, but I never thought things would get... well... I never thought." Shawn spent a few moments taking in Gordon's haggard appearance. "You know, I'm worried about you, Gordon Lake."

"Why's that?"

"You're a chronically distracted person. Your head's always in another region somewhere, thinking about who knows what."

"I've been busy."

"Doing?"

"Things."

"Which brings me to concern number two: your ambiguity. I

appreciate the helping hand you've offered to Cedric and me, but you... I really know nothing about you."

"There's not much to know," said Gordon.

"Something tells me there's *a lot* to know," said Shawn. "Let me review the scant details I've gathered during your brief stay in Intolerance Manor." He ticked off the facts using his fingers. "You're from Chicago. Mid-twenties. You're a freelance editor, though your bedroom contains absolutely *nothing* related to the field of editing. No computers, no books, no paycheck stubs, nothing. You've hinted at a female presence in your life, but without giving a name. Is she your girlfriend? Business partner? Dominatrix? I simply don't know. You drive a rented car with no sign that you ever intend to actually get a car of your own. You used to dress nice when you first moved in. Now you show up looking like you slept on the sidewalk. And that's about it." He held up his hands. "Six fingers worth of knowledge."

"You can't expect to really know a person after a few months," said Gordon.

"True," said Shawn. "I suppose you'll remain a mystery to me."

"We'll keep in touch."

"I doubt it. Calls are always a pain in the ass, and you don't seem like the social networking type, seeing as you don't own a computer."

"Been looking in my room?"

"I was born a Lookie-Loo. Can't help it."

Gordon smiled and ran his hand through his hair. "I better get—"

"Going, yes," said Shawn. "Plenty of things to hide away in those bags. Least it's not Alan and me. That's a relief."

Head on Shawn's shoulder, Alan waved goodbye to Gordon.

Chapter 64

ANOTHER RESIDENCE. Another pair of trash bags.

Gordon walked into Dean's apartment to gather his stuff and found Naomi in the living room, organizing books on a shelf. She stepped back when she saw him, frightened. Gordon had hoped to pack his things without running into anyone at any of the locations, but that was turning out to be a pipe dream.

"Why didn't you tell me?" asked Naomi.

"Tell you what?"

"Fuck you."

"Naomi… tell you what?"

"That you attacked Dean."

Gordon looked to the floor.

"He said you leapt out of some girl's car and started a fight. Is that true?"

"It was a skirmish."

"I saw the marks on his face."

Gordon shut up, having no defense.

"After what you did, how could you then come to my work, knowing what you did, and feed me all this, this…" Naomi gestured, her hands grasping the air as if the right word hung before her, "… *shit* about the flowery feelings you have for me, about caring about me, about wanting the best for me?"

"Because I do," said Gordon.

"You made me stand there and listen to all your heartfelt emotions like I was supposed to be overcome with the power of the moment and give myself to you…"

"I didn't expect that."

"… and you conveniently fail to mention that you *attacked Dean.*"

"I don't—why're you here anyway?"

"Where?"

"In his apartment," said Gordon.

"I'm getting some stuff for him," said Naomi. "He didn't want to see you."

"Why?"

"His lawyer told him to avoid you."

"Lawyer?"

"You can't go around pummeling people," said Naomi.

"Great," said Gordon. "He got a lawyer. Is he suing me?"

"He's weighing his options," said Naomi, unsure of how much to reveal. "He doesn't want me talking to you."

"You two back together?"

Not at all defensive, Naomi spoke with a touch of pride. "We're working things out."

"After what he did?" Gordon touched his face at the same spot Naomi had her stitches.

"Glass did that. It was an accident," said Naomi. "Accidents happen. He's apologized for it."

They stood there in silence like two strangers stuck in an elevator.

"What about school?" asked Gordon.

"Dean and I are no longer your business."

"Some people learn the hard way I guess."

"But not you, right?"

"No. *Especially* me."

"Yeah," she said, "learning is hard sometimes. Like who to trust and who to stay away from."

"You soulmates don't gotta worry about me anymore. I'm clearing out for good."

"Please don't come near us anymore, and please don't come to the restaurant. If you sit in my section, I'll have the manager move you."

"To a section with good service?"

"I mean it."

At that moment, Gordon realized he didn't know Naomi. He never did.

From the second he first saw her, he'd taken her pretty face and plastered it onto a fantasy personality, rubbing out the air bubbles to make it smooth, to make it fit. She was never that person, though. It had taken months for the face to peel off, to curl at the edges, to crack with the dryness of a cheap sticker left to bake in the sun. Now it had finally broken free and drifted to the ground as Naomi told Gordon to leave her and Dean alone.

Gordon's perfectly compatible, female counterpart had no identity again. No features. No name.

He wondered if she ever would.

Chapter 65

WHERE THE FUCK was Ash?

All Gordon wanted was to crawl inside the carpeted, air-conditioned incubator that was room 116. He wanted to sleep for the next three days. He wanted to surf through bad TV. He wanted to order in food. He wanted to get lost in his thoughts.

But before all that, he wanted to find out where the fuck Ash was. He didn't want the distraction lingering in his head.

He went by the loft, but she wasn't there. He went by every little spot he'd been to with her. He even stopped at Serrick's apartment to make sure he wasn't offering her sanctuary. Serrick insisted he wasn't (and with the stuffy, moldy smell emanating from inside his place, Gordon wasn't about to stand there and argue).

Then the answer hit him.

He wondered why he didn't think of it sooner.

***

Gordon banged on Myron's front door. Nobody answered.

He wasn't going to stop there. He hopped the fence, landing squarely on top of a patch of half-dead daffodils. The hose was rolled up around the arm of a lawn chair, dripping. No one was around.

Gordon looked through the glass door, cupping his hands to his face.

And there was Ash. Lying on the couch, wearing Myron's old, tattered robe.

Gordon tapped on the glass. She glanced his way. He was about to start screaming for her to let him in when the door suddenly slid open.

"Thought you'd call first," said Myron, dressed in a black suit and tie, his shoulder-length hair combed back with a rigid styling lotion.

"I didn't have your number," said Gordon.

"She's resting, to answer your next question."

Gordon pushed by Myron and walked to Ash, who wasn't wearing anything under the robe. He caught a glimpse of a breast as she sat up.

"I've been looking everywhere for you," said Gordon.

"I wasn't hiding," said Ash.

"What're you doing here?"

"Resting," said Myron.

"I didn't ask you," said Gordon.

"I reserve the right to offer answers in my own home, son."

"Ash…" said Gordon, trying his best to ignore Myron.

Ash looked at him like he was a stranger. "Is your name really Gordon Lake?"

"Of course it is."

"Don't say *of course*. You could've easily created three different names."

"Well I didn't."

It dawned on Gordon that Myron probably knew everything too. Ash must have regaled him with the nasty details.

"Nice diary, by the way," said Ash. "You got a talent for writing. Doesn't match your aptitude for outright lying, though."

"You weren't supposed to see it," said Gordon.

"No shit."

"I'm trying to figure things out. Surely you can appreciate that."

"I can't appreciate someone shitting on my trust."

Myron checked his watch. He wasn't going to let this go on forever.

Gordon said, "I had other parts of my life you didn't know about, but that didn't mean I didn't believe what we were about."

"And what were we about?" asked Ash.

"Lots of things."

"Rough sex and fast food?"

"More than that."

"Why'd you come here?"

"I was worried about you."

Gordon expected a trademark Ash-laugh when he muttered the word worried, but she just looked away.

"I don't feel guilty being here," said Ash.

"I'm not trying to make you feel guilty," said Gordon. "I wanted to know you're all right."

"Since when have I ever been all right?"

"What you wrote… the things you said…"

"Set off alarm bells, did it?"

"You didn't sound like yourself."

"See earlier statement. When have I *ever*?"

She lit a cigarette and leaned back against the giant cushions. The robe was too big for her. It resembled a burgundy shroud that someone had draped over her corpse. Only she was still breathing, still blowing out light streams of smoke. She'd always been fucked up in her own disconnected way, but this was a different Ash. A weaker Ash. The fight had been taken out of her.

"I don't mean to interrupt," said Myron. "But I need to be rolling along, son. I'd appreciate it if you let her relax by herself."

"You wanna be by yourself?" said Gordon to Ash.

"Yeah," said Ash, snuffing out the half-smoked cigarette. "I mean… I'm gonna nap. If you wanna talk to me while I sleep, that's up to you. Maybe you believe in the theories that say my brain will still be able to hear you." She stretched out, adjusting the robe.

"Son?" said Myron.

Ash turned on her side, away from Gordon.

***

Myron walked Gordon down the steep driveway. Myron's car was parked at the top, but he wanted to escort Gordon down, an effort to show he was serious about letting Ash be alone.

"I don't owe you this, but," said Myron, "I didn't sleep with her."

"Hey, whatever you two—"

"Like I said, I don't owe you that nugget of information. But circumstances are screwy, and the way she looked in there, I can tell you suspect we were intimate. We weren't. Thought you should know as much." Myron looked at his watch as they trudged down the driveway. "Beautiful day."

Gordon hadn't noticed.

"I got a service to attend," said Myron. "Friend passed away."

"Sorry."

"When you get to my age, you tend to have one of these a year. Still, Jack was one of those fellas who thought he'd live forever." He sighed, part mournfully, part frustrated at the inconvenience. "His wife wanted me to say a few words, but I declined. All I ever did was talk to this guy about everything from Egypt and back, but now that he's dead, I don't feel inclined to say anything."

They reached Gordon's car.

"Look," said Myron. "Ash up there, she's in a new place. She'd bludgeon me for telling you this, but tomorrow she's being admitted to Cedars."

It was a complete surprise and not a surprise at all.

"Why?" asked Gordon.

"Exploratory surgery," said Myron. "Something's afoul in her abdomen, but they can't tell what from the tests."

"They don't have any idea?"

"They got plenty. Just don't know which is right."

"How long she gonna be in?"

"Depends on what they find. They got ways of going under the skin that they never did before. Those tube-cameras, whatever the hell they're called." Myron scratched his beard. "I hate suits." He turned and started the long haul back up the driveway. "Gonna leave instructions in my will to make the dress code for my funeral casual. Beach attire. Shirt optional. Why should others suffer 'cause I'm gone? Margaritas for all."

Chapter 66

THE NEXT DAY, after spending the night in the loft (which now felt disturbingly hollow and foreign without Ash, leading to a night of fitful sleep), Gordon drove to Cedric and Shawn's.

He counted out the remaining rent in cash at the small table in the kitchen. Once he made the final payment, he'd officially be done dealing with their world. In the same way he handled it with Dean and Ash, he was paying for the time he wouldn't be around, since he neglected to give thirty days notice, but he didn't care. As long as he was out.

It's funny how one day you can be so excited about arriving somewhere, and the next, you just want to leave.

He left the rent money in envelopes for Dean and Ash and thought about doing the same for Cedric, but knowing his luck, one of Cedric's illiterate cohorts would swipe it. So he'd agreed to meet with Cedric one last time to handle the transaction. Gordon was early, so he paced a bit, looked in the fridge, looked through the mail. And lo and behold, there was something in the mail for him.

A red envelope with no return address.

His name was written on the front, and he recognized Shawn's handwriting immediately. Gordon tore open the envelope and pulled out a greeting card. He lifted it into the sunlight. On the cover was a little boy in a straw hat enthusiastically licking a round lollipop that appeared bigger than his head. Under the picture were the words: *Lick Up the Good Times!*

He opened the card and read the message scrawled in red ink:

To the Mystery Man,

I hope this card reaches you well and before you've completely moved out of the House of Expressed Resentment. Otherwise, I'm wasting ink.

Ah well, the chances we take. May you find a home that shelters you and welcomes you. I wish the same for my belongings, since they seem to have made a life without me.

I didn't get a chance to say this when we said goodbye in the shell that used to be my bedroom, but for what it's worth, you were there for me.

You listened, you shared, you cared. What goes around, comes around, Mystery Man, and you got a lot coming to you.

Lick it up!

XOXOXO,

Shawn

Gordon pocketed the card when he heard Cedric enter the house. Right on schedule. Cedric was always punctual when he knew money was coming to him. He strolled in, still basking in the fact that Shawn was gone for good.

"Peace and quiet, peace and quiet. Should've done this months ago," said Cedric.

"Ever tell him where you put his stuff?" asked Gordon.

"Don't know why I waited so long."

"That a no?"

"His stuff is his stuff. Ain't my problem."

Cedric opened the cabinet and removed the container of protein powder.

"Wanna pay rent, right?" said Cedric.

"My last." Gordon handed the money to Cedric who immediately flipped through the bills.

"It's always cash with you," said Cedric. "You runnin' from something?"

"Nah."

"Don't like checks?"

"You complaining? Cash cuts out the middle man, right?"

"Amen to that," said Cedric, cracking open the lid to the protein powder. He reached in for the plastic scoop. He always reached in, digging his unwashed fingers directly into the powder. How many shakes had Cedric drank that contained toilet handle bacteria?

Cedric dumped two heaping scoops of protein into a Lakers mug, then poured in milk, mixing it with an unwashed spoon from the sink.

"That stuff taste good?" asked Gordon.

"Not McDonald's good, but it's all right. You should drink some yourself." Cedric looked him over. "Want some?"

"No thanks."

Cedric put the mug to his lips and tilted his head back—drinking,

drinking, drinking every last drop. He slammed the mug down on the counter, let out a breath of satisfaction, then belched.

"Lost two roommates in one week," said Cedric, wiping his mouth.

"What're you gonna do?"

"Find more, I guess. Bitches this time. House bitches. Or move out. Go closer to the beach. I dunno. I should. People on this block suck."

It figures Cedric would consider moving out now that Shawn was gone. Before, the very notion was an impossibility. Gordon had floated the idea of Cedric leaving more than once, and Cedric had reacted each time with a fierce resistance, as if this was the house his grandfather built by hand. But now that he'd essentially thrown Shawn out, he was thinking of moving. Fucking figures.

Cedric reached for the roll of paper towels, but as his fingers touched the paper, they withdrew and clutched the kitchen counter for support.

Cedric coughed, bits of spit hitting his fist as he raised it to his mouth. He calmed, exhaled.

"You all right?" asked Gordon.

Cedric looked to him as if he wanted to answer, but began coughing again. He stopped for a moment and spit in the sink, a look of distaste playing across his face as the coughing resumed, becoming more strained. It was unlike anything Gordon had ever seen. The color left Cedric's face within seconds.

He dropped to one knee, his jaw locking open in a series of spastic coughs. From his mouth came a weak, wheezy sound.

Gordon made a move toward him as Cedric collapsed on his back, both hands around his neck. His legs flailed, then locked at the knees.

Gordon dialed 911, rushed the information to the operator, then crouched to Cedric's side, dropping the phone on the tile. He tried to wedge his arms under Cedric to lift him.

Eyes bulging, Cedric arched back and looked at Gordon.

Fucking do something, his eyes were saying. Help me.

"I'm trying to," said Gordon.

Gordon managed to sit up Cedric and scoot behind him, stomach to back, like two Olympic racers in a luge. In an effort to perform the Heimlich Maneuver, which he'd only seen in movies, Gordon clasped his hands in front of Cedric's belly and pulled in with a strong jerking motion. Cedric's muscles were rigid, making it difficult.

Cedric again looked back.

Fucking help me.

Gordon pulled in again in an effort to dislodge the chunk of food he didn't think even existed. Cedric didn't eat any solid food, only six gulps worth of shake.

Saliva ran down the corners of Cedric's mouth, drawing a sloppy grin on his face.

***

The assessment that Cedric needed to be rushed to the ER didn't take long for the paramedics to make, and soon after, Gordon was standing with a pack of curious neighbors on the edge of the driveway, watching Cedric get loaded into an ambulance.

Stabilized, but in bad shape. Stabilized from *what*, Gordon didn't know.

Already, rumors were swirling amongst the neighbors.

"Gang shooting," said one. "Ever notice the types that pull in and outta here? It was a gang hit. Someone snuck in and shot him."

"Heroin overdose," said another. "Fella's in the record business. One outta three people in the record business has a serious dope addiction. Heard it on the radio."

"My money's on a heart attack. Heart attack from cocaine," said another. "People these days snort that stuff more than ever. Can't understand it. Kids of my generation used to smoke weed. Now it's coke. Sends 'em into cardiac arrest. Happened to that basketball player, what's-his-name."

Gordon nodded with each theory.

It wasn't a shooting, of course. There were no bullets whizzing through the air before Cedric hit the deck. As for drugs, well, Gordon couldn't rule them out, but Cedric didn't have any addictions as far as he could tell, discounting the occasional bong hit.

The ambulance pulled away, wafting a puff of exhaust toward the neighbors.

"Carbon monoxide poisoning," said a neighbor.

"For him or us?" said another, waving away the smoke.

Maybe it *was* poison. Not carbon monoxide. Something in the powder. Put there on purpose. Put there to kill. Put there... by Shawn?

Gordon didn't know what to think. Anything was possible at this point. What's a war without an assassination attempt?

"Faulty pipe," said a neighbor. "These houses are old. Things crack. Things leak."

"Who called the ambulance?" asked a woman with a suspicious whine. "They might know a thing or two about a thing or two."

Gordon didn't take responsibility for the call in front of the neighbors. Doing so would turn the focus on him, and that's the last place he wanted it.

Everyone else in the pack of would-be sleuths shrugged, equally ignorant, and the crowd soon lost interest and dispersed, returning to whatever was consuming them before this little drama interrupted their day.

Gordon wasn't so lucky. There was no idle hobby to return to. No brainless chore. He went from one drama to the next.

But he was close to a new life. So close. He just had to tie up a few loose ends.

Room 116 was calling him. Begging him to crawl back in its belly. There was only one stop he had to make before it got its wish.

Chapter 67

THE SMELL OF FOOD combined with the scent of clean linen made Gordon want to gag. An odd reaction, but he was in a hospital where smells were always a little off, where a unique mixture of odors added to a visitor's sense of displacement.

When Gordon located Ash's room on the eighth floor, she was in bed, dressed in a cotton gown identical to the one she refused to take off a few weeks prior. The covers were drawn to her waist, her sock-covered feet poking out. An IV ran into her hand, its needle taped down.

"Private room," said Gordon as he strolled in. "Nice."

"Rather it wasn't," said Ash.

He dragged a chair next to the mattress and sat.

"I get my own room because of the fluids," she said.

"Fluids?"

"From my stomach. They're going to put a tube down my nose. Prevents vomiting." Ash nodded to a transparent container on the wall. "Tube empties into there."

"That's pleasant," said Gordon.

"I'll see if they can save some stomach bile for you."

"Will you?"

"I'll see what I can do."

"Even if it's just a little, that'd be cool."

"You're a sick man."

"Aren't you proud? I'm not denying my urge to use morbid humor."

"That's my boy." She rested her head against the pillow.

They sat in silence. A cart was wheeled by the door.

"Myron told you where I'd be?" said Ash.

"Yep."

"Knew he would."

"That piss you off?"

She shrugged. "He's got a good heart."

Gordon nodded.

"I didn't sleep with him, y'know," said Ash.

"He told me."

"Really?"

"Yeah."

"He tell you I gave him the most intense head of his life?"

"I'm gonna assume you're joking and leave it at that."

"Best you do."

More silence. Another cart was wheeled by in the opposite direction.

"When do they take you in?" asked Gordon.

"This afternoon."

"Scared?"

"No."

"Not at all?"

"I'd rather know what was wrong, than not know."

"What if it's something bad?"

She let out a long sigh. "I need a cigarette."

Ash glanced at the button attached to a cord near the bed, "They make you feel like the hospital's safe, but it's not. They had me sign a consent form before giving me a CAT scan."

"They made you sign a waiver?"

"A consent form. Sounds less dangerous. Much to the nurse's annoyance, I read it. It said a contrast agent was going to be injected into my blood to enhance the quality of my exam. Said most patients experience a sensation of warmth after the injection. Not too bad, right? Even welcomed. Then it said nausea may occur. No biggie. Nausea occurs for me most of the time anyway. Then it listed difficulty breathing as a possible side effect. Then it casually dropped in the fact that the contrast agent had a one in forty thousand chance of *killing me*."

"It gave the odds?"

"One in forty thousand. And that has nothing to do with the massive dose of radiation I'd be subjected to *after* surviving the contrast agent. I don't remember that being discussed. And this was all for a test to help see what's *really* wrong."

"You survived it."

She reflected on the dubious accomplishment. "The warm sensation was kinda nice. Would've been a lot nicer if I wasn't half expecting death."

Silence. Another cart.

"Gordon."

"Yeah?"

"Is there anything else I don't know?" asked Ash. "Anything that *wasn't* in your diary?"

"Like what?" asked Gordon.

"You tell me."

"Does it matter?"

"You mean, like... have you reached your lie maximum?"

"Something like that."

"You could always be a serial killer."

"Would you hold it against me?"

"I'm serious," said Ash. "Is there anything? Anything I should know?"

"I think you got the whole picture," said Gordon.

"I don't think so." She looked up at the ceiling. "This is my life. In a hospital with a stranger."

"You know me."

"I don't even know myself."

"I'm glad you read it in a way."

"Makes you think," said Ash. "How many other diaries are out there? Filled with secrets never meant to be read. You wonder why they're written down to begin with."

"Can I tell you something?" asked Gordon.

"What?"

"It's a *journal*. Stop calling it a diary. You make it sound girlie."

"'Cause it is. *Girlie* -man."

A nurse came in to take Ash's temperature and blood pressure. Her vitals, as the nurse called them. They were normal. The nurse smiled and walked out.

Gordon wished there was another bed. He wanted to sleep, but he wanted to stay with Ash. He was sure she wouldn't mind if he grabbed a little shut-eye.

"You don't gotta stay," said Ash, as if reading his mind. "It's only a few hours before they slice me open."

"That's what I'm here for," said Gordon.

"The slicing?"

"Your body is my next target. My next expansion. I'll let the doc cut the incision and whatnot, then I'll complete it. I'll poke around, rearrange some things. Remove some things. Sign the E on your belly. Myron's gonna love it."

"Knock yourself out," said Ash. "If I could trade in my body, I would."

Ash tossed aside the bed sheet, swinging her sock-covered feet onto the tile. She locked her hand around the IV pole and pushed it forward on its squeaky wheels, walking to the bathroom.

Gordon stood up. "I'll come by... after..."

Ash wheeled the IV into the bathroom, turned back, and said, "See ya, girlie-man."

The door closed.

Gordon took in the room for a moment, thinking about how unnatural it felt. He wondered if he'd die in a room this sanitized. This boring.

All the fuss and fury of everyday existence only to end up in a place like this. He didn't want to be hooked up to machines for weeks on end, waiting to die. He wanted his exit to be sudden, unexpected. That was the way to go. Not wasting away in a bleached room with a container on the wall collecting your stomach fluids. With a nurse peeking in every few hours to see if you're still breathing. With a trained staff ready to transfer your corpse to the morgue.

What's the name of this one? Gordon Lake? Oh yeah, he's been rotting away for months, screaming at all hours, begging for relief. Barely conscious toward the end. Body was a mess. Stunk like hell. Nurses picked straws to see who'd change his sheets. 'Bout time he went.

Fuck that.

Gordon made his way to the elevator, allowing himself to glance into rooms along the way, taking in split-second images.

An old woman sleeping.

A doctor speaking to a family.

A nurse taking the pressure of a teenage girl.

An empty room, waiting for its next occupant.

Staying in a hospital was like moving to a new place. New neighbors to get used to, new bathroom with new faucets to figure out, new window view, new telephone number. Some might say it's more akin to an unexpected vacation. But not really. Not if it's the last residence of your life.

The worst thing had to be not knowing if your hospital stay was going to be your last stay anywhere.

Ignorance is bliss? Not in a place like this.

Chapter 68

THE STARLIGHT INN was busier than Gordon had ever seen it.

He hoped it didn't translate into increased noise drifting into his room. If it did, he'd counter-attack with white noise from the air conditioner and even a large fan if he was forced to buy one.

Parking in the hotel lot, he felt drained, as if he'd just completed a sixteen hour road trip. He killed the engine and swung his feet out the door and sat there for a few minutes. He couldn't remember the last time he had a decent night's sleep.

The room. He had to get to the room.

Gordon forced himself to get up and made his way across the lot. Strangers were coming and going, and he didn't make eye contact with any of them. His fingers found the room key as he reached his door.

Breathing a sigh of relief that he was finally at his destination, he looked up and saw a maid standing next to a cart of cleaning supplies and towels, about to open room 116.

"Hey…" said Gordon.

Her hand turned the knob. The door started to open.

"*Hey.*"

The maid turned.

"Please don't go in there."

"Excuse me?"

"I told the manager to—don't go in this room."

"I'm cleaning—"

"I know you're cleaning, but this room's off limits." Gordon looked for the Do Not Disturb sign that he hung on the doorknob, but it was missing. "There was a sign, but I shouldn't need one. I have an arrangement with the manager. I don't want my room cleaned."

"He didn't tell me, sir."

"It's been months now. This happened before, and… it's been

months. That's all."

The maid apologized again, and Gordon let it go. It was his last weekend, he didn't recognize her, and to hell with it.

He entered the dark room and locked the door.

The air was nice, the way he liked it. Not bothering to flick on a light, he stripped down to his boxers and climbed under the covers. He wanted a dreamless rest. He wanted it to be like death.

***

Gordon didn't wake for the next thirteen hours. When he eventually stirred into consciousness, he couldn't think straight. Waking up after a sleep like that felt like being resurrected.

Shrouded in blackness, he sat up in bed with a headache and a hunger.

For a moment, he didn't know where he was. Cedric's? Ash's? Dean's? He didn't know. But the chill of the air soon keyed him to the fact that he was in the cocoon of room 116. The realization was comforting and made him smile. But he had to get something to eat.

Not bothering to shower, Gordon dragged himself to the grocery store. He pushed the cart up and down aisles without any real direction. He had no shopping list. Items were tossed in the cart on impulse. Stuff that required no heating or refrigeration.

He felt drugged, like his brain had turned to mush. He'd been analyzing his life nonstop for so long. He'd been breaking down experiences, flipping them, holding them under the light, trying to be different things to different people.

Every little task. Every little cause and effect. All judged. All measured. All processed.

If a brain ever needed rebooting, it was his.

Now it was time to let instinct take over. Time to listen to intuition.

No more journal entries, no more analytical breakdowns, no more long conversations with himself. If he was going to step onto this planet as someone else other than the blank Gordon Lake that landed in LA, he had to go with his gut. He would behave as he saw fit from moment to moment, not in a prescribed manner, not in a style that had to fit into a mold.

People weren't molds. They were fluid. He had to let his true nature come to him. He had to.

A brightly colored box in the snack aisle caught his attention. Peanut Butter Cookies 'n' Cream Berry Bite Bundles with Shaved Almonds.

Shit, he had to get a box of those. Talk about a snack for the indecisive.

***

Gordon took a detour back to the hotel.

At the supermarket, he'd seen a cardboard standee of a girl on a surfboard promoting a sweepstakes for some diet drink. The image of the ocean had stuck with him. He felt the need to see it. The wide open water had a way of clearing his head, and he found himself driving west.

Trudging through the sand, he plopped down, just a few feet from where the tide reached. He ripped open the box of the multi-flavored Bite Bundles and shoved a few into his mouth and stared at the waves.

Watching. Chewing. Breathing. Being.

Already the ocean had him under its spell.

He thought about walking out into the water. Letting it rise around him, letting the tide push and pull him wherever it pleased, letting the undertow drag him under, letting the saltwater rush into his mouth and fill his lungs, letting his body be washed against the rocks.

When a person is battered against the perforated surface of a reef, the person's clothes are often shredded, ripped, then pulled clean off. When a corpse washes up on shore, it's not uncommon for it to be completely nude, as if the ocean claimed its clothes as the price for its intrusion.

If Gordon could choose how to be found, it would be like that. Naked and dead on a beach. His flesh sampled by a hundred species. His collared shirt, pleated pants, checkered boxers, crew socks, and faux leather loafers swallowed by the sea.

Clothes make a man. Fine. But what if the man has no clothes? What if he's clad in nothing but his birthday suit, shriveled genitals exposed to the wind? How is that man judged by the morning jogger who discovers his body resting against an eroded sand castle?

Such a fate would be fitting for Gordon, after switching clothes back and forth for months to reflect different personalities. Ironic? Maybe. But fitting.

***

An hour drifted by, and there sat Gordon. Cross-legged and barefoot on the beach, with an empty box of Bite Bundles in his lap. Mouth slightly open. Eyes fixed on the churning Pacific.

The foamy tide touched his legs for the first time, soaking his pants. The cutting cold of the saltwater jerked him back to reality.

He felt tranquil. Centered, even.

Gordon picked up the box and slowly made his way back to the car, the muscles in his leg feeling stiff. He was glad he delayed taking a shower. The hot water would feel good when he got back.

Chapter 69

WALKING ACROSS THE LOT of the Starlight Inn, Gordon stopped in his tracks. He could feel his pressure rise, his fists clench, a rage and frustration welling.

Son of a bitch.

He couldn't believe what he was looking at. After the talk with the maid, after he made it crystal clear he had an arrangement, after he once again hung a Do Not Disturb sign, he simply couldn't believe what he was looking at.

The door to room 116 was open.

Open.

His explicit request had been ignored. Someone was inside.

Gordon marched toward the room, ready to scream at whatever maid was unlucky enough to be changing the sheets. He kicked the door open.

But there was no maid.

There was only a man with his back to the door. A man that spun around the moment the door banged against the wall.

Gordon's anger vanished.

It was Mike.

Confusion.

Mike from Chicago.

Disbelief.

Mike from Chicago was standing in his hotel room in Los Angeles.

"Gordy?" said Mike, stepping forward.

Gordon couldn't answer. His brain was still processing who was standing before him, the same brain that had worked *so hard* at shutting out memories of Chicago. But here was one of them. In the flesh.

"The fuck is all this?" asked Mike.

"All what?" said Gordon.

Mike extended his hands toward the collages on the walls. *"This."*

"Nothing," said Gordon.

"Jesus Christ, Gordy... I..." said Mike, trying to make sense of it all. "You realize what you've been puttin' people through back at home? What you—you disappeared. One day, you don't answer your phone. You're not at home. You're not anywhere. Thought you got in an accident. We called the hospitals. The police. What the fuck's goin' on?"

Gordon shrugged. Where would he begin?

"You know what I went through to find you?" said Mike. "Do you? It was easy enough to learn you flew to LA, but fuck, it's LA. I mean, the rental car place gave me an idea you were still around... maybe."

Gordon broke Mike's stare.

"What're you runnin' from?" asked Mike.

Gordon shrugged.

"You've been livin' in a fuckin' hotel while we're all back home worried sick?"

"No one's gotta worry about me."

"The fuck they don't," said Mike. He looked Gordon over. "You fucked up or something? You on drugs?"

"No."

"You can tell me if you are."

"I'm not."

"I hear drug addicts lock themselves in hotel rooms for weeks on end."

"I don't take drugs."

"Then what is it?" Mike turned to the strange collection on the walls. The pictures, the notes, the souvenirs, the fragments of Gordon's lives. "What the fuck *is* all this?"

"Personal stuff."

Mike plucked off the piece of paper with FUCK OFF FAG scrawled on it, the one Cedric taped to Shawn's door way back when.

"Personal stuff, huh?" said Mike. He crumpled the paper into a ball and dropped it. He then tore a line of photographs from the wall. "Who're these people?"

"People I know."

"Who?"

"Does it matter?"

"The fuck's the matter with you?"

"What d'you care?"

Mike let the pictures fall from his hand. He stepped closer to Gordon. "What do I care?"

"Yeah."

"What do *I* care?"

"It's nobody's business 'cept—"

Mike grabbed him by the shirt and shoved him against the wall. Gordon clutched Mike's arms, trying to pry them off, but Mike was stronger than him, always has been.

"You know the shit we went through with your father dyin'?" said Mike. "Then you pull this shit?" He let go. "People know you're depressed."

"I'm not depressed."

"Your pop died, Gordy."

"I'm fine."

"You two were closer than any father and son I ever knew. 'Course his death's gonna fuck you up."

"I said I'm *fine.*"

Mike opened his arms to the collages on the wall. "You call this fine? 'Cause this ain't fine." Mike exhaled, wanting to stay calm. "I dunno. Maybe I could've done better as a friend. I should'a had this talk when… what I'm sayin' is—Ollie's passin' ripped our hearts out too."

"Stop talking about him." Gordon didn't want to hear another word about his father. About Chicago. About the past.

"I know what his passing did to you."

"It didn't do anything to me."

"You two were peas in a pod. I know it left a hole in your heart."

"*There's nothing.* You get it? It left nothing. I feel nothing. He's gone. Stop talking about him. He's gone, and I don't care. I'm not gonna be *him.* I'm not gonna grow old in a warehouse doing what *he* did. Being what *he* was. I'm not him. FUCK HIM!"

It came all at once.

The pressure that had been building ever since that day in the snow, the moment his father left. It had been accumulating, but Gordon never acknowledged it. He pretended he couldn't feel it. Yet it was always there, growing, and now it was finally bursting free.

Gordon tried to fight it back, tried to suppress it like he always did, but it was too much.

The tears came.

Mike watched in silence as Gordon dropped to his knees and started to cry. And cry. And cry.

Gordon crumpled to the floor, covering his face with his hands, tears wetting his palms. It was getting hard to breathe, but he couldn't stop.

Gordon kicked his leg out and knocked a chair over, as if a single, concentrated burst of anger could halt the flow of tears, as if one emotion could push another emotion aside, as if rage could dispose of grief like a bouncer throwing a drunk patron out of a bar.

But the human psyche is far too complex for that, and Gordon was learning it was more than capable of weathering two surging emotions simultaneously. He couldn't tell where the anger ended and the sadness began, and he was sure—positive, even—that the sadness wasn't there before. He'd gotten rid of it back in Chicago. Banished it.

Now it was back and stronger than ever.

Where'd it come from? Why was he feeling it now? His father died months ago. He was over it, beyond it. His father was dead. This was the new Gordon. It wasn't supposed to be like this.

Gordon wept.

Mike sat on the edge of the mattress and watched his friend. He'd come far to find Gordon. At least he was still alive. Not in good shape. But alive.

Mike turned to the collages on the walls. He'd never seen anything like it and didn't know what to think. He could discern separate sections with similar photos and names within each, but he didn't know who the hell these people were. All of Gordon's friends and family were back in Chicago, people that loved him, people that pushed Mike to go look for him, but there weren't any pictures of *them*.

When Mike first made the manager open the door earlier that day (insisting it was an emergency and lying that he was Gordon's brother and demanding action or else he was going to call the police), he thought it was a mistake. He thought the manager had opened the wrong door. Then he saw Gordon's handwriting on a pad near the phone and knew, as strange as the condition of the room was, it wasn't a mistake.

From the ground, Gordon said, "I'm not like him."

Mike looked to Gordon whose hands had dropped from his face. His eyes were red.

Gordon sniffed and said again, "I'm not like him."

"Gordy…"

"That's not who I am."

"He was a good man. You should be proud to be like a man like that. My dad was an asshole that ran out on me. Ollie was a stand-up guy. He was everything."

"If he was everything, what does that make me?"

Mike looked down, shook his head. "Everyone's worried sick about you. You gotta call 'em. Let 'em know you're okay. Then we're gettin' you back. Your vacation's over."

"This isn't a vacation," said Gordon.

"If you ain't where you live, it's a vacation."

"I live here."

"In a hotel?"

"I'm getting a place."

"Your life's in Chicago."

"No."

"We've been holdin' down the fort best we can, but we need you back at the warehouse. Busy season's gettin' close."

"I'm done with that."

"We need you back."

"I can't."

"You're just depressed. You'll feel better."

"Stop saying I'm depressed."

"Your dad built that business for you."

"I don't want it."

"Your dad—"

"I don't want it."

"Then what d'you want?" Mike stood and glared at Gordon. "What d'you fuckin' want? You disappear, you hole yourself up in a hotel, you turn your back on everything and everyone who loves you. Tell me the big plan. What d'you want?"

At that moment, as Mike spoke, the chill of the air conditioner felt like falling snow.

Chapter 70

Then

SHIELDING HIS FACE from the sleet, Oliver Lake jogged to the back of the building, deftly navigating deep puddles.

Standing under a thin strip of aluminum awning, Gordon watched his father approach, admiring the fact that he was still nimble enough at his age to be hopping puddles.

"God damn," said Ollie, joining Gordon under the awning. "God damn this weather."

"Where is he?" asked Gordon.

"Supposed to be here. Said three o'clock."

"How we gonna get in?"

"We ain't 'til he gets here."

"Should leave it outside."

"Something tells me he wouldn't appreciate seeing his two thousand dollar desk getting soaked."

"Serves him right."

"Customer gets the benefit of the doubt. Always does. Who knows why he's late? Could be anything in this weather. Let's hope it's nothing serious."

They stood side-by-side, trying to stay warm and dry, and did the only thing they could do. They waited.

"Should we sit in the truck?" asked Gordon.

"Nah," said Ollie. "Been stuck in that thing all day. This ain't too bad. You wanna?"

"I'm good if you're good."

"I'm good."

Gordon pulled up the collar of his jacket and pulled down his cap.

His breath was frosty. He tucked his gloved hands into his pockets and hopped a few times in place.

Ollie glanced to him. "I know it's miserable."

"Ain't too bad."

"It's wet, cold, and shitty. The exact words the weatherman used, I believe." They laughed. "Or somethin' like that."

"Partly shitty with a forty percent chance of freeze-your-ass-off."

Ollie smiled, looked to his son. "It ain't always gonna be like this."

"It'll clear up in a few months," said Gordon, glancing at the grey sky.

"I mean… havin' to go through this. Waiting outside for a customer in dreary weather. Lifting and hauling. Loading and unloading."

"Job's a job."

"But when it's *our* job, it should be different. We're gonna have people working under us one day. A lot of people. No more deliveries like this. Especially you."

"Especially me?"

"When you're running things. Down the road. You'll have a nice, heated office with hot coffee, a leather chair, a computer, a TV to watch the ballgame when times are slow. You won't be out in this freezin' shit. This is temporary is what I'm sayin'. We gotta do what we gotta do now. But if things grow, *when* things grow, we'll get a staff, get more orders, get another truck."

"Tell me more about the heated office," said Gordon.

"It'll be so damn hot, you'll be in shorts and a t-shirt. You'll be drenched in sweat, givin' orders to some young secretary."

"I get a young secretary?"

"Damn right."

"Blonde?"

"Any type you want," said Ollie. "But you know what I'm sayin'."

"I know."

"This is just the beginning. What I create, you'll continue. You got a big future with this. A stable one. I'm working for that. I'm working for *you*."

"Hey. It's for you, too. We'll both have heated offices."

"I won't need one. I'll be retired in Miami."

"And leave me alone with all the work?"

"You won't be alone. You'll have the young secretary."

"Good point. Enjoy Miami."

The wind picked up, and they edged closer to the wall.

"I tell ya, you're gonna have a life better than mine," said Ollie, looking out at the relentless sleet pounding the pavement. "You got a better life ahead of you already. No need to worry about it. No need to think about the future. It's already there. You just gotta wait for it. It's there. All planned out for you. Just gotta wait for it," said Ollie, patting his son on the back.

They stood there. Father and son.

Waiting.

Chapter 71

Now

GORDON HUNG UP the phone, ending a short conversation with his Aunt back in Chicago. He didn't say much, only enough to let her know that he was okay and coming home.

During the time Gordon was talking, Mike had begun tearing down the collages. Gordon's Los Angeles lives were being shredded before his eyes. But they were already destroyed. He thought about stopping Mike, about insisting he keep the collages intact, but it was better to do away with them.

This much Gordon knew: It was easier to destroy than create. It was during that thought that it dawned on Gordon that it was the last day of the experiment.

The ninety-three days were over.

This was the day of his decision, or at least the day that was supposed to bring about a decision. But instead it of being the fresh start that Gordon envisioned, the day had suddenly become a clean-up day. A take-out-the-trash day. A boy-have-you-been-fucked-up-lately-but-we're-takin'-you-back-where-you-belong day.

Mike had suggested to Gordon that he see a therapist when he returned to Chicago. It was the first laugh Gordon could remember having in a long time. A therapist! Gordon had done more introspection in the last three months than most human beings did in a lifetime. He wasn't about to start over from scratch with some half-ass shrink. He'd rather spite everyone and start drinking heavily or gambling heavily, anything to make them feel guilty for bringing him back.

But that wouldn't be right. He was above that now. To do those things would be to bury his life and he was through burying his life.

It didn't matter anyway. You didn't need alcohol or blackjack to throw a shroud over who you were. You could do it as he had done it his whole life. You can bury it in your job, in television, in music, in sports, in the internet, in mindless conversation, in anything that distracted you. That's what most people did whether they realized it or not.

But not Gordon. Not anymore.

Mike could lure him back to Chicago, but he couldn't make him live the life he once led. The truth was, all his friends and family wanted him back for *them*, not for him. They wanted him back in their presence to make *them* feel better.

But it was his life. So with all due respect, *fuck them*.

The walls of room 116 were clean. Just like that. A little damage here and there from tack holes and areas where tape had ripped off paint, but otherwise, it was clean.

Empty.

Mike got some trash bags from the maid and made Gordon accompany him, believing he was some sort of flight risk. Gordon then watched as Mike loaded the trash.

Soon after, Gordon watched as Mike checked him out of the Starlight Inn.

Soon after that, Gordon watched as Mike returned the rental car at a branch different from the one Gordon had originally rented it, a spot closer to Mike's hotel. The manager broached the subject of excess mileage fees, drawing Mike into a thorny debate. After a few minutes of sorting through contract jargon, the manager reached the limits of her patience and implied that Mike didn't have the capacity to understand the rental agreement. Not good. Anytime Mike's intelligence was called into question, he flipped out.

During the altercation, Gordon found himself edging to the door. Found his hand reaching to push it open. Found himself holding his breath when the door's chime sounded.

Mike and the manager didn't notice.

Gordon eased out. The moment the sunlight hit his skin, he was gone. Like a convict clearing the prison wall.

Gordon sprinted down the street, feeling Mike's eyes on his back, though he never turned to see if he was actually being watched.

At the intersection, the red hand on the crosswalk sign was visible, but he crossed anyway. A car swerved. He kept running, leaping over the legs of a homeless man in front of a video store, dodging a woman handing out postcards, colliding with a guy talking on a cell phone. The guy fell. The phone shattered. Gordon didn't stop.

As he ran, the wind on his face, he felt the urge to cry again and tried to hold it back. But he couldn't.

He raced ahead with no destination. He just wanted to create distance. He wanted to move forward to somewhere. Anywhere. It didn't matter. It was about distance. He had to separate himself. He had to escape.

He crossed another street, then another, passing stores, cafés, bars, porn shops, fast food joints, parking lots.

He felt the dry wind, felt the tears stream from the corner of his eyes toward his hair, felt his chest constricting.

The noises were varied and mixed. Car horns, people yelling in Spanish, music, engines.

His own footsteps, his own breathing.

Then a siren.

Cutting through the air with a sudden, high-pitched volume. A fire truck passed Gordon, heading in the same direction. The sunlight changed colors on the street, becoming an orange haze. He looked at the sky and saw a plume of black smoke rising a few blocks away.

As he approached the smoke, his speed slowed. He recognized the landmarks and realized in an instant where he was and what was burning.

Gordon pushed through the crowd, not wanting to reach the front, but the middle where he'd be surrounded with a layer of bodies like a protective blanket. His sight locked on the flames before him.

The Column of Light Cathedral was on fire.

Gordon stared, already piecing together what happened.

The charges. The charges that Ash and him had set on the church's roof had finally ignited. The tiny explosives that had been up there for weeks, dormant, had somehow gone off. But instead of unveiling the banner (their sole purpose) the charges had started a fire. The banner itself was destroyed, Gordon figured.

The whole point, the whole message, was lost.

The smell of the smoke, the heat of the fire, the sweat on his face… they slowly stole his urge to escape. Standing in the pack of locals and tourists, Gordon's mind switched its focus.

The church faded away, and in its place was set a single image.
The face of Ash.
He was through running.

Chapter 72

GORDON TOOK THE ELEVATOR to the eighth floor.

He wasn't sure if you had to be a family member to visit, so he didn't ask. He just walked to her room without making eye contact with anyone.

When he opened the door, Ash was asleep.

An array of machinery surrounded her, as if keeping vigil.

The transparent container on the wall held some of her stomach fluid, its thin tube leading to her nose where it was held in place by a strip of white tape.

Gordon pulled up a chair and sat next to Ash.

Her face was pale. Even with her eyes shut and her body still, Ash seemed agitated. He didn't like seeing her like this.

Gordon noticed something on the table next to her bed. It was a wooden figurine. The one she made of the little girl holding the tiny white flag.

A child surrendering.

He had once asked what the little girl was surrendering from, and Ash said it didn't matter. But it did. And here it was, next to her. Though he saw her drop it in a trash bag, she hadn't thrown it out. Ash had brought it with her, perhaps to draw strength from it, perhaps to remind her of something, perhaps to serve as a piece of home to comfort her. Gordon didn't know, and he couldn't ask her now. But he was glad to see it.

Its presence indicated its importance. Ash had declared it irrelevant not too long ago, a piece of art that wouldn't be seen or appreciated. But she was wrong. The little girl with the white flag was here. To be seen by her.

Gordon knew it would be a while before Ash woke up, but he didn't mind. He had no intention of leaving her. He found the remote control and turned on the television with a low volume.

On screen was a live news report of the burning church.

It was a view from a helicopter hovering above the burning building, the crowd, the fire trucks. From what the reporter could gather, the fire had started on the roof and spread quickly. The cause was unknown.

The report indicated that the church had been gutted. The view switched to a handheld camera as it neared the scene.

Firemen were blasting a steady stream of water over the blackened steeple. Smoke continued to rise, twisting high above Hollywood and toward the valley. The camera got close to a fireman as he pulled something out of the smoldering debris.

He held what appeared to be the corpse of a baby.

The reporter gasped, but the fireman quickly brushed it off, and what first appeared to be human was revealed to be a doll.

A charred baby doll.

A familiar one at that. It was from the group of plastic dolls that Gordon and Ash had attached to the banner. The other babies would surely be discovered as well, and the media would ponder what it all meant.

He wondered if Myron was watching the same report right now, wondered if he felt a shred of responsibility. He could be ecstatic. Even though the message was lost, Myron got what he was looking for.

Exposure.

Gordon muted the television and reached out and took hold of Ash's hand. He tried to think of what he had learned the past three months.

It was the last day of the experiment, so maybe he should force himself to come to some conclusion. Not too long ago, he thought he had come to one.

Give in to what it is, but desire to make it better.

That sounded good at the time, and it had a nice way of tying his lives together, but what did it really mean?

From what he could figure out, *give in to what it is* meant to accept reality and not look away from the truth.

Okay, fine. Fair enough. That seemed like a good thing. But what's reality? Everyone had their own reality.

Then there was the other part of the apparent conclusion— *but desire to make it better.*

Fine, again.

This seemed to mean that he should see life for what it truly is, but want to improve it. Create a better planet for everyone, blah, blah, blah…

admirable shit to be sure, but was that really what it was all about?

After three months of exploring, of being different people, of being different things to different people, of thinking and acting differently… where was he?

He was in a hospital room next to Ash.

This is where his path had led him. Not to some philosophical conclusion, but to a place.

After wrestling with his mind for so long, it started to feel right. It wasn't about what to think. It was about where to be.

There would always be confusion, apprehension, anxiety, depression. Fear. It was like that for everyone. Gordon had managed to shrink the world into a place where only he struggled.

But after ninety-three days, where was he?

By someone's side.

Sitting there, next to Ash, he watched the news report.

With her hand in his, he watched the church burn.

Chapter 73

Ash and Gordon

THE LAST TIME GORDON worked on an art project, he was five years old.

The preschool class was assigned the task of converting empty, eight-ounce cartons of chocolate milk into snow covered cabins. He remembered being undaunted by the creative endeavor, even enthused. The five-year-old Gordon taped construction paper around the milk carton, drew windows and a door with crayons, and layered the top with cotton balls applied with Elmer's glue. When he took the completed piece home, it was celebrated and sat on display for years.

Working on an art project *now* felt impossible, and he let it be known. Ash told him his first problem was thinking of it as work. He wasn't fixing a bicycle spoke or stacking bricks. He was creating, and creation shouldn't be work.

Gordon bought into this notion as much as he could. He returned to shaping the copper wire with pliers, bending it around a ragged ball of clay.

He was sitting next to Ask on the Indian rug that served as her shop on the Venice Beach Boardwalk. The ocean behind them winked intense flashes of sunlight. A dozen sources of music blended into a single, almost subliminal beat. Foot traffic was heavy. The vibe was edgy, but good. As good as edgy gets.

His hands ached. He used the pliers to scratch his beard, a growing sprawl of unkempt facial hair that Ash insisted was his first true stab at art since that milk carton day in preschool. Gordon had given up shaving much as he had given up everything else that didn't feel essential.

It had been months since Ash's operation, and life was different.

Things were stable. Gordon had found out the best way to deal with an onslaught of problems was to simply let go. To take the beating. Life would eventually grow tired of punching. And so it did. Problems retreated like the tide. Things were easier. Maybe life was only taking a breather, resting up in the corner for the next round when it planned on delivering the knockout blow. Gordon didn't know and didn't care. He was enjoying the peace.

Communication with people in Chicago was sporadic, enough to let family and friends understand he had no plans of returning. One day maybe. Maybe not.

He hadn't seen Shawn, Cedric, or Dean since he moved out of their places. He had no intention of changing that. He had left them behind. He had let go.

He was fine with his current life with Ash. Cool nights in the loft, adrift in a sea of art supplies. Warm days on the boardwalk, selling handmade figurines to tourists.

Toby was still located next to them, but he no longer sold bags of bath salt. There had been persistent and concerned grumbling that people were using bath salt to get high. A cheap, dangerous thrill achieved through smoking, snorting, or shooting. Toby couldn't keep the stuff in stock even when he priced it up. He finally discovered why. A few visits from the local police and an enraged addict made him rethink his inventory. Thus the switch to incense. Simple and safe. He specialized in giant, thick sticks of it, more suited for basketball arenas than one bedroom apartments.

Ash was doing okay, although she appeared slightly gaunt. She had shed an alarming amount of weight during her time in the hospital and had only regained half of it. An adjusted diet and a regimen of legally obtained, responsibly ingested prescription pills maintained her otherwise good health.

Gordon showed her the piece he was creating. He expected her to snort a laugh at its crude nature, but she beamed a proud smile. She took it from him and set it down on the rug. Only then did it occur to her to ask, "Is it done?"

Gordon wondered. "I don't know."

A tourist picked it up.

Gordon started to say something, but just as quickly, the tourist set it back down and moved on to the collection of Toby's broom stick incense.

"Ah, well," said Ash.

"If a person buys it, does it mean it's done?" said Gordon.

She raised an eyebrow. "That's profound, Mr. Lake. And I have no fucking idea." She looked at the piece. "What is it anyway?"

Gordon retrieved it from the rug and held it up. He thought about the question. The realization nourished him. "Pure."

About the Author

Brad Keene is a screenwriter and author residing in California. His second novel is VIRTUAL PET CATCHERS, a high tech adventure.

Follow Brad Keene on Twitter and Instagram for more info.